# VENGEANCE ZERO

## (AN AGENT ZERO SPY THRILLER—BOOK 10)

## JACK MARS

# Jack Mars

Jack Mars is the USA Today bestselling author of the LUKE STONE thriller series, which includes seven books. He is also the author of the new FORGING OF LUKE STONE prequel series, comprising six books; and of the AGENT ZERO spy thriller series, comprising eleven books.

Jack loves to hear from you, so please feel free to visit www.Jackmarsauthor.com to join the email list, receive a free book, receive free giveaways, connect on Facebook and Twitter, and stay in touch!

## BOOKS BY JACK MARS

**LUKE STONE THRILLER SERIES**
ANY MEANS NECESSARY (Book #1)
OATH OF OFFICE (Book #2)
SITUATION ROOM (Book #3)
OPPOSE ANY FOE (Book #4)
PRESIDENT ELECT (Book #5)
OUR SACRED HONOR (Book #6)
HOUSE DIVIDED (Book #7)

**FORGING OF LUKE STONE PREQUEL SERIES**
PRIMARY TARGET (Book #1)
PRIMARY COMMAND (Book #2)
PRIMARY THREAT (Book #3)
PRIMARY GLORY (Book #4)
PRIMARY VALOR (Book #5)
PRIMARY DUTY (Book #6)

**AN AGENT ZERO SPY THRILLER SERIES**
AGENT ZERO (Book #1)
TARGET ZERO (Book #2)
HUNTING ZERO (Book #3)
TRAPPING ZERO (Book #4)
FILE ZERO (Book #5)
RECALL ZERO (Book #6)
ASSASSIN ZERO (Book #7)
DECOY ZERO (Book #8)
CHASING ZERO (Book #9)
VENGEANCE ZERO (Book #10)
ZERO ZERO (Book #11)

# Agent Zero – Book 9 Recap

*A foreign president is murdered. A convincing doppelganger takes his place. When the American president is lured onto foreign soil under the pretense of a historic peace treaty and taken hostage, there is only one man who can get him back: Agent Zero. But the president's captors have laid a clever web of deception, leaving a trail of breadcrumbs, diversions, and clues in the hopes that only Zero can unravel them. A deadly game of cat and mouse reveals their ultimate plan: to assassinate not only the president, but Zero alongside him.*

Agent Zero: After proposing to Maria, Zero made a new friend out of Seth Connors, the only other agent to have had a memory suppressor installed in his head. But Connors could offer him no clues about a potential cure for his failing memory. Zero thwarted the body double of the Palestinian president and his faction in their efforts to spark a war and rescued the president, but at the cost of his friend Agent Chip Foxworth, whom Zero had recruited personally. As Chip's sacrifice weighed heavily on his mind, he discovered that Connors had taken his own life—but not before leaving behind a single clue for Zero to follow.

Maria Johansson: The soon-to-be Mrs. Zero continued to struggle with her newfound domestic life—not only the pending wedding and being the stepmother to Maya and Sara Lawson, but also the recent adoption of Mischa, a twelve-year-old (at the time) former spy, all of which Maria must balance with being the leader of the newly formed Executive Operations Team.

Maya Lawson: Having returned to West Point to finish her studies, Maya was catching up and on track until the dean of the academy put her on the case of a campus forger who was providing fake but convincing documents to cadets. After following a dangerous trail, Maya found the forger—only to learn that it was all a test from Dean Hunt to see if she was ready for an experimental CIA junior agent program. Having passed her test, Maya is returning to Virginia for the program and the pursuit of her dream to be the youngest agent in CIA history.

Sara Lawson: Finding the women's trauma group Common Bonds provided Sara with a plethora of abusive men to find and seek vengeance on. Being charged with babysitting Mischa while her dad and Maria were away seemed like a disadvantage, but when Sara got in over her head with a gun-wielding abuser, Mischa swept in to save her. Now knowing more about her future stepsister's sordid past, Sara and the younger girl have bonded, with a promise from Mischa to teach her how to defend herself.

President Jonathan Rutledge: The president's ongoing quest for peace between the US and the Middle Eastern countries was nearly sidelined by his capture by the fake Palestinian president, but his rescue at the hands of Agent Zero and the EOT only strengthened his resolve to unite these divisive fronts—even if it requires a show of force to do so.

Chip Foxworth: The former pilot turned EOT agent was recruited by Agent Zero for their new team, rounding it out to five members. He proved to be a valuable asset in many ways, but none so much as his own sacrifice to save Zero's life.

Stefan Krauss: Little is known about the German-born mercenary and assassin, other than his disdain for Zero and desire for vengeance. But Krauss doesn't do anything for free, and as a master manipulator, Krauss has found a way to get what he wants while also making it a job—by uniting fractious dissidents in their fear and hatred of Rutledge's executioner, Agent Zero.

# PROLOGUE

"There can be no peace!" said the Tall Man, for what must have been the fifteenth time. But this time he punctuated it with a sharp slap of a fist on the table, causing the ashtray to jump, as if he was tired of making the point over and over—all the while not offering any viable solution, Fitzpatrick noted.

The Tall Man was lanky, his limbs spindly, a long beard elongating his angular face. Fitzpatrick pegged him to be in his early fifties. There were nine others in the room, including himself; mostly Iranians as far as he knew, certainly Arabs. They'd tried sharing their names, all of them Ahmad This or Mohammad That—the Johns and Williams of the Middle Eastern world. He'd given up trying to even remember. Instead they were the Tall Man, the Scrawny One, the Ugly Guy, Scar Man.

Scar Man was by far the most interesting; he stood in the corner, sullen, his arms folded, a dark shadow over his face and a pink scar running beneath his left eye, sweeping across his cheek to his ear like a fishhook. Men who looked like that had stories. Whether they were real or not didn't matter. It could have been that Scar Man's scar was from a knife fight or a combat mission. It could have been from tripping over his own two feet or getting kicked in the face by a donkey. The truth didn't matter; Fitzpatrick would bet money that whatever story he might share would be more aligned with the former anyhow.

Men who looked like that had stories, and he knew because he was a man like that. His own face, his body, was a roadmap of cicatrices, though the truth behind it was far less interesting than anyone might guess.

"Our resources are limited," said Ugly Guy, apparently picking up on the Tall Man's habit of stating the obvious. Ugly Guy's face was pockmarked, pitted, and his nose came to a bulbous end bright red with burst capillaries. "We lack time, we lack manpower—"

"The greatest attack on US soil was carried out by fewer men than we, armed only with box cutters," argued another, his appearance so unremarkable that Fitzpatrick had not yet come up with a nickname for him yet.

1

"They planned for years!" Ugly Guy argued. "We have but days. And since then security measures have been significantly increased. You know this. What we need is ingenuity. We need—"

"Money." This came from Scar Man, the first word Fitzpatrick had heard the man utter, and he had to resist the natural urge to raise an eyebrow, to show that he was listening. "That is what we need, is it not? We lack time, and we lack people. The obvious solution is money."

Fitzpatrick scratched idly at his beard, pretending he did not understand. The nine other men in the room had been speaking in Arabic, under the assumption that he did not understand. But he did. He'd picked up some of the language on tours in Iraq and Iran years ago, but it wasn't until he'd founded the Division that he'd realized the necessity of it. Much of his former group's work had involved the Middle East and North Africa; staging small coups, putting down rebel uprisings, assassinating troublesome tribal leaders.

He understood every word, but he pretended not to, and instead lit a cigarette from the crumpled pack in the breast pocket of his black T-shirt.

This place, this ramshackle building in which they had set up a temporary headquarters, used to be a food-processing plant and still smelled like it. It sat in a small industrial complex not three kilometers from the Sabzevar bazaar, a city formerly known as Beyhagh, in the Razavi Khorasan Province of northeastern Iran, approximately six hundred sixty kilometers from Tehran.

Sabzevar was a pleasant enough city, as far as cities in this shithole of a country went. Fitzpatrick had certainly been in far worse. At least here he could walk the streets freely, even identify as an American, without much trouble. Though that could speak as much for his muscled, six-foot-four frame as for the relative safety of the city.

Yet this place, the former food-processing plant, this was not a pleasant enough place. It stank. It was poorly ventilated. Too hot in the daytime and drafty in the night. Scar Man was, unfortunately, right; the group had no money. What little funding they had was from a sheikh whom the Tall Man had blackmailed for certain indiscretions that involved underage boys, the details of which Fitzpatrick had not asked and did not want to know.

He had few scruples. But fucking around with kids was unforgivable. The less he knew about the sheikh, the better, or he'd be inclined to put a bullet in the man's head.

"The obvious solution, you say." Ugly Guy raised a thick eyebrow at Scar Man. "If money is so obvious, how do you propose that we procure it? And what would we do if we had it?"

Scar Man's lip curled. Clearly he had no plan but was simply frustrated at their situation. "We would be unfettered!" Scar Man argued. "We could buy weapons! Drones… explosives… We would not be sitting around and bickering about what paltry scheme we might be able to perform under these limitations!"

The Tall Man pointed a crooked finger at Scar Man. "There is nothing paltry about what we are doing here—"

But Scar Man just pointed one right back. "You least of all should have a seat at this table!" He was shouting now, his face reddening. "We talk about resources? You wasted our funds on this… this American *dog*! You dare to bring him here, to discuss our plans with him? You expect us to put any trust in him?"

"He knows things," said the Tall Man, and Fitzpatrick held back a chuckle.

But Scar Man did not. "Ha!" he spat derisively. "Of what does he know? He is a contract killer. A fighter-for-hire. And by the looks of it"—Scar Man sneered in Fitz's direction—"he lost his last fight."

He said nothing, just continued to stare down at the tabletop. Scar Man wasn't wrong; Fitzpatrick hadn't always been this handsome. He kept his beard trimmed short these days because of the long white scar that intersected his chin, where hair refused to grow. From around his right eye and orbital bone spider-webbed a network of lines, creases in his face that would never go away.

And those were just the visible ones. Beneath his black T-shirt and dark cargo pants were more, many more, where the doctors had surgically reset bones and put his insides back where they belonged.

Fitz took a long drag on his cigarette and stubbed it out in the ashtray before speaking. And then: "I'll tell you the story of my scars," he said in near-flawless (though heavily accented) Arabic, "if you tell me yours."

No one spoke. The Ugly Guy's mouth fell slightly open, revealing a few empty sockets. Scar Man narrowed his eyes, seething, as he slowly took a step forward.

3

There was nothing overtly threatening about the way in which he advanced, but his body language spoke volumes. Shoulders back, elbows slightly cocked, jaw clenched.

Fitz had been expecting some pushback to his presence since the meeting had begun. His left hand rested on the hilt of a black-handled Ka-Bar. He pulled it, making sure that everyone in the room heard the sound of unsheathed steel before he set the wickedly sharp knife down on the table before him.

"You may be thinking you have something to prove," said Fitzpatrick, his gaze boring holes into Scar Man, "but I promise that if you try, I'll make your face nice and symmetrical again." He drew a line across his own cheek, swooping around to his ear, miming the line of the man's long scar.

Scar Man said nothing. He tensed—but after a moment he slowly set himself down on a wooden stool.

"Good." Fitz switched to his native Oklahoma dialect. "Now then, I'm gonna go ahead and speak in English for a while, 'cause nothing personal but your language makes me feel like I'm chewing on a sunbaked goat turd. I know not all y'all speak it, but you can translate for your buddies later."

He glanced around, again expecting some contentious words, but none came. He had his audience, at least the ones who could understand him.

"Y'all have paid a pretty penny to have me here, and I haven't been sitting on my thumbs. I've been thinking. As I understand it, y'all want to put the fun back in fundamentalist, is that right?" He was playing on his southern roots, exaggerating it almost to the point of parody, but it was worth it; these men were likely cringing internally at the very notion of listening to an American, let alone a yokel.

"The Ayatollah is misguided," said the Tall Man in English. "His peace with the US is a grave error. Already we have witnessed trade agreements and economic sanctions that threaten to bring westernization to our country to the point of—"

Fitz held up a hand. "I get it, man, one McDonald's in Tehran is one too many. Y'all don't want a Walmart coming in next, or there goes the neighborhood."

"We want to strike a blow to the psyche and pride of their nation," the Tall Man said forcefully. "While simultaneously demonizing Iran in the eyes of Americans again. There can be no peace!"

4

"You mentioned that," Fitz mused. "Right, so whip up some good ol'-fashioned Islamophobia like back in the early aughts." It sounded so strange on the surface; these men wanted to vilify their own country in order to save it. They, a small contingent of less than a dozen, assumed they were the mouthpiece of a nation, the true heroes that would do what they needed to do, whatever was necessary to keep Iran from becoming anything like the Big Bad West.

That sort of loyalty could easily be seen as unfounded, even insane. But Fitzpatrick could understand it. After all, he'd been a Marine for more than a decade.

*Oo-rah.*

"And you know how to do this?" Ugly Guy asked.

"I got an idea. Pass me that tablet."

The Tall Man slid the tablet toward him and Fitzpatrick navigated to YouTube. He typed a keyword into the search bar and waited—"Wi-Fi sucks here," he muttered—and then tapped on a video thumbnail. It took an irritatingly long time to buffer, but when it finally played, he turned the screen so everyone present could see. They drew in closer, the nine of them, bunching up shoulder to shoulder as their brows furrowed in confusion.

On the screen was an old man. He sat in a preschool classroom with a picture book in his lap and a circle of children seated around him as he read a story about a family of ducks trying to cross a busy street. The old man wore a US Army ball cap and a checkered flannel shirt and jeans. He had deep laugh lines creased around his still-bright blue eyes, though his hair had long since gone white. He hunched over the book and read slowly, all the while keeping a genial smile on his weathered face.

"Now for the ten-thousand-dollar question," said Fitz. "Anybody here know who this is?"

The nine Iranian faces glanced at each other and then back at him, some shaking their heads, all silent.

"Didn't think so. That right there is William Preston McMahon. Or I should say, former President of the United States William Preston McMahon. Goes by Bill these days. Or Billy, to his wife. Grandpa Bill, to his litter's litter. He is eighty-four years young. Served two terms in the White House, from 1981 to 1989. Grandpa Bill spends his golden years reading to preschoolers and volunteering at animal shelters. He runs a scholarship for inner-city kids, pays five full rides every year.

5

Most recently, Bill has been doing a lot of press. He's been on talk shows and news shows and all that, a very vocal ally of President Rutledge's peace efforts."

"And what use is this old man?" asked Scar Man impatiently. "Why are you showing us this?"

"Well," said Fitz, "because as your tall friend said, I know some things. For example, I know that Grandpa Bill owns a ranch out in rural West Virginia. I know that he's guarded by a couple of retired Secret Service agents that spend most of their time watching *The Price Is Right*, shooting pool, and not expecting any trouble. I know that Bill is still very much beloved by the people, possibly more so now than when he was in office. And finally, I know that for the price of a plane ticket, a rental car, and a few bullets, we could get to him."

The Tall Man shook his head slowly. "I... do not understand."

Scar Man threw his hands up. "This is what our money has gotten us? A plan to kill an old man?"

"Not exactly," Fitz countered. "Look, you want to hurt the American psyche? Wound our pride? You could take out a building. Go for body count. Or—you could go after an icon. And Bill here is the least guarded icon I can think of. It'll hit 'em where it hurts. But that's not enough. So we're gonna go in there and we're gonna kidnap ol' Bill. Take him hostage. Blame Iran. We'll demand a ransom. The US government, they won't want to negotiate with terrorists, but they might cave for Bill. The American people will put them under a ton of pressure. It'll be damned if they do, damned if they don't; either way it'll cause a lot of dissent. But that's not even the best part. 'Cause whether they pay up or not, we're still gonna put Bill out to pasture."

To the Tall Man's confused expression he added, "Kill him. It means we'll still kill him. And the beauty of it is, most people are pretty simple folks. Even if the government catches on that it's not actually Iran behind this, the people will believe it. The tensions are still fresh in their minds; they'll *want* to believe it. They'll rally around that. You'll get what you want, and all it'll cost is Bill McMahon. You dig?"

It seemed to take a few moments for the plan to fully sink in. Fitzpatrick thought it was quite brilliant, if he could say so himself; in fact, he'd gotten the idea from an incident that unfolded about six months ago, when President Rutledge had been briefly held hostage by Palestinians, one of whom was masquerading as their president. He had

6

seen firsthand how quickly the country screeched for war, for bombs to strafe the West Bank from the face of the Earth.

This group could never get to President Rutledge. But Bill McMahon? And with Fitzpatrick at the helm?

Easily.

To his surprise, it was Ugly Guy who nodded first. A jack-o'-lantern grin lit on his face, stretching his pitted face as he said, "Yes. I dig."

The Tall Man nodded silently. As did the Scrawny One, and the unremarkable one (who Fitz decided on the spot would henceforth be the Drab Arab), and the others.

All except Scar Man. He frowned deeply, eyes locked on the tablet screen.

"What do you say, Scar?" Fitz prodded.

"You would do this?" the man asked somberly. "To your own former president?"

Fitzpatrick shrugged. "I ain't got any ties left there. That country chewed me up and spit me out. My loyalty is for sale, and the money you're paying will set me up nicely in a non-extradition country. I'm thinking Moldova. I hear Eastern European girls dig scars."

Scar Man contemplated it for a moment further, and then nodded once. "I still think you are an American dog," he muttered. "Though maybe... more like wolf."

Fitzpatrick grinned at that.

Two and a half years ago he had been the head of his own company, leader of the private security organization called the Division. At least that's what the general public and IRS thought they did. In reality, they ran covert ops that even the CIA wouldn't touch. They loaned themselves out to any banana republic government with an open wallet and in need of a few guns. He and his men toppled regimes and turned the tides of wars.

Then came that day in New York City, a fairly unremarkable afternoon just before the attempted bombing of the Midtown Tunnel. All Fitz and his guys had to do was stall Agent Zero for a little while. But then that Israeli bitch had crashed the party. The Mossad agent with the lesbian haircut had hit him with a car.

He suffered seventeen broken bones that day. A punctured lung. A loss of vision in his right eye that had only partially returned. He was laid up for four months. He had to relearn how to walk. How to shoot a gun. There was permanent nerve damage in his spine and limbs. The former deputy director who had hired him, Ashleigh Riker, had disavowed any connection to the Division and was later imprisoned. Fitz had been lucky in that regard; he avoided prison, but the medical bills bankrupted him. The few remaining members of the Division abandoned him. For the last two years he had no one and nothing.

Except... he still had connections. People still talked, and that chatter had led him here, to a group of people who couldn't be more different from him but still shared at least one thing in common. They too were willing to do whatever was necessary to regain some sense of control, to salvage whatever they could of what used to be.

They would take lives if they had to. Just like he would. Just like he had before.

After everything he'd done for his country, they had turned their back on him. Dissolved his company, disavowed him. He'd lost everything. But this... this was a way to get it back.

Was taking one life worth getting back what remained of his?

*Yes,* he told himself. *It certainly is.*

# CHAPTER ONE

"Fascinating," Dillard murmured as he examined the CT scans of Zero's brain, clipped to a horizontally mounted illuminator box on the otherwise white wall of the examination room. "Simply fascinating."

*Real glad my rapidly deteriorating brain has your interest,* Zero wanted to say. But he held his tongue; the man was only trying to help.

"Look here." The neurologist pointed at one of the backlit scans, to (what looked to Zero to be) a nebulous blob in the southeastern quadrant. "This is a scan from April, your third visit with me. And this," he pointed to the same spot on the scan beside it, "is from yesterday's scan. As you can see, the cholinesterase inhibitors seem to be working."

It wasn't exactly apparent to Zero, but he nodded anyway as if it was.

"They're not stopping the progression, mind you," Dillard said, "but they do seem to be slowing it."

"I must admit, I am a little embarrassed," said Dr. Guyer from the computer screen on the table beside them. The Swiss neurologist was joining them via video conference from Zurich. "I had considered a course of treatment akin to that of an Alzheimer's patient, but wasn't confident in the efficacy without further tests. I see now that it was well worth the attempt."

"Don't blame yourself, Doctor," said Dillard, "this is as unique a case as it gets." He removed a pen light from his white lab coat pocket and shined it in Zero's left eye. "Follow the light, please. Any episodes lately?"

"None," Zero said honestly as tears formed in his eye from the blazing light. On any other day, to any other person, he might have lied when he said "none"—but this time it was the truth.

"Any impediments to motor function?" Dillard asked as he blinded Zero in the other eye. "Physical dysfunction of any kind?"

"None," Zero told him, and again it was the truth. Frankly, he felt great. "Well… there is the one impediment." He held up his right wrist and shook it, jangling the silver medical alert bracelet he wore there.

Dillard smirked. "As long as you're my patient, you'll be wearing that at all times. Especially in your line of work. The last thing I need is for you to be unconscious and have someone try to administer benzodiazepine. And you're taking the memantine regularly?"

Zero nodded. "Like clockwork."

"Good. That regulates the activity of glutamate, which is important for information processing and retrieval in your brain. Any headaches, constipation, dizziness lately?"

"Yes, no, and no."

"On a scale of one to ten, how bad are the headaches? One being a minor inconvenience and ten being you've been shot in the head."

"Hard to say, I've never been shot in the head," Zero quipped. *Only everywhere else.*

Dillard gave him a pointed look.

"I'd say never worse than a four or five."

"Good. Very good." Dillard made some notations on a clipboard chart.

Dr. Eugene Dillard was easy to like. He was only forty-eight, less than a decade Zero's senior, yet held himself with confidence and was highly respected in his field. He had a shock of dark curly hair that hadn't even begun to gray, and kept his face clean-shaven. Despite his age he ran daily and spoke of it often; Zero was made aware on more than one visit that Dillard ran at least one marathon annually and never twice in the same city.

Five and a half months ago, in mid-March, Zero had been devastated to find Seth Connors dead. Connors had been the only other CIA agent to have the memory suppression chip installed in his head, and even though they had really only had one conversation Zero had started to think of him as a friend—or at the very least, a kindred spirit.

But ultimately Connors had been unable to reconcile the man he thought he was with the fragmented memories of his former life that were constantly invading his thoughts, especially that of the untimely death of a daughter for which Connors blamed himself. It was Zero who had found him, as well as an apologetic note that ended with a cryptic one-word sign-off: "Dillard."

Seth Connors would never know it, but his second-to-last act, just before the self-inflicted gunshot wound, would represent a new beginning for someone else.

It hadn't taken long to find Dillard. Two days after finding Connors, Zero followed the lead and discovered that Dr. Eugene Dillard was the head of the Department of Neurology at the George Washington University School of Medicine in Washington, D.C. Dillard and Connors had never met in person, but had spoken on the phone a few times, and the doctor had tried each time to have Connors come in, to no avail.

By Zero's third visit to Dillard he realized that the doctor could be trusted, and he divulged his full story. To his credit, the neurologist took it all in stride and never once doubted it as the truth. Perhaps the doctor was used to bizarre medical anomalies, or perhaps he'd heard this song before. A tale as old as time, Zero's: CIA agent blames himself for wife's murder; best friend steals an experimental chip from an agency lab that suppresses memories; two years later Iraqi terrorists kidnap him and tear it out of his head with needle-nose pliers.

A real classic.

After that they looped in Dr. Guyer, the Swiss neurologist who had installed the memory suppressor in Zero's head in the first place (at Zero's behest). And now after five months, many visits, innumerable scans, a *lot* of medications, and a few bouts of vomiting and dizziness while they got the dosage just right, they were seeing results.

And more importantly, Zero wasn't lying. He wasn't lying to the doctors when he said he felt great; he wasn't lying to Maria or Alan when he said he hadn't had an episode in two months. He wasn't lying to himself when he said he'd be fine and he'd beat this. In fact, he felt sharper, keener somehow as of late.

Maybe that ridiculous medical alert bracelet was a good luck charm.

"Well," said Dillard with a click of the pen. "While you still have a long road ahead of you, I don't think I need to tell you that this is all very promising. I would even say reason to celebrate."

"I'll be doing plenty of that anyhow," Zero said. "Tomorrow is my wedding." Just the mention of it aloud made butterflies flutter in his stomach. In little more than twenty-four hours he and Maria would be exchanging vows in front of their closest friends and family.

Dillard smiled wide. "You don't say. Well, don't do *too* much celebrating. This is the part where I tell you that you shouldn't be drinking alcohol, but… let's just take it easy on the alcohol."

"I will." Zero stood, the white paper under him crinkling. "Say, Doc, you should come. Bring the wife. It's a very small gathering, but it'll be a good time. The more, the merrier." And he meant it; between him and Maria they had less than a dozen people coming.

"I appreciate the thought," said Dillard, "but I'm afraid I have a speaking engagement in Baltimore tomorrow. Best of luck, though."

"Thanks, Doc."

"And I will be seeing you next week?" asked Guyer through the computer. "Here in Zurich, yes?"

"Of course." He had long promised Guyer the opportunity for another hands-on examination. But first he had to get married. And then he needed to spend a week on a beach in the Bahamas with his bride. But right after his honeymoon he'd be boarding another plane to Switzerland. He'd made a promise, and he intended to keep it.

"I'll be there." Zero chuckled. "Pending disaster, of course."

# CHAPTER TWO

Maria opened the basement door just a few inches and peered down the stairs. It was pitch-black down there; last year, when Sara had made it her bedroom, she'd covered the only window with thick gray fabric. Despite the morning hour no light permeated the basement, which was just how Sara wanted it.

Of course she was still asleep. If sleeping were an Olympic sport Sara would be a medalist. It didn't help that Maria had been awoken the night before by the sound of the security code being punched in at the front door. She'd checked her phone—it was nearly three in the morning when Sara had finally come in. It had become something of a regular occurrence, at least twice a week, sometimes more.

Maria didn't think it was drugs again. Sara was alert, looked healthy; her comebacks were as snappy and sarcastic as ever. So what was it? A few weeks prior Zero had sat his youngest daughter down and asked her to be honest with him. Sara had claimed she'd been attending a support group for women lately at the community center. She attributed the late nights to helping out some of the women who didn't feel safe in their own homes.

But Maria was dubious about that claim. Nothing against Sara, but she couldn't imagine that an aloof, emotionally stunted seventeen-year-old would be anyone's ideal support person.

Still, she didn't ask or say anything about it. As long as the girl wasn't back on drugs and the police weren't knocking at their door, she would keep silent. It wasn't her place, and her and Sara's relationship was strained enough as it was.

Because after tomorrow, Maria would be... well, she'd be Sara's stepmother.

*Jesus.* She sighed as she gently closed the basement door again. *The wedding is tomorrow.*

Almost six months had passed since Zero had proposed to her. The wedding would be small—*very* small—but that was more than fine with both of them. They had planned it casually, taken their time, and now everything was done; all the preparations had been made. Save for the urge to try on her dress again and admire herself in the mirror, there was nothing more to do but keep herself busy and her mind occupied.

*Because tomorrow, you'll be* Mrs. *Maria Johansson.*

She and Zero had already discussed it, and she wouldn't be changing her name. She'd already done it once, legally from her birth name to the name she now carried. Mischa was a Johansson too, by virtue of the US citizenship documents that the CIA had cooked up for the girl. Not to mention the added detriment, whether imaginary or not: Maria couldn't help but think that changing her name to Lawson might make Sara and Maya feel some kind of way, and the last thing she wanted them to think was that she was trying to be their mother. They were pretty much adults.

And besides, she didn't need it to be any easier for anyone to connect her and Zero in more ways than they could already, considering their line of work.

*Our line of work.* Funny, despite being in a field that put her life in danger regularly, the seemingly paltry problems she had in her head now still gave her a flutter in the stomach.

She heard the clacking of shoes on tile and turned to see Maya enter the kitchen, dressed smartly in black slacks and a white blouse. She'd been growing out her dark hair again from the boyish pixie cut she'd maintained during her time at West Point, and it was long enough now for her to tie it up into a neat bun. She rarely wore makeup, but today she had on eyeshadow and some lightly feathered foundation that made her face more angular, mature. All in all she could have passed for mid-twenties instead of her nineteen years.

"Morning," Maya said as she reached for the coffee pot.

"Aren't we looking sharp this morning?" Maria noted. "Where are you off to?"

"The program," Maya said simply as she stirred some sugar into a travel mug.

"Right. The *program.*" Back in March, Maya had announced that she had been allowed to "test out" of her final year at West Point—something that neither Maria nor Zero had known was possible—and had been invited to an "advanced training program" in D.C. On the one hand, it meant that she was living with them again and commuting daily, which meant they got to see a lot more of her.

On the other hand, she was extremely vague with what she was training for and what this alleged program would do for her career

14

trajectory. Hell, neither of them could even confirm that there really *was* a program. They didn't know where she went or how she spent her days. Maya liked to joke that it was "above their security clearance."

*As long as the police aren't knocking on our door...*

"Hang on a sec," Maria said. "It's Saturday."

"Yeah. Just a little... extracurricular activity today," Maya replied simply. "And they asked that we dress professionally. Speaking of, do you have a black blazer I can borrow?"

"Sure. Left side of my closet. Help yourself." Maria poured herself some coffee while Maya vanished for a moment and then reemerged shrugging into a blazer.

"Thanks. So, big plans today? Considering that by this time tomorrow you'll be—"

"Uh-uh," Maria cut her off. "I don't want to hear about it, don't want to think about it. Today is going to be a fun and relaxing day free from worry, stress, and doubt."

"Fair enough," said Maya with a chuckle. "Then what do you have planned for this completely ordinary day that may or may not be the eve of a particular event?"

"I am taking Mischa back-to-school shopping." Maria beamed; she couldn't help herself. Mischa was such a unique girl, and independent, that there were few things Maria could do for her that she would consider "parental." But this, back-to-school shopping, this was certainly one of them, and Maria actually found herself kind of excited about it.

But Maya frowned. "I think she would have had to be in school at some point to be *back*-to-school shopping. For her it's just school shopping."

"Pedant," Maria murmured with a smirk. But Maya was right—and that cat was out of the bag anyhow. The eldest Lawson girl had not for one second bought Mischa's fake adoption cover story, so Maria and Zero had decided the truth was easier than another attempt at a fable. Now both girls were aware that their soon-to-be stepsister was a former spy and child soldier for the Chinese who had been trained by a Russian sparrow expat.

*Never a dull moment under this roof.*

"Speak of the devil," said Maya as the youngest member of the household entered the kitchen. Mischa was still in her pajamas, which today were comprised of sweatpants and a pink Sailor Moon T-shirt

15

and fuzzy bunny slippers. Considering her demeanor, the girl's choice of apparel was, for lack of a better term, amusing. Her bright blonde bed-head and cherubic, youthful face only completed the ensemble— and completely betrayed what might have been going on behind her green eyes.

"Good morning," she said politely as she reached for a glass.

"Morning," Maria replied. "You slept late; you're normally up with the sun."

"I'm sorry."

"It's okay." Maria chuckled. "You're allowed to sleep in."

Mischa poured herself some orange juice and replaced the cap. "I was up late finishing the book Maya lent me."

"Oh? And what book would that be?"

"*The Crucible*," Mischa replied.

Maria shot Maya a look.

"What?" the older girl protested. "She wanted to learn more about American history—"

"And you thought the witch trials were a good place to start?"

"Maria, she's read every other book I own," Maya muttered.

It was believable; Mischa was a voracious reader. She'd started with the volumes of European history texts on the shelves of Zero's study and quickly moved on to assail Maya's modest library. It had actually been one of the nicest things about having Maya around this past summer; the two girls got along famously, as long as the topic of conversation was political dissidence, war, rebellion, or assassination (be it attempted or successful).

Mischa perched herself upon a stool at the counter, and Maria leaned on the counter with both elbows. "So, what's with the sudden interest in American history?"

The girl shrugged. "Nothing much. I just thought I should educate myself before executing my plan to overthrow your government."

Maria's eyes widened. Behind her, Maya choked on a sip of coffee.

The blonde girl in the Sailor Moon shirt looked between them. "That was intended to be a joke. Did I not do it right?"

Maria found herself remembering how to breathe. "Oh… yes. It was perfect. It's just, sometimes something is so funny that… we forget how to laugh."

"Nice save," Maya muttered.

"Anyway!" Maria said, louder than she needed to. "Today you and I are going to go out. School starts next week. We need to get you some school supplies and some new clothes."

The girl frowned. "I have clothes."

"You have Sara's hand-me-downs."

"They are serviceable."

"Sure, for bumming around in the summer. Don't you want nice clothes? That are yours?" Mischa was really killing the school-shopping buzz Maria had going. "And a backpack, and notebooks...?"

"Notebooks." Mischa nodded. "Yes."

"Great." Maria held back a snort. "We'll start at notebooks and work our way to sweaters."

"Okay, I'm off," Maya announced. She squeezed Mischa's tiny shoulder. "Have a great one, kiddo."

"Maya," said the girl, deadly serious. "You must know that I was only joking about overthrowing the American government."

"Oh, but if anyone could." Maya winked, and then turned to Maria. "I'll be back in time for our, uh, 'not at all wedding-related gathering.'"

Maria smiled. "Appreciate it." Maya had offered to throw her a bachelorette party—the nature of which Maria could not begin to guess—but she'd politely declined in favor of a perfectly dull evening at home with her adopted daughter, her soon-to-be stepdaughters, a bottle of red wine, and a couple of epically cheesy rom-coms.

She glanced over her shoulder as Mischa carried her orange juice into the living room to turn on CNN. "Are you sure you can't skip the extracurriculars and join us today?" Maria asked in a low voice. "I could use another pair of hands, and I'm sure Mischa would enjoy having you along..."

"Sorry, no can do. Afraid she's your burden to bear today." Maya smiled as she headed toward the door, shoes clacking as she did. "Enjoy it. And... maybe make sure she's not *actually* plotting anything?"

Maria let out a small laugh. "Yeah." In the living room, Mischa sat on the sofa and watched a report about growing tensions in the Iranian army. Her feet didn't even reach the floor and the plush heads on the fuzzy bunny slippers bobbed slightly as she kicked her legs gently. "If anyone could."

# CHAPTER THREE

*No more pencils, no more books…*

It was a silly thought, a silly song to be running through her head, but Maya couldn't seem to shake it as she entered the lobby through double glass doors. The place was busy, filled with rigid men in stiff suits. The atrium beyond was equally packed, mostly men, shaking hands and speaking amongst each other in groups of four or five. The hotel bar was beyond that, and would even be in her line of sight if not for the number of people between it and her.

"Jeez." Her partner stepped up beside her and wrinkled his nose. Rather, her "partner," as she'd come to think of him, quotation marks added, because calling him a partner added a level of legitimacy that he simply didn't deserve. "The air in here is like fifty percent cheap cologne."

"Focus," she said sharply. "It's the business conference."

Coleman just looked at her blankly.

"The textile manufacturers' conference?" Maya's exasperation was growing. "From the notes I sent you? The whole reason I said 'dress professionally'? So we can blend in?"

He shrugged. "I skimmed."

Maya's jaw clenched instinctively. "Forget it. We need a distraction so I can get behind the desk and find out what room he's in…"

"Come on, Maya. It's obviously the penthouse suite. Don't you watch movies? It's *always* the penthouse suite—"

"This isn't a movie," she said brusquely. "And when we're out here, it's Agent Lawson to you."

"Whatever you say." He grinned. "*Junior* Agent Lawson."

Her teeth clenched again, so hard it made her jaw ache. Of the fourteen people in the program, of *course* she was partnered with him for this.

Trent Coleman had won the genetic lottery. He was tall, a few years older than Maya, with brown hair that was never out of place, high cheekbones, and a strong jaw. He was intelligent, funny, charming, and had been his high school's star wide receiver for three years. His father

18

was an attorney at a firm that counted half the Senate as their clients. His mother was a former Miss Maryland who could have won the title of Miss America had she not graciously dropped out of the competition when she was accepted to her top-choice med school. She was now an internist at Kaiser Permanente.

Maya had, obviously, read his file.

And she had decided, even before being partnered with him, that she loathed Trent Coleman.

She'd known this type of guy before. In high school, and again in West Point. The kind of guy who had skated by because he had good looks and half a brain. The kind of guy who considered a bad day to be one in which his sports car got a flat or his Wi-Fi wasn't working. The kind of guy who could melt problems away with a wink and a smile.

Trent Coleman had a damn perfect smile. It showed off both rows of white, symmetrical teeth. It made guys trust him and made girls weak in the knees.

God, she hated that smile. Seeing it made her jaw clench so hard she feared she'd crack a tooth.

The two of them couldn't be more different. Trent Coleman had never once had to worry if he was going to get abducted in the night—again. He'd never had to learn that his mother's untimely death was a murder at the hands of a man he'd once trusted with his life. He'd never been kidnapped and sold to traffickers, drugged, and nearly raped. He'd never watched a girl his own age get gunned down right in front of him.

No, Trent Coleman had gotten by on money and a modicum of intellect and that smile. That rage-inducing, oh-so-punchable smile.

"Are you going to take this seriously?" Maya asked him somberly as they stood in the lobby of the Hilton Grand in downtown D.C. "Because if this ends up being like the water rescue training…"

Trent chuckled. Maya stuffed her hand in her pocket to keep it from flying across his cheek of its own volition. "Look, that was just a dare." Last week, Trent had shown up to their water rescue training wearing a snorkel and a large inflatable pink inner tube with a flamingo's head. Everyone had such a laugh at his antics. Even the former Navy SEAL the CIA had brought in to teach their junior agents in the program had a little chuckle.

And Maya, she'd seethed, and she'd clenched her jaw, and she'd worried about cracking a tooth.

"I get it, Lawson. I'm clearly the last person you want to be here with," Trent said. "I can tell by that thing you're doing with your face. That's going to give you little lines in your forehead, you know." *Don't hit him.*

"But I'm just glad to be out of that stuffy facility and getting some real action," he continued. "So let's get it done, huh?"

"Fine," Maya relented. "But we're going to do it right. So we need a distraction so I can get a look at their check-ins. You seem to be good at attracting attention."

"That's true," he agreed. "What'd you have in mind?"

Maya glanced left and right. No one was looking their way. So she stepped slightly in front of Trent, cocked an arm tight against her side, and in one smooth, quick motion she jerked her hips around, throwing most of her body weight as she drove her elbow into his solar plexus.

Hard. Really hard.

"*Ooph!*" The air left Trent's lungs in an instant. Both hands grasped at his midsection as he fell to one knee. Maya allowed herself to flash him a smile, for just a millisecond.

And then she screamed as loud as she could.

"Oh my god, someone help! Help, please!" Suits appeared at her side and huddled around in concern as Trent's red face and bugged eyes stared at her. "I-I don't know what happened, h-he just grabbed his stomach and collapsed!"

More men huddled around as Trent struggled to breathe. The woman at the front desk scurried over in small steps and precipitous heels, crouching beside Trent. "Sir? Sir, what's happened? Do you need an ambulance? Sir?"

"Please, help him…" Maya took a step back, and then another, and broke through the small crowd of do-gooders that all wanted to later tell the story to a rapt audience at the hotel bar about the young man whose life they saved. Maya crouched low, low enough that she couldn't be seen over the granite check-in counter, and silently thanked the God of Squats as she duck-walked to the hotel's computer.

She put her fingers to the keys and quickly typed: S-M-Y-T-H-E.

No results.

*Think. Probably didn't use his real name. What sort of pseudonym would make sense for a man like…?*

*Aha.*

S-M-I-T-H.

There were five Smiths registered at the hotel that day. Two were women. One was a Bradley. Another was a Hunter. The fifth was a Jimmy.

Jimmy. Jimmy Smith. James Smythe.

*Got you.*

And the room he was checked into was…

"Son of a bitch," she murmured. Then she duck-walked back out from behind the counter and hurried over to the crowd of onlookers, putting on her terrified face again. "Is he okay? Honey, are you all right?"

The front desk woman was helping Trent to his feet. He breathed shakily and stared daggers at Maya, but nodded. "I'm okay… *honey.* Just some… indigestion."

"Thank you," she gushed as she gripped the front desk clerk's shoulder. "Thank you so much for your help."

"I'm not sure I did much of anything—oh my." The woman was taken aback as Maya pulled her into an emphatic hug.

Her left hand tugged the woman's key card from the lanyard clipped to her belt.

"Are you certain you wouldn't like me to call anyone?" the clerk asked.

"No, no, I think he's fine. Again, thank you." Maya smiled as she tucked the key card into her own pocket.

Without a spectacle, the crowd dispersed quickly as Maya thanked them and gripped Trent's arm in fake concern.

"Come on," she said, and pulled him toward the elevators.

"You got a hell of an elbow. Did you enjoy that?"

"Made me weak in the knees," Maya said with a smirk.

"Terrific. Let me guess. He's staying in the—"

"Shut up," Maya snapped. "Let's just go."

They rode the elevator to the penthouse level in silence. Or relative silence, as a Muzak version of "The Girl from Ipanema" played as background noise to Trent's occasional cough.

Maya knew from schematics that the Hilton Grand's penthouse level was a luxury apartment that took up the entire top floor. It was also only accessible by the current guest or hotel staff—so the front desk clerk's keycard had come in handy when Maya was required to swipe it before pressing the penthouse button.

Her heart rate almost doubled as they ascended. This was it, her first real op as a junior agent. She wondered briefly if she should have told Maria where she was actually going, just in case something happened today. But what good would it do? For one, the CIA would thoroughly deny it, even to one of their own agents. Furthermore, she'd come this far without her dad or Maria even knowing what she was up to, let alone getting involved. She didn't want their help or intervention.

Besides, this was a low-impact operation, even compared to some of the things Maya had done before her time in the program.

Five floors to go.

"You remember the objectives?" she asked Coleman.

"Of course. Locate the briefcase, neutralize Smythe, not necessarily in that order."

She nodded once. Had it been anyone else in the elevator with her there might have been a more thorough plan, one zigs while the other zags, but she couldn't count on Trent to follow through. As far as Maya was concerned, she'd take care of this and just hope that this idiot didn't get in the way.

According to the brief, James Smythe was a former NSA peon who had somehow fallen in with the Croatian mob. (Before today, Maya hadn't been aware that there *was* a Croatian mob, but it stood to reason that just about any country could conceivably have a mob, so why not Croatia?) Yesterday Smythe had packed a briefcase with classified US intelligence and was holed up here at the Hilton Grand awaiting a red-eye flight to Zagreb.

It was unfortunate he'd be missing his flight.

*Idiot.* What sort of aspiring criminal used such an uninspired pseudonym and stayed in the penthouse suite for only a single night? Someone like Coleman, she reasoned, who had watched too many movies. Smythe might as well have hung a bright neon sign from the balcony.

Funny, she thought, how her heart rate had jacked up. How her palms were starting to sweat. This operation was so low-threat that not even the Department of Homeland Security wanted to deal with it. Even the FBI had shrugged it off, tossed it down the ladder until the CIA junior agent program scooped it up.

"Good training," they'd called it.

"This is our stop," Coleman murmured as they reached the top floor. He reached into his jacket and pulled out the Glock 19 holstered under his shoulder.

She did the same. It felt heavy in her hand, real steel filled with real rounds that had no place in this hotel or this elevator.

The elevator doors dinged and slid open. The two of them stepped out into a contemporary foyer with long windows, lots of natural light, white walls, and a six-foot-three ape in a black jacket built like a linebacker who looked just as surprised to see them as they did to see him.

"What the f—" was all he managed before Maya launched herself forward. She took two leaping steps and jumped, wrapped an arm around his neck and using the momentum to swing herself around behind him, her legs locking around his elbows and midsection as her arms snaked around his neck in a chokehold.

There were two types of chokeholds, with slightly different arm positions; one that would cut off a person's air supply, and one that would cut off the blood supply to the brain. Maya chose the latter, not only because the victim would typically pass out quicker but also because an overzealous stranglehold could cause permanent damage to a trachea. And while she had no compassion for whoever this man was, he was merely an obstacle, and she wished him no more ill will than she might a speed bump.

It took fourteen seconds for his knees to buckle, and she set him down as gently as she could. Coleman had acted in precisely the capacity that Maya had assumed he might—which was to stand there slack-jawed as she did all the work.

"There wasn't supposed to be anyone but Smythe up here," he said at last.

"Quiet. And I know. Just stay alert. Be ready for anything. And… maybe stay behind me." She faced the door to the penthouse proper.

"Uh… yeah. Good idea."

She nodded to him and counted silently, moving her lips. *One… two… three.*

Then she kicked out a foot, striking the door just above the knob. It flew open and she was through it in an instant, tracking the barrel left to right in a quick arc as she announced loudly, "CIA! James Smythe, come out with your hands up!"

*Damn, that feels good to say.*

But she saw no movement. Coleman swept in behind her, and then moved past her to clear the kitchen and dining room.

"Clear!" he called.

She turned right, into a wide den with a flat-screen television, a mahogany coffee table, and a black leather briefcase.

"Briefcase!" she called out.

"On it." Coleman hurried past her and knelt on the floor to check the contents as Maya swept the rest of the apartment.

*Maybe he's not here?* she wondered, until she saw the closed door at the rear of the penthouse.

She put an ear to it but couldn't hear anything.

*Soundproof?* If Smythe was in there, he might not have heard them bust in.

She took a breath and kicked open the door.

"CIA!"

And she froze.

She had seen photos of James Smythe in the briefing package. He was a man as bland in appearance as anyone would expect from someone who chose to go incognito as "Jimmy Smith." He was short, a bit chubby, his boyish features only belied by the jowls in his cheeks. He wasn't anyone that anyone would look twice at if they passed him on the street.

She had seen photos of James Smythe, but presently he stood at the foot of a king-sized bed in nothing but plaid boxer shorts, his mouth agape, his body frozen. There was something in his hand—what was that?

A riding crop. He had a brown leather riding crop in his hand.

On the bed was a girl, slight-framed and small. Wearing only white cotton underwear, she looked back at her just as wide-eyed as Smythe, but her expression wasn't one of shock. It was fear.

And if this girl was a day over thirteen, Maya was next in line for the throne of England.

"Lawson, we got it." Coleman's voice drifted to her from somewhere outside her field of vision, somewhere beyond the bed and the man and the riding crop. "Did you find... oh. Damn."

In that moment, Maya forgot a lot of things. She forgot what James Smythe's offense was in the first place. She forgot why it was important that they were there at all. She even forgot about Coleman's inadequacies. She forgot anything that didn't matter.

24

But there were two things she knew. One was that she had a gun in her hands. The second was the definition of "neutralize."

*To render someone or something harmless by way of opposing force.*

"Lawson," said Coleman carefully from his far-off place, "let's just arrest him…"

*Render harmless.*

She looked down at the Glock 19 in her hands.

*By opposing force.*

James Smythe shook his head. "Please. Just not in the face…"

"Lawson, wait!" Coleman shouted.

Maya raised the gun and fired two shots. They were quick—*pop-pop*—and both center mass, right around where his heart would be if he had one.

Smythe's body flopped backward and hit the carpet hard.

"Jesus…" Coleman breathed. "Christ."

Maya holstered her gun. She held both hands up, palms out, toward the girl. "I'm not going to hurt you. You're safe now."

"I know," the girl said plainly. "Well done."

Maya frowned. "…What?"

A door opened to her right. One she hadn't even noticed was there, thanks to Smythe and his own extracurriculars. Beyond the door was another room—a dressing room or sitting room of some sort. All Maya noticed were the three people in it, all in suits.

Two of them she didn't recognize. But one she did.

"Agent Bradlee?"

Their handler at the CIA junior agent program stepped into the room, her hands clasped behind her back. Bradlee was semi-retired, her hair entirely white now and cut short, styled to one side with pomade. She had the habit of holding her chin high so that when she nodded—as she did now in Maya's direction—it was a deep nod, almost reverential.

"Lawson, Coleman. Excellent job."

Maya blinked. She was fifty percent confused, and fifty percent certain that she knew what was happening here—and that she didn't like it at all. "Ma'am?"

Bradlee prodded Smythe's body with a foot. "Come on now."

To Maya's shock, Smythe sat up, or at least halfway, propping himself on his elbows. He grimaced deeply. "I think I need… a hospital."

25

Maya could hardly believe what she was seeing. She should have noticed it sooner, when there had been no blood spray across the pristine white sheets of the bed. Neither place where she'd shot Smythe had penetrated skin; instead, they'd left large welts, already raised on his skin, a horrid red color that was spreading out from the impact site and rapidly turning purple.

They'd handed her the gun that morning at the briefing. She'd felt the weight of it in her hand as they'd said, "It's already loaded." Of course she had ejected the magazine to check for herself, and seeing it full she'd pushed it back in.

Had she inspected any of the rounds themselves she would have noticed.

"Rubber bullets," she murmured.

"Correct," Bradlee said. "There is no James Smythe, former analyst of the NSA absconding with US intelligence to Croatia."

"Thanks," said not-Smythe with a groan, "for not shooting me in the face."

This had been another exercise. Training and nothing more. They had let her believe that she had made junior agent and would be taking on her first op, only for it to be a ruse.

No; not a ruse.

"A test," she murmured.

"Indeed. And you passed," said Bradlee. "You caused an excellent distraction—no offense, Mr. Coleman—and located Smythe. You found the briefcase. And... I probably shouldn't be saying this, but I may as well. The two of you were the only team to effectively neutralize the target, despite the emotional impediment."

*Emotional impediment.* She meant the girl on the bed, too young and mostly naked. Others had come before them, others in the program, and they had failed. How had they failed? Perhaps they had demanded an explanation, or merely detained Smythe, or rushed to make sure the girl was okay first.

But not her. She had shot first with no intention of questions later. Funny—an emotional impediment, when her emotions were all that had dictated her actions.

"You wanted us to kill him?" asked Coleman behind her.

"What else would you expect 'neutralize' to mean?" Bradlee asked candidly. "You can't honestly expect us to put 'kill' in a briefing."

26

The girl rolled off the bed and stretched before pulling on a robe that hung on a hook on the back of the door. The action was so casual, but still Maya looked away.

"I know what you're thinking," said Bradlee, "but Ms. Lindt here is actually twenty-two."

*Is that supposed to make me feel better?* Maya thought bitterly. But she held her tongue as Smythe groaned in pain and muttered again his desire for a hospital.

"Of course," Bradlee replied. "In just a moment." She turned to Maya. "Congratulations, Agent Lawson."

Maya blinked. "You mean...?"

"Yes. This was your final exam. Out of fourteen candidates, two have just become junior agents." She looked past Maya to Coleman and nodded to him as well. "Welcome to the CIA."

Maya held her head high, keeping herself straight-faced as possible as she said, "Thank you, ma'am." It was as if everything that had just happened dissolved, simply faded into the background.

Because she'd done it. She was an agent now.

# CHAPTER FOUR

Zero pushed into the foyer of the one-story bungalow he now shared with four women and punched in the six-digit security code. *Four against one,* he thought with a chuckle. He'd always been outnumbered by the women in his life, ever since Kate had given birth to Maya—actually, before even then. He'd been outnumbered as soon as they'd found out that it was a girl, while Maya was still in the womb, and Kate would say things like, "I know it's two in the morning, but your daughter needs chocolate peanut butter ice cream..."

He smiled at the memory. A simpler time. But one there was no going back to. His daughters were grown; he was getting remarried, and to a woman who had adopted a brainwashed child spy.

Still, he wouldn't trade it for anything.

"Anyone home?" he called out. Maria's car was gone; she had taken Mischa school shopping today. He wondered if Maya had gone with them. It would be nice for them to spend more time together.

"Mm," came a grunt from the kitchen. He found Sara there, in pajama pants and a T-shirt, her blonde hair tousled as she slowly stirred a spoon in a cup of coffee.

Clearly, she'd just woken up.

It pained him sometimes, as she grew closer to adulthood, how much she looked like her mother. The angle of her jaw, her button of a nose, her soft blue eyes. While Maya had taken on much more of his features, Sara had Kate's genes, through and through.

He wondered then what she thought of that, when she looked in the mirror. He'd never thought to ask.

"That must be ice cold by now," he remarked, gesturing to the coffee cup.

"I'll microwave it." Sara yawned.

"Maya around?"

"No one's around. I woke up and the house was empty."

"Gotcha." Zero very much wanted to share his news of how well his appointment with Dillard had gone, but something told him that Sara wouldn't exactly jump up and down. She'd been increasingly standoffish lately, distant. He couldn't help but feel like a gap was growing between them these past few months; up until just a few weeks ago it had felt small enough to jump, but now it yawned like an impassable chasm even when she stood only a few feet from him.

*Don't push her,* he told himself. *She's been through a lot, and she needs to process it in her own time, in her own way.*

It was like someone else's voice in his head, because the next thing he knew his mouth was moving. "You got in late last night."

"Mm-hmm." Sara stuck the coffee cup in the microwave.

"...Another friend from therapy?" he prodded.

"Yup." She watched the mug make lazy circles through the glass door.

"They okay?" he asked, trying to sound empathetic and not like he was fishing for something, anything, an indication of what was going on under all that bed-head.

"No." She finally turned to face him, one hand on her hip and the other picking idly at a cuticle. "They're not okay. They're terrified every day and every night that their abuser is going to show up in their life again and do something awful to them."

Zero blinked at her candor. "And... do you feel like you're helping them?"

Sara nodded once. "I do. I make sure their abuser isn't coming."

He frowned at that. His younger daughter had seemed to find some sense of purpose in this group, these women, but at the same time he didn't like the idea of her putting herself in the path of anyone potentially dangerous.

"Long as you're staying safe," he said, for lack of anything better to say.

She smiled at him, but there was no mirth in it. "When are we ever really safe?"

The microwave beeped. Sara took her coffee out and headed for the basement. "I have to get changed, I've got a meeting in half an hour."

"Um... okay. I guess I'll see you later." But the door was already closed behind her.

Zero retreated into the living room and sank into a recliner. Was he losing her again? At fifteen, Sara had legally emancipated herself after learning not only the truth about his career, but also that her mother's death had been a murder and not a sudden stroke. At sixteen she had come back to him. And now at seventeen, he felt her slipping away anew.

He knew that the answer wasn't to tighten his grip. He'd never been all that authoritarian of a parent anyhow. He could only hope that giving her space didn't come off as apathy on his part.

A few minutes later he heard the beep of the security keypad, and then the front door opened and closed. Gone without so much as a goodbye.

Zero sighed, sinking deeper into the worn armchair and closing his eyes. *One thing at a time,* he told himself. Tomorrow was the wedding; they would all be together and happy. And then the honeymoon. And then the trip to Switzerland, where he hoped Dr. Guyer would agree with Dillard's positive prognosis.

*One thing at a time...*

His eyes snapped open as he heard the front door close. Or he thought he heard the front door close. But there were no footfalls, no warning sounds from the security system or telltale beeps of the code being entered.

"Sara?" He rose from the chair. Maybe she'd forgotten something...

But there was no one in the foyer. No one in the kitchen. The basement door was shut. Zero stood there for a long moment and just listened. There was only silence and the dim sound of his own blood rushing in his ears.

He stepped closer to the security keypad and squinted at it.

It was disabled. Why was it disabled? He'd only arrived home himself not fifteen minutes ago, and he'd punched in the code. Had Sara disabled it on her way out? Why would she do that?

And the front door was unlocked. So either Sara had disabled the alarm and left the door unlocked, or...

He pulled open the coat closet to his right. Hanging there was an old brown leather jacket that he didn't wear anymore, and in the left pocket of that jacket he kept a revolver. A small black snub-nosed .38, hammerless, loaded with six rounds. Point and shoot.

*Just hang on.* The weight of the gun in his hand made him feel ridiculous. He thought he'd heard the door close but there was no one here. He was being paranoid. He slipped the revolver back into the coat pocket and closed the closet door.

In the kitchen, Zero poured a glass of water and laughed at himself. "It's the day before your wedding," he told the glass. "You're nervous. You're high-strung. That's all."

As he brought the glass to his lips he saw the movement reflected in its side.

His heart leapt into his throat as he dropped the glass and darted left. It shattered on the floor as his assailant lurched for him and grabbed nothing but air. Zero spun and threw out an elbow, but his balance was off and the blow glanced weakly off a shoulder.

The man was large, as tall as Zero and twice as broad, wearing a ski mask and gloves but had nothing in his hands. At first this seemed foolhardy, to attack someone like Zero unarmed—but then the man grabbed his arms, just above the elbow, in a viselike grip and lifted him clear off the floor. Zero pulled his knees in, planted both feet on the larger man's hips, and pushed off as hard as he could. He felt the tight grip slip away as his body catapulted backward, landing on the small island. He rolled off of it and put it between him and the assailant.

Then he put up a hand. "Wait," he said breathlessly. "Just wait…"

Suddenly he was thrown into darkness, his breath stifled. A second man, behind him; a bag over his head. A drawstring tightened around his neck. Zero spun and swung his right arm but hit nothing. Strong hands grabbed his arm and held it still. Then another pair, the first guy, grasped at him. The two held him tightly as he shouted and writhed and was dragged across the floor. He heard the front door open, and then more dragging, and then—

*Is that beeping?*

If he wasn't mistaken, his would-be kidnappers were resetting his alarm system.

"Hang on—" he tried to say, but the hood over his head was thick, and then he was dragged again, half-stumbling as he tried to get his feet under him. A car door clicked open and he was tossed across a back seat.

At last his arms were free and he clawed at the drawstring. It was knotted at the back of his head. The engine turned over and he felt the vehicle moving. At last he clawed the bag off his head, sat upright, and sucked in a breath.

"Son of a *bitch*," he hissed at the two men in the front seat.

Todd Strickland drove—Zero was in the back seat of his Jeep—while Alan Reidigger rode shotgun, the ski mask perched on his forehead while he laughed and slapped at his knee.

"That is not funny!" Zero shouted. "I could have killed you!"

"Maybe, but worth it." Alan wiped a mirthful tear from his eye. "You should have seen your face. I can't believe you tried to tell a kidnapper to 'just wait.'" He laughed again.

Zero felt his face grow hot. "And why in the *hell* are you kidnapping me?"

"Bachelor party!" Strickland winked in the rearview.

"I told you I didn't want a bachelor party!"

"We know," said the young agent. "That's why we kidnapped you."

"I…" Zero shook his head, but now that the adrenaline of the moment was waning, he couldn't help but laugh. Not only at himself, but at the whole ridiculous situation. "I can't believe you guys. Wait—did Sara know? Was she in on it?"

"How else do you think we got in?" Reidigger tugged off the ski mask and replaced it with his frayed red trucker's cap, sweat permanently staining the brim.

Zero shook his head. Sara had intentionally disabled the alarm and left the door unlocked, knowing that her dad's two best friends were going to attempt a kidnapping.

"Betrayed by my own offspring," he muttered.

"Well, you'll be pleased to know that we didn't actually plan anything," said Reidigger.

"Except the kidnapping part," Strickland added.

"Right, except that. So where we go from here is your choice—"

"Can I choose to go home?" Zero asked.

"No," said Reidigger flatly. "Now let's see. We could hit up a strip club…"

"Absolutely not."

"A karaoke bar?" suggested Strickland.

"No way."

"We could do Vegas," said Reidigger. "I know a guy who can have us back by dawn…"

"We are *not* going to Vegas!" Zero protested.

"Then I'm out of ideas," Reidigger conceded. "What do *you* want to do on your final eve as a somewhat-eligible bachelor?"

Zero thought for a moment. "Honestly?"

"All right, I'll give it to you," said Reidigger with a sigh as he kicked his feet up on top of the cooler. "This was a good idea."

Forty minutes later, the three of them sat in an open garage bay at Third Street Garage, reclining in lawn chairs Alan had pulled out, enjoying the late August sun with a cooler of domestic beer between them and two large pizzas on the way.

"For what it's worth," Strickland noted, "I was against the strip club idea too."

Zero laughed. What a strange trio they made; Todd Strickland the clean-cut, thirty-one-year-old former Army Ranger; Alan Reidigger, the burly and bushy-bearded operative who'd spent more than two years of his life incognito as a mechanic called Mitch. And him, Zero, a former professor of European history who had tried (and failed) to erase his memory as a CIA agent.

He thought of Sara and her group, and smirked to himself as he realized that the three of them, they were like their own little trauma support group. And they'd all had more than their fair share of it.

"To Zero." Alan held up his beer can in a toast. "And to Maria. May your union be blessed with half a dozen babies, not half as screwed up as the ones you've already got."

Zero snorted at that.

Strickland raised his can. "To Zero and Maria."

He raised his own drink. "To Chip."

Neither of the other two moved. They sat there, the three of them, staring at the oil-stained concrete floor of the garage for a long moment, no doubt all replaying the scene in their heads.

Not six months earlier, the newest member of EOT, Chip Foxworth, had taken a bullet that was intended for Zero.

"Yeah," said Strickland quietly. "To Chip."

He deserved to be there tomorrow. He deserved to have gone home that day with the rest of the team. He hadn't deserved to die in a desert with his last words still lingering on his lips: *I'm Agent Zero.*

"To Foxworth," said Reidigger. "He was the best of us."

At the wedding tomorrow, there would be an empty chair for Chip. If it was up to Zero, there'd be more than one.

Strickland and Reidigger tilted the cans to their lips and drank, but Zero held his just a little longer.

*To Shawn Cartwright.*

*To Karina Pavlo.*

*To Seth Connors.*

And then he drank, to everyone who should have still been there but wasn't, while he was starting a new chapter of his life.

For some reason, the last thing he'd said to Guyer flashed through his mind: *Pending disaster, of course*

.

# CHAPTER FIVE

A part of Sara wished she had stuck around long enough to watch Alan and Todd try to kidnap her dad as she pedaled her bike across town. The plan itself sounded funny as hell, but she could think of a hundred ways it could go sideways, any one of which she would have loved to see unfold for herself. But she had work to do.

Sara steered into the parking lot of a gas station with an attached convenience store, and she slowed her bike. Just outside the glass storefront she stopped, staying on her bike, putting one foot down instead of the kickstand, and stared through the glass. Inside, a woman bought two sodas from the dead-eyed clerk behind the counter, a twenty-eight-year-old man, Sara knew, named Craig.

The woman paid, and Craig handed her the change, and the woman left. As she pushed out of the doors the clerk glanced up after her, and then he saw Sara, and his flat gaze went wide.

His right eye was still blackened, bruised to a dark shade of purple. Sara flashed him the slightest of smirks, and then she pushed off again, pedaling out of the lot and on her way.

She wanted to see him—but more importantly, she wanted him to see *her*. To know that she was still watching.

She had told her dad she was going to a meeting. But there was no meeting for her, and there likely wouldn't be ever again. Sara couldn't show her face at Common Bonds anymore, the therapy group for women who had endured trauma from a variety of sources. Because despite the variety, the source was almost always a man, and somehow those men kept getting hurt lately, and the ones who saw her face—and the ones who could still talk afterwards—started describing a petite blonde girl. It was getting too easy for anyone who knew her to trace the deeds back to the quiet girl who never shared in group.

So two weeks ago she had called it quits on Common Bonds, and was forced to find other means by which to find her prey. And after just a cursory amount of searching, she'd nearly smacked herself in the head for not thinking of it sooner.

35

Arrest records were public information, published to an online database after processing. But not all arrests led to jail time, especially if their offense couldn't be proven in court. Realizing this gave her no shortage of options. It was outright incredible—and equally infuriating—how many men accused of abuse, or harassment, or stalking, or even rape were able to get off the hook for a lack of evidence or testimony that couldn't be proven.

It wasn't just a treasure trove; it was a dragon's hoard. So much so that Sara had to choose them carefully, be very discerning in whom she picked and how she went about it. Getting a last-known address was easy enough, but she had to make sure she had the right guy. Know what he looked like, what kind of car he drove, where he worked, what hours he kept, who he lived with. And then—figure out how she was going to strike.

Just last night she had visited one of those men. A guy by the name of Javier Gutierrez who lived in an apartment in the suburbs of Annandale, a twenty-minute Uber ride from her own home. Javier had been accused of stalking his sixteen-year-old neighbor, had even shown up at the girl's school and tried to coax her into his car.

He'd been arrested, he'd been warned, he'd been released. There was even a restraining order, but what good was that? He lived next door to the girl—shared a wall with her, for Christ's sake.

So Sara had paid him a little visit. She'd waited until the lights went out in his apartment and then she'd waited a little longer. Eventually she'd rung his doorbell. She had done enough snooping to know that his building didn't have security cameras and that no one on his floor would be awake at that hour.

When Javier had answered the door, rubbing sleep from his eyes, Sara had kneecapped him with a tire iron. It was often her weapon of choice, thin and easy to swing while still having some weight behind it.

She figured she had thirty seconds, maybe less, of Javier's pained howling before she'd be spotted, so she quickly made it clear why she was there and what Javier would stop doing. Between his sobs, she managed to get a choked "okay" out of him before hightailing it out of there.

Maybe he called the cops. Or maybe someone else in the building did. But she wasn't worried. What was he going to say? "Yes, Officer, like I said, it was a blonde teenage girl with a tire iron. Why yes, I am

36

that gentleman who was arrested three weeks ago for stalking my teenage neighbor. Do you think they're somehow related?"

She chuckled at the thought.

The act itself was a rush like none other. It was better than any high she'd gotten from any drug or pill. And she was addicted.

But she was not out to hurt anyone today. For one, it was broad daylight, and she made sure to strike at night when it would be harder for anyone to get a good look at her or follow her. And secondly, she hadn't done enough research on any recent marks to do it today.

Instead she was making her rounds. That's what she called them in her head, her "rounds," like a doctor checking in on their patients. But she checked in on her victims. She rode her bike slowly past their houses. If they worked in a public place, she visited it. The purpose was for her to see them, but sometimes they saw her too—and if they did, it was incredibly satisfying to see the look on their faces. When they saw her but could do nothing about it. When they knew that she hadn't vanished but was still around, still watching.

Today was a little different, though. Today there was a small detour to take. She hadn't been entirely lying to her dad; there really was a meeting, even if she wouldn't be attending. But ever since she'd stopped going to Common Bonds, she still liked to stop by now and then. She'd get there just as the meeting would be getting out. She'd look for new faces, and she'd see if the familiar ones were still coming. If they weren't, she would follow up with them on social media, to make sure they were alive and hopefully thriving. It helped her think that what she was doing was working, even if that wasn't always necessarily true.

But today as she pedaled her bike toward the community center, she noticed there were a lot fewer cars around than usual. Almost none, in fact. Sara frowned and pedaled right up to the double glass doors, affixed to which was a small sheet of paper with a few large printed words: CLOSED FOR FUMIGATION.

"Lice outbreak," said a female voice behind her.

Sara turned to see a tall, slender blonde woman walking toward her. Maddie—the organizer and coordinator of Common Bonds. She was some sort of strange hybrid, part model and part soccer mom and part therapist. She had eyes that looked like she was smiling even when her mouth wasn't. Her makeup was always so perfectly blended it was hard to believe she was wearing any at all. She was the kind of woman that most women would think they could talk to easily, which just made her all the more difficult for Sara to talk to.

How many times had Maddie asked Sara if she'd like to share in group? Too many.

"One of the summer day-care kids brought it in a couple of days ago," Maddie continued. "They're spraying the whole place, just to be safe."

"Good thing you didn't catch it," Sara remarked. "It'd be a shame to have to shave all that perfect hair."

Maddie smiled at that.

"If it's closed, why are you here?" Sara asked.

"Looking for you, actually."

She frowned. "How'd you know I'd be here?"

Maddie's smile didn't waver. "At the end of every meeting I watch from the window to make sure the ladies get to their cars safely. After you stopped coming to group, every now and then I'd glance out the window and see you out there, at the edge of the parking lot on your bike. I was hoping you would show up today. So we could talk."

Sara resisted the urge to roll her eyes. "Talk about what? My feelings?"

"No. The men you're hurting."

*Oh, shit.* Sara's jaw clenched. Her first instinct was to run, to jump on her bike and pedal away from there as fast as she could. But another part of her was curious; Maddie clearly wasn't an airhead, and Sara wanted to know just how much the Queen of Soccer Moms had put together.

"Don't know what you're talking about," Sara said as casually as she could.

"Mm," Maddie said in reply. "So you don't know who Roger Black is?"

Roger—that was a special night. That was the night that Sara realized how well her fighting lessons with Mischa had been paying off. Roger had caught her vandalizing his house in the middle of the night and made a grab for her, and Sara had shoulder-flipped him through a glass table without thinking twice.

"'Fraid not," Sara said with a shrug.

"Huh. And I'm guessing you've never heard of Gavin Douglas either?"

38

Sara bit the inside of her cheek to keep from smirking instinctively. Gavin was another feather in her cap, a serial girlfriend-beater who worked second-shift packing boxes at a warehouse. Sara had confronted him in the parking lot at his job one night, near his car, and Gavin thought a perfectly reasonable reaction would be to throw a punch. Sara had ducked it—or mostly, his knuckles had just barely grazed her cheek—and responded by breaking his arm at the elbow.

"Sorry, who?"

Maddie sighed. "I'm not an idiot, Sara. The girls talk. And after the fourth or fifth story of an ex or a dealer ending up in the hospital, I started looking around. And do you know who I ended up looking at?"

Sara clucked her tongue. "The troubled teen who never talks in group? Careful, Maddie, sounds like you're stereotyping."

The older woman scoffed. Some part of Sara admired her for figuring it out; another part of her enjoyed seeing something resembling frustration on her face.

"Look," she said, "all I'm going to say is that if it *was* you doing this, you need to stop."

"Sorry?" Sara felt a flame light in her chest, a sudden warm sensation that fueled the conviction in her voice. "I *need* to? You don't know a thing about what I need. You're not my mother. My mother is dead. She was murdered on the street by someone my family was supposed to be able to trust."

Maddie's mouth fell open a little. Her eyes were no longer smiling. "I… didn't know that."

"No. You didn't." The flame roared larger, warming her neck, her face. "You always wanted me to share, right? Okay. I'll share. I'm a recovered drug addict who left home at fifteen. I used to run drugs for a guy before I stole his stash and OD'd so hard I almost died. You want to know more? See this?" She turned her arm over so that Maddie could see the two small round scars just above her elbow. "That's where doctors put pins in my arm after I broke it. See, me and my sister were trafficked, and to get away I jumped off of a moving train. Do you want to know more, Maddie? Because believe me, there's more."

Sara was inches from the woman's face now, hadn't even realized that she had stepped up to her until all she could see in her field of vision was Maddie's horrified expression. She'd said too much; revealed too much about herself to someone she didn't even really know.

She backed off and looked away.

"Is that…" Maddie said after a long moment. "Is all that true?"

"Does it matter?" Sara muttered.

"Of course it does. If it is, you should be seeking help—real help, more than I or Common Bonds could give you—"

"Help." Sara scoffed. "What would you know about 'real' help? What's the worst thing that's happened to you, breaking a nail? Soccer practice runs late? How come *you* never share, Maddie?"

The woman looked down at her designer flats. "You're right. I don't share. Nothing bad has really happened to me. Except the one." She drew a long breath. "I had a sister. A few years younger than me, and just… the *total* opposite. She just wanted to have fun. Fell in with the wrong crowd. Always with a not-so-great guy. And even though we were so different, I was always the one she felt she could talk to. Not the police, or our parents. Me. And she did have fun… until she didn't anymore."

Maddie looked up and met Sara's gaze. "After she passed, I formed Common Bonds to help women like her. I figured if I was good enough for her to talk to, maybe I could be for others too." She chuckled. "And it's just crazy how much you remind me of her."

Sara's nostrils flared. Was that supposed to sway her, some sob story about losing someone? Someone needed to lay off the Lifetime channel.

"I'm not your dead sister."

"No," Maddie agreed quietly. "You're not. But it's not too late for you to turn right where she turned left."

Sara said nothing to that. She wanted this to be done, to get back on her bike and away from there and lice and Maddie's eyes.

"I've said what I came here to say," Maddie said at last. "So… where do we go from here? What am I supposed to do with what I know?"

To Sara, it sounded like a threat. Her first instinct was to snap back. *Keep it to yourself if you know what's good for you.*

But no. She wouldn't hurt Maddie, so she wouldn't threaten her either. A threat was like a loaded gun; you didn't point it at someone unless you were planning to use it.

"You do whatever you think is best."

Maddie nodded. "I just don't want to see you get hurt. I don't want to see anyone get hurt."

Sara scoffed at that. What an empty, saccharine sentiment. People got hurt every day; there was no stopping it. All she was trying to do was make sure the right people got hurt and didn't hurt anyone else.

This conversation was over. She wasn't going to convince Maddie to see things her way any more than Maddie's dead-sister story would change her mind. Sara swung one leg over her bike and planted a foot on the pedal. She had her rounds to make.

"You don't want to see anyone get hurt? Must be nice to have that choice. All you have to do is look the other way."

# CHAPTER SIX

Bill McMahon had always considered himself a simple sort of fellow. He took pride and pleasure in the little things. Stripping and refinishing the pair of rocking chairs on the front porch. Talking to his grandkids on the phone, now well into adulthood, and even the great-grandkids, of which there were two so far and hopefully more on the way. The start of the NCAA football season; go Mountaineers.

Or the taste of a good bourbon on the back of his throat on a late-August evening as he stood on the deck of his home in Six Springs, West Virginia, not two hours from D.C. as the crow flies but so much a world apart. He had twenty-five acres here, mostly field, a stretch of woods, the house he'd had built to spec fifteen years ago. He had met Gwen here in this town, had started his political career here; it only made sense that they would retire here and, if he had his way, die here someday.

Gwen. What an incredible woman she was. Seventy-nine years young and still ever the butterfly, flitting from charity auction to tea with the Ladies' Auxiliary to volunteering at hospice without needing a break. He was amazed by her daily, as the aches crept into his old bones and getting out of bed each morning got a little tougher.

Still, her absence afforded him an occasional sin, since he was not, in fact, supposed to be drinking bourbon. At least that's what the doctors said. But what did they know? That was just a recommendation based on his age. He was a very healthy eighty-four, all things considered, and still quite capable for such a ripe old coot.

About a hundred and fifty yards out he saw Sadie and Bruce tearing across the field, chasing each other. Those dogs practically lived outside these days, except on the coldest of nights. They slept in the shed and caused mischief all over the property, coming in now and then for chow and ear scratches. They'd been a gift, those two rascals, from Gwen for their fiftieth wedding anniversary four years ago. She had a wicked sense of humor—since gold was the preferred anniversary gift for a fiftieth, she had gotten him two golden retrievers.

Bill stuck two fingers in his mouth and blasted out a long, sharp whistle. "I'm locking up, you two! Come on in, or you'll be sleeping in the shed!"

He heard a playful yip in the distance, and a flash of cream-colored fur dashing for the tree line. That would be Sadie, the fairer-haired of the two, and a few seconds later Bruce trotted along after her, his golden fur shining in the setting sunlight.

Bill chuckled. "All right then, you feral mutts. Go chase some squirrels." He headed inside, slid the glass door closed, and locked it behind him. "I really shouldn't," he told his empty glass, and then went into the kitchen for an ice cube and two more fingers of Jim Beam.

He had always considered himself a simple sort of fellow, who took pleasure in the little things. Former president or not, he didn't need any fancy, expensive liquor when the good stuff came cheap.

The sharp clack of billiard balls rang from the rec room, and then a groan of disappointment. Bill grinned; Tony was awful at breaking, and always managed to blame the table, the cue, the chalk, or anything under the sun except how bad he was at the game.

"Hey now, Bill," said Jim as Bill entered the rec room.

"Boys." Bill sank into a recliner in one corner. The rec room was practically where the boys lived these days, when they were here in Six Springs. Jim leaned against one end of the pool table while Tony lined up a shot on the opposite side.

"Watch this," Tony announced. "Three ball, corner pocket."

Jim scoffed. "Yeah, yeah, I'm watching."

Tony took the shot; the cue ball bounced off the rail, missed the three ball entirely, and sank into the opposite corner. A scratch.

Jim laughed and slapped the table. "Should have put money on that."

Tony grunted. "It's the table. Balls aren't shooting straight. You saw it."

"I just re-felted that table myself last month," said Bill teasingly. "Did I do it wrong, Tony?"

"Course not, Bill," he muttered. "Jim was leaning on it. I bet that was the problem…"

Tony and Jim were good guys—"the boys," as Bill liked to call them. Secret Service agents usually had a shelf life of about twenty years max, if that, so it wasn't all that strange that these two were semi-retired in their early fifties. They could have taken the pension and settled down, but neither wanted to call it quits just yet, which was how they came to be Bill McMahon's personal security in his golden years.

It was, to him, a little amusing to even think that he needed security. He hadn't been president for thirty years now. His time in the White House felt like a lifetime ago. Hell—neither of the boys were even old enough to vote when he took office.

But he liked having them around. Since Gwen kept busy and his no-good dogs were fond of abandoning him in favor of romping through the trees and digging up gophers, it was nice to have the boys and their constant chatter filling his home. Funny, in the beginning they were Agent Kopchak and Agent Sloan, and wore ties and black blazers and carried their guns in hidden holsters and called him "Mr. President." Now he was just Bill, and they spent most of their days shooting pool, watching whatever sporting event was on, bumming about in denim and flannel, and getting love handles off of Gwen's country-style gravy and biscuits.

At least that's how they conducted themselves when in Six Springs. When they were out there, out in the world, the blazers and ties were back and they were all business. Professionals, these two were—but chummy and casual behind closed doors.

"Busy day tomorrow, Bill," Tony noted as Jim lined up his shot and sank it easily.

"Busy week," Bill replied. "Enjoy it, boys; this is your last evening of beer and billiards for a little while." Tomorrow they would be embarking on an eight-day circuit, starting with a press conference in D.C., then on to Baltimore for a speaking engagement, and up to New York to appear on a morning show. From there they'd be flying west, out to Michigan, to lend their efforts to Bill's favorite charity, the Home Again Foundation, which built houses for the homeless out of recycled construction materials. They'd be there for three days; Bill had never been a photo-op kind of guy and he wasn't about to start now. He liked to put the work in, and to work with his hands while he was still able to. Tony and Jim would be there, griping and ribbing each other the whole time, but working right alongside him.

Bill hadn't been this active in the public spotlight since he left office. But these last several months had seen significant change, brought about by the man currently sitting behind the Resolute Desk, President Jonathan Rutledge.

44

Rutledge had, at first, seemed a bit timid to Bill. After all, the man had never even run for the seat; he'd been promoted from Speaker of the House straight to the top rung when his predecessors were impeached. But after a period of acclimation, Rutledge started to show some real spine. He appointed a brilliant young woman as his VP, and he set about keeping the promise that he had made to bring peace to the Middle East.

What he had achieved so far was staggeringly impressive, and while Bill had once promised himself that he wouldn't get back involved in politics, he couldn't very well keep silent. After an all-night discussion with Gwen, he decided to publicly lend his support to Rutledge and his efforts in whatever way he could.

Bill McMahon didn't have a publicist, but he didn't think he needed one. He could handle his own appointments—or so he had thought. Shortly after a phone call with the White House to announce that he would be making himself available, his own phone started ringing off the hook with requests for appearances. Tony had become an unwilling receptionist of sorts when Bill simply couldn't tolerate the sound of a ringing phone any longer.

After their stretch with Home Again, Bill and the boys would be flying to California for four more press appearances. The thought of spending three days building houses outdoors was invigorating; the thought of spending three more days wearing a tie and talking to pundits sounded exhausting.

Jim lined up a shot carefully, but failed to sink the twelve. "Bill, you want winner?"

"Much as I'd love to," said Bill, "the game's starting soon. We're playing Texas Tech, I think. Besides, I don't think either of you boys needs to be embarrassed by an old man."

Jim laughed as Tony staked a claim on the seven. "Watch this now, Jim, you're about to get an education…" He drew back the cue stick, gave it a couple of slow practice strokes—

And the lights went out.

"Dammit!" Tony hissed as he miscued, the white ball merely spinning in place. "Not fair, I should get another shot!"

"What's that about?" Jim frowned.

Bill rose slowly and craned his neck. He couldn't hear the refrigerator running, or the hum of the air conditioning unit. It wasn't just the lights.

"Power outage. Nothing to worry about, boys. I'm sure it'll be back up in a few minutes, but if not we can power up the genny. Can't have the freezer spoil—"

From elsewhere in the house, a window shattered. Bill froze—*did a storm whip up suddenly?* was his first thought—but the two other men turned instantly into professionals.

In two long strides Jim was at the mini-bar, behind which was a Sig Sauer P229, loaded with .357 rounds, and a twelve-gauge Remington shotgun. Tony went to the door of the rec room, keeping his body out of sight as he silently but quickly closed it.

Jim tossed him the shotgun and Tony caught it deftly, racking a round into the chamber. "Stay with him," Jim ordered. "Get out the back door if you need to."

Tony retreated, walked backward until he was positioned directly in front of Bill. "Stay behind me, Mr. President," he said in a solemn whisper as he brought the shotgun to his shoulder and aimed it at the door.

Jim's white teeth flashed in the darkness as he counted softly. "One... two... three." On three he yanked the door open and raised the pistol.

*Bang!*

A single shot rang out, impossibly loud in the otherwise silent house.

Jim's head jerked backward, and his body followed. Dark blood spattered against the far wall, across the felt of the pool table, almost black in the darkness.

Bill's stomach turned. What was happening? *Was* this really happening? A minute ago they'd been laughing and shooting pool. And now...

Tony kept his composure perfectly. He didn't jump at the sound of the gunshot or budge as Jim's body fell. Instead he aimed the Remington squarely at the open door, waiting for the moment. "Back door, Bill," he said quietly. "Check it first. If there's no movement, I want you to—"

Something came through the door. Not a body, but an object, something small and round that clattered across the floor.

"Grenade!" Tony dropped the shotgun and wrapped both arms around Bill. Before he knew what was happening, the larger man was pulling him down, covering him with his own body. Bill barely had

46

time to process the word, let alone realize that this man was willing to give his life for him, to sacrifice himself, and was about to be shredded by an explosive that had been tossed into his rec room…

But no explosion came. Five seconds went by, and then seven, and nothing happened. At last, after what felt like a minor eternity, Tony pushed his weight off of Bill.

"A dud." He let out a sigh of relief as he reached for the shotgun again. "It was a dud—"

A second shot hit Tony in the side of the head, and he fell dead in an instant.

*Tony.*

*Jim.*

Bill's hands shook. When he looked up again, he saw he was not alone in the room; five others had entered. Four of them were dark-skinned men with beards and wraps around their heads in a fashion that told him they were Muslim.

The fifth was Caucasian, his face scarred, wearing tactical gear and a lopsided smirk and carrying a pistol, no doubt the pistol that had ended the boys' lives.

"Not a dud," said the white man. "A prop. Comes in handy for distractions."

"You sons of bitches," Bill murmured. His hands shook, but not from fear. From anger—an anger unlike he'd had reason to feel for years, an anger that he felt bubbling up in his chest, consuming him totally.

"Yeah," the man sighed dismissively. "On your feet, Bill."

He complied; not because the man had told him to, but because if he was going to die, it was going to be on his feet. He stood, refusing to look down at the mess that was now Tony's head, and he faced the five armed assailants.

"Take him," said the commando.

The four Islamic men advanced. One of them pulled a pair of handcuffs from his belt.

They didn't mean to kill him. They meant to kidnap him.

The one with the handcuffs grabbed Bill's arm roughly. He responded by shaking off the grip and cutting across the guy's chin with his other fist. The shock of the impact sent pain shooting through his hand and up his arm, but it was worth it.

Bill was old, but he was far from helpless.

47

The man snarled at him, blood eking from his lips, and then there was a gun in Bill's face as the man spat something vitriolic in a language he didn't understand.

"Hey!" shouted the commando. "Alive, remember? We need him alive."

Bill stared down the barrel. His gaze met the eyes of the man pointing it at him. This man, Bill could tell, had killed before and would do it again. But not today. He was under orders… from this American, somehow.

Finally the man lowered the gun, and two others grabbed Bill roughly. He squirmed and fought and protested, but they were younger, stronger than he was, and after several seconds of expletives and writhing about, the handcuffs clicked around his wrists.

The commando grinned. "Not your first time with a gun in your face, huh, Bill?"

Bill stared back at him. "Not my first time being kidnapped, either. Though it is my first time by an American. Is that Oklahoma I hear?"

The commando grinned wider. "Good ear. Let's go." He led the way, two following him, stepping over Jim's body, and the other two half-dragging Bill along. His feet brushed against Jim's boot.

*You deserved better, my friend.*

They dragged him out of the rec room, right out the front door, and into the back seat of one of two waiting SUVs, where he was flanked by two of the Islamic guys. The American commando rode in the front passenger seat.

"What'd I tell you fellas, huh?" he laughed. "Easy-peasy."

Tires squealed and the two SUVs raced down the long driveway. Bill thought he heard a familiar sound, and he twisted just enough in his seat to see two shapes in the dim red glow of the taillights. It was Bruce and Sadie, barking and chasing the SUV that held their master. But they couldn't keep up, and soon the dogs vanished from sight.

They were good dogs. Loyal. But they couldn't save him from whatever fate these men had in store for Bill McMahon.

# CHAPTER SEVEN

"Okay." Maria stood in front of the full-length mirror. "Okay." She turned sideways and inspected her profile. "…Okay."

"Sorry, what was that last part? Didn't catch that," Sara said with a smirk, leaning against the doorframe of the master bedroom. "Little nervous?"

"Little bit, maybe." Maria turned—and she did a double-take. "Wow. Sara… you look amazing."

The girl just shrugged, but the thin smile on her lips said that she knew it too. She wore the powder-blue dress that Maria had chosen for the girls—her bridal party—to wear, a simple number with a skirt just past the knees and an appropriately conservative halter neck. Her blonde hair was up in small ringlets, perfectly framing her face. And while she'd gone just a *little* heavy on the eye shadow, the look was a far cry from the sweatpants, tousled hair, and raccoon eyes that Maria was used to seeing on her.

"You don't look so bad yourself," Sara remarked.

"Thank you," she murmured. Her dress was simple enough—a white satin off-the-shoulder A-line gown, no lace or beadwork, just smooth fabric. Her own blonde hair was thick and tended to be unruly when shoehorned into any style other than a ponytail, so Maria opted to let it hang down, cascading around her shoulders the way that Zero had so often mentioned he liked.

In less than an hour, she was getting married. This was happening. She looked at herself once more in the mirror, and this time she nodded at her reflection. "Okay."

"Okay," Sara parroted. "We should get going soon—"

"Wait." Maria turned to her again. "Before we go, I just wanted to say, um… thank you. Not just for the compliment. For everything… you know? For… letting me in."

She was babbling. Hadn't she rehearsed this over and over in her head? And now it was all falling to pieces.

Sara held up a hand. "Yeah, no problem. Don't get all sappy on me or your mascara will run." She turned away from the doorway and

49

added, "And maybe don't thank me just yet. You haven't seen your daughter."

"What?" Maria frowned. "Sara? What does that mean?" She hurried to the doorway, but Sara was already gone. "Mischa?" She turned the corner to Mischa's room. "Are you in here?"

"Yes?" The girl was sitting on her bed, though she stood at the urgency in Maria's voice.

"Oh my god." Her hand flew over her mouth, and she told herself not to cry. Sara was right; it would ruin her mascara. "Did you let Sara put makeup on you?"

"Yes," the girl admitted. "She told me it was necessary. Is that all right?"

"It's… yes." Mischa wore a miniature version of the same blue dress Sara wore, and her hair was in a tight, neat bun atop her head. On her cheeks was just a little bit of blush, and thankfully Sara had been much more conservative on the eye shadow than on herself, but the effect was staggering; it added contour and angles to Mischa's usually cherubic face that made her look all the more like the young woman she was quickly becoming than the child that Maria saw her as.

"It's perfect," Maria said. "You look stunning."

"Thank you." Mischa looked down at the dress. "This is certainly the nicest thing I have ever worn. It's not exactly functional, but it is surprisingly comfortable."

Maria laughed. "I'm glad. And I'm going to hug you now." She wrapped her arms around the girl, and felt small hands on the small of her back.

"I quite like your dress as well. I once saw a picture in a book, a portrait of a princess. You look just like that today."

*Oh, dammit.* Now the tears came; she could feel them brimming, so she pulled away from the hug before they could spill over. "I have to go fix my makeup," she said breathlessly, and she hurried back to the bedroom to dab at her eyes with a tissue.

Funny how such a strange, even offhand comment could send her over that emotional edge. Funny that it came from someone who, only a few months ago, could barely understand the concept of hugging and had the emotional range of a carrot.

*Funny,* she thought, *that it takes such a screwed-up little family to realize just how perfect everything is.* And today, everything was perfect. It would be perfect.

"Knock knock," said Maya as she entered the bedroom with a small spray bottle. Maya being Maya, she'd been dressed for two hours, her short brown hair straightened, marching about the house reminding everyone of the itinerary she'd written up, which included specific wake-up times, check-in intervals, dress and hair inspections, and departure time. "We have to leave in eighteen minutes. Close your eyes, let me spray this on your face."

Maria frowned. "What is it?"

"Setting spray. It'll keep the makeup in place. I picked some up the other day assuming at some point you'd become a sobbing mess. I just didn't think it would be this early. Close, please."

Maria obliged, and Maya lightly misted her face with the spray. "*Et voila.* Perfect."

They stood there for a long moment, facing each other, Maria sitting and Maya standing. Just like with Sara, she found the words she'd rehearsed failing, evaporating in her mind like wisps of smoke, here one second and gone the next.

*Screw it. Just wing it.*

She took both of Maya's hands in her own. "Maya... there's something I need to say. It's been on my mind for a long time now, and if I don't say it now I might never—"

"Wait," Maya interrupted gently. "I know what you want to say, and honestly... we don't need to do that. I know you're not trying to replace my mother. I know you love my dad. You've never put any undue pressure on me or Sara to do or be anything other than what we are. I already know all of that."

Maria smiled; that was part of it, to be sure, but not the whole thing. "Thank you. But there's something else. I... I realized that back when your dad proposed to me, I said yes right away. I should have talked to you first. Gotten your blessing. I'm sorry I didn't."

"Are you asking me now?"

Maria smiled. "I guess I am."

"Hmm. Wow. Big moment." Maya's head pendulumed left and right in faux deliberation. "First, what exactly are your intentions with my father?"

Maria laughed. "You Lawson girls are trouble."

"Yeah, well, you're about to be one of us."

Her smile faded. "You should know I'm not changing my name." Maya just shrugged. "That's up to you. All the same—you're about to be one of us."

Maria squeezed Maya's hands and tested the limits of the setting spray, dabbing at her eye with a tissue. No mascara lifted off with it; that was good.

Maya inspected her printed itinerary. Then her eyes went wide. "Oh... *shit*."

"What?"

"Uh... I made a typo," Maya said gravely. "We have to go. Right now."

Maria blinked. "Right now?"

"Yes, right now!" Maya hurried out of the bedroom as fast as she could, teetering in her white pumps. "Sara, Mischa! It's go-time! Time to get married!"

# CHAPTER EIGHT

President Jonathan Rutledge drummed his fingers atop the Resolute Desk in the Oval Office. It was the only sound in the room, but he was not alone.

Sometimes... sometimes this job was worth it. Other times, perhaps even most of the time, it aged him years with each day.

Opposite him sat his Chief of Staff, Tabitha Halpern. She'd been doing something different with her auburn hair, which was usually styled in a bob. Growing it out, it seemed. It was a good look for her. Tabby didn't meet his gaze, not because she was afraid to—she had never been afraid to speak her mind or even butt heads on occasion if the situation called for it—but because she knew that this was a pain point for him.

Was he showing pain in his eyes? He certainly felt it.

"But why?" he asked at last.

"We just don't know yet, sir."

Rutledge rubbed his temples. What terrible news to wake up to. Even worse that he had to wake up to it, and that he had not been woken for it because it hadn't been deemed a situation worthy of waking the president.

"Tell me again."

Tabby pursed her lips. She'd already been through it twice, but still she read from the report in her hands. "At some time between seven thirty and nine p.m. last night, armed assailants cut the power to former president McMahon's West Virginia home. They gained entry through a broken window. His security detail, Agents Anthony Kopchak and James Sloan, were both found armed, but dead. Single gunshots to the head." She lowered the report slightly and added, "They didn't suffer."

"And Bill was gone."

She nodded. "We rushed forensics. None of the blood on the scene belonged to him. It was all..."

"The agents'. I get it."

"Right. Their protocol dictated a check-in to HQ every twelve hours; it would have been due by nine p.m. but the call never came. Police were dispatched and arrived at the house only minutes before…"

"Oh, god. Gwen." Rutledge shook his head. That poor woman… to arrive home to that scene. "Is she all right?"

"No, sir," Tabby said candidly, "I'm told she's not. But her daughter came to get her from Virginia, and three agents have been assigned to her. So she's at least safe."

*We thought Bill was safe too,* Rutledge thought.

"I just don't understand," he said. "Bill was—"

*Not was.*

"Bill *is* such a sweet man. A gentleman. Any feuds he might have had are decades old by now. Who would want to do this?"

"We don't know, sir. But the FBI and Secret Service are both working diligently to find him."

He appreciated that she spoke like Bill was still alive. He must be, Rutledge reasoned. Why else would these people go through the trouble of kidnapping him when they could have killed him right there, like they did the two agents?

"He was coming to Washington today."

"I know, Jon."

"We were supposed to have lunch." Rutledge sighed. "Tabby, tell me the truth. Is there any hearsay or theories of political motivation behind this? It can't be a coincidence he was supposed to be here today. With me."

"Nothing suggests that. But… it's not out of the realm of possibility. No one has yet come forward to claim responsibility or make any demands, either. The media has the story, of course, and they'll say what they will. But right now? We simply don't know, and conjecture won't help the situation any."

"You're right," he conceded. Of course she was right. But that wasn't going to stop the thoughts swimming through his head. Bill had been a huge proponent of his these last few months, going on talk shows and battling the talking heads in his honest, southern way.

There were a lot of people out there who still felt a different way about what Rutledge was doing. There was still a lot of unease; 9/11, the War on Terror, and the ensuing wave of Islamophobia weren't all *that* long ago, after all.

"If you're really that concerned," Tabby said, "you know there are others you can bring in on this."

True. He knew without saying that she meant EOT, the Executive Operations Team led by Agents Johansson and Zero. They'd saved his life back in March, had run down his own kidnappers to the end of the earth to get him back.

Remembering that experience made his heart break all over again for Bill, so much so that he almost reached for the phone. But no; today was Zero's wedding day. He knew that because he'd been invited. It was, of course, a token invitation; they knew that he wouldn't attend, and he knew that he couldn't. They wanted a small, private affair, and nothing the President of the United States attended was small or private.

"Let the FBI and Secret Service do their jobs," Rutledge told her. "I have every faith in them. And like you said—there's no reason to believe this is political just yet. No reason to sound the alarm any more than it has been."

She nodded. "Yes, sir." It seemed like meeting adjourned, but Tabby hesitated. "Would you like me to sit with you for a little while?"

He smiled. "Thanks. But no, I'll be all right. There are other things to attend to, after all. I want to be kept up to date on everything though."

"Of course, Mr. President." She rose and hastily made her way out of the Oval Office.

Rutledge loosened his tie and eased back in the chair. Bill McMahon was out there somewhere, in the hands of captors who had proven they would kill for their quarry. He knew firsthand what that was like. Harrowing. Life-altering. Even months later he sometimes woke in a cold sweat, at least once a week, in fact, jolted out of a nightmare about his time in captivity.

And that was just what it was like for one man... but what of the nation?

Bill was a beloved former president. Probably more so now than when he held office. If he was found dead... Rutledge didn't want to think about that. The blow would be a lot for America to handle. And depending on the perpetrators, could be extremely divisive for an already divided country.

\*

55

Bill McMahon had no idea where he was.

After handcuffing and shoving him into the back of the SUV, they drove for two hours, maybe a little more. It was hard to tell; there was no clock on the dashboard and he wasn't wearing his watch. His phone had been on the deck when he'd been taken; he forgot to bring it in with him, thanks to Jim Beam.

He thought of Bruce and Sadie, and their desperate bid to chase down the car that had taken him, their shapes fading in the red taillights. He hoped they were all right.

Few words were spoken between his captors. Occasionally there was a terse exchange in what he figured was Arabic, in which the Oklahoman commando seemed to be fluent.

After a while his wrists became sore, handcuffed behind him as they were, and his legs began to cramp. Bill had never really been one to sit still for long, and in his old age the aches just set in quicker. He dared to speak, if for no other reason than to distract himself from the growing pain in his limbs.

"I wonder," he said, "what would make someone so desperate as to betray their country like this."

The man to his left snarled something foreign at him, which he assumed was some form of "shut up," but the Oklahoman just chuckled.

"Betray," he repeated. "This country betrayed me plenty well before I betrayed it."

Bill scoffed. "That's a coward's excuse. There are more than three hundred million people in this country. It takes every single one of us to uphold the liberties and freedoms that we enjoy as American—"

"Oh, save the podium speech, there ain't no cameras here." The commando turned slightly, and Bill could see the network of scars spreading from around his left eye. "I fought for this country for a lot of years. Other countries too. I saw how quickly those so-called liberties can be taken away. You ever fight for this country, Bill?"

"If you're asking if I served in the armed forces, no. I didn't." The commando chuckled. "A career politician. Some might say you're braver than me. At least smarter, that's for damn sure. But there's still one thing I know that you don't."

"And what's that?" Bill dared to ask.

"Those liberties and freedoms you preach about? That Constitution y'all like to cling to like a life preserver and wave in the air when things don't go your way? It's not as sacred as you might think. In fact, all it takes is a gun and a boot heel, and they can vanish pretty quick."

"And if the other side has a gun too?"

"Come on now. That's war, Bill. You're talking about war." The commando chuckled again. He seemed to find the conversation, or maybe the whole situation, thoroughly amusing. "And to answer your question—what would make me do this? It's money. A great big pile of money."

Of course it was. This Oklahoman was the kind of man who could be bought. Most could, in fact. Bill had seen it himself firsthand, lobbyists and senators and all manner of corruption in the name of dollar signs.

"Funny," said the commando, "for a second there I would've thought you were a vet. When you clocked Bonehead there in the jaw—that's what I call him, no idea what his real name is and I probably can't pronounce it anyhow—there was a fire in your eyes. It was impressive, Bill."

"I boxed in college," Bill muttered. "Some things never quite leave you."

"Ain't that the truth." The commando stretched. It seemed he was now in a talkative mood. "You know, I was just a boy when you were in office. I knew your name, but I didn't really understand who you were. My old man, though? Man, he loved you. Worshipped the ground you walked on. Hung on your every word. 'Best president we'll ever have,' he would say. When you left office, he says, 'That's it. Whole country is gonna go down the shitter, just you watch.' But then again... they say that every time there's a new one, huh?"

"They certainly do," Bill agreed quietly.

"Yeah, but they don't make 'em like you anymore, Bill. I like you. You seem like a straight shooter, and that's why I'm gonna shoot straight with you." The Oklahoman twisted in his seat and propped his forearms on the headrest. "We're going to kill you, Bill."

Bill took a deep breath, in through his nose and out through his mouth, in a vain attempt to keep his heart rate down. "Yeah. I assumed as much when you killed my boys." Still, it didn't make it any easier to hear.

He was supposed to die in Six Springs, in his home, ideally holding Gwen's hand, with his family around him. That was the plan.

"We're going to kill you, Bill," the commando repeated, "but how much longer you live depends entirely on you. If you try to run, we're going to kill you quick. If you do something stupid, we're going to kill you quick. If you cooperate, and do what we ask, you'll last for as long as we let you last."

Bill thought about that for a moment. "Knowing that you plan to kill me anyway, why wouldn't I try something stupid?"

The commando grinned. "Because, Bill. You strike me as the kind of guy that doesn't want to die on the run with six bullets in his back."

Bill McMahon's throat ran dry. "Yes." The word came out as little more than a whisper. "You're right about that."

The commando nodded deeply. "Like I said—I like you. You're a good leader. You're a good man. But good men die every day. Sometimes for no reason at all. You? There's a reason. A purpose."

Bill dared to ask the question, the one he'd begun speaking to discover. "And what purpose is that?"

The commando flashed his lopsided smirk. Then there was darkness as a bag was pulled over his head. The SUV slowed and came to a stop at some new destination. And Bill realized the commando had obliged him, had kept him talking just so he wouldn't notice wherever they'd arrived.

And then he was dragged out of the back seat, and they were moving again.

# CHAPTER NINE

Zero kicked off his shoes, peeled off his black socks, and stepped out onto the warm sand in his bare feet. He curled his toes into it and let out a small laugh.

His first wedding had been in a church with ninety-five guests, along with four groomsmen all in tuxes. His second would be on a small peninsular stretch of private Chesapeake Beach, owned by someone Alan knew—a "friend of a friend," allegedly—in front of eight seats, not all of which would be filled.

He knew it wasn't fair to compare. In fact, he felt it immensely gratifying that the two events would be so dissimilar that they were hardly worth comparing at all. He was appreciative at how small and intimate this would be. When he married the first time, holding Kate's hands in his and promising himself to her, he thought he would never do it again.

Now, here on the Chesapeake Beach with the first hill of the roller coaster just barely visible on the boardwalk to the north, he told himself again that this would be his last time.

Unless, of course, the call came from Jennifer Connelly's people that she was available and interested.

They had no trellis or arch or decorations of any kind; just eight white chairs arranged in a single row, four and four, with space in the center where Zero would be standing. He stood there now, in the spot he'd be when Maria came walking down the aisle—or rather, across the beach, as there wasn't really an aisle to speak of.

Alan stood behind him. He had also kicked off his shoes, and had even rolled up his pant legs a bit, which just made the shirt and tie he wore all the funnier a getup. Zero had nixed the tie for himself, opting instead for just a white shirt and black slacks. The top two shirt buttons were undone because Maya and Sara had agreed it was a suave look.

"In a couple of minutes," Alan said gruffly, "it's going to be too late for you to run. If you go now, I'll stall them as long as I can…"

Zero chuckled. "I'm good. Thanks." He clapped Alan on the shoulder and squeezed. "Glad you're here."

The first time he had done this, Alan hadn't been formally invited to the wedding. They weren't supposed to know each other outside of the CIA. But he had still shown up, his face clean-shaven back then and unmistakable at the rear of the chapel, where he had smiled warmly and nodded only to Zero before vanishing.

And now, he would be up there with them. Front and center where he belonged.

Just beyond the small stretch of beach, standing between it and the homes that lined it, was a thin copse of pine trees. From between two of them came Todd Strickland, wearing a full brown suit, with a fetching young woman on his arm wrapped in a hot-pink chiffon dress.

"Penny." Zero hugged Dr. Penelope León, the twenty-seven-year-old CIA engineer and friend. "Thanks for coming."

"Are you kidding? It gave me an excuse to break this number out." She smiled and took a seat at the edge of the row next to Todd.

Alan leaned in and whispered, "You think those two are...?"

Zero shrugged. It wasn't his business, but they'd be a hell of an odd couple if they were.

Another shape pushed through the trees. A woman in her late forties, with curly brown hair and a conservative maroon dress, made her way across the sand in heels. "Wasn't sure this was the right place!" she exclaimed.

For a moment Zero froze, because the sight of Linda was jarring, almost painful. They looked so much alike, she and Kate, save that Linda was four years older than her sister, and it had been nearly four years now since...

He felt a pang in his heart, because he couldn't help but think that Linda was how Kate might look now.

She crossed the sand carefully and then wrapped Zero in a hug. "Reid. It's been too long."

"It's very good to see you, Linda." She had said yes the instant he had invited her, had even traveled from New York to be there. Some might think it odd, him inviting his late wife's sister to his second wedding, but Linda was family. She was the girls' aunt and the only relation they had left on their mother's side. The only one *he* had left of her either.

Linda took a seat next to Todd and set about introducing herself and shaking hands as another guest arrived, pushing a branch out of his way and gingerly stepping past it, careful to avoid getting anything on his pressed gray suit, which matched his salt-and-pepper hair.

"Wow," said Alan in a low murmur. "Can't believe he came."

Zero didn't say anything, but he couldn't either.

David Barren was the Director of National Intelligence, one of only two men that EOT answered to—the other being the president. He was also Maria's father, and their relationship had been less than close for the last few years. He hadn't confirmed whether or not he would be coming today, but had responded with, "I'll see if I can move things around."

"Does she have any idea?" Alan asked.

Zero shook his head. "Not a clue."

Maria had written him off as a guest. She would be shocked to see him—whether it would be good shocked or bad shocked remained to be seen.

David Barren did not approach them, but rather hung back, standing near the tree line with his hands clasped in front of him. He looked Zero's way and nodded once, and Zero nodded back.

Alan's phone chimed. "It's time," he announced. He nodded to Todd, who reached down and pressed play on a portable stereo near Alan's feet and cranked the volume. The opening notes of the "Bridal Chorus" began—or, as most people knew it, "Here Comes the Bride" or "The Wedding March," though the original name was the official one, a song from a Wagner opera written in 1850…

*I must be more nervous than I thought.* He chided himself and pushed nineteenth-century music trivia out of his head.

A moment later, he forgot about anything else anyway.

The branches shifted and a figure emerged. Maya came first, smiling and taking each careful step one at a time. She locked eyes with her father and he swelled with pride. What an incredible young woman she was becoming. No, not becoming; she *was*. She'd already become one.

When she reached the front she kissed his cheek and sat beside Linda, giving her aunt a brief hug.

Sara came next. She was stunning, his youngest, his baby girl. She winked at him and sat. Mischa was after her, almost unrecognizable in a dress and makeup. Zero took a small amount of pleasure in David Barren's confused frown; the DNI knew that Zero had two daughters and he could see the man was trying to do the math in his head when a third had appeared.

Maria hadn't told her father that she'd adopted the girl. *That* would be a fun conversation for the reception. He could only hope that it would be left out that their ceremony was taking place about ten miles from the Calvert Cliffs nuclear reactor, where they had detained Mischa after she had tried to kill them.

Mischa stood in front of the seat beside Sara as the other five guests stood, Alan already standing behind Zero, and Maria came through the trees.

The sight of her took Zero's breath away. Her strong, bare shoulders; her unruly hair cascading over them. Her gray eyes that still sparkled in the sunlight. Her gown, elegant yet understated. It was all her, all there, and it was all Zero could do to remember to keep his jaw from falling.

And then Maria noticed the man standing there, waiting for her. She looked at her father, and he looked at her, and as far as Zero could tell no words were exchanged between them. She simply offered her arm, and he took it, and the two of them walked in step to the song until they reached Zero.

David Barren took his daughter's hand, put it in Zero's, and clasped his own over them both. "You'll take care of her," he said. It wasn't a request or an order; just a statement, and a true one at that. And then he sat, between Mischa and the empty seat for Chip Foxworth.

Zero turned to her, and she to him, and there was nothing else in the world at that moment.

Except for Alan Reidigger. "Dearly beloved," he said, louder and clearer than anything Zero had heard him say in the last two years. "We are gathered here today to make this quick. It's been a long time coming, and let me be the first to say—about damn time."

Their guests chuckled. Maria rolled her eyes but smiled.

"Reid. Do you take this woman to be your wife, to live together in holy matrimony, to love her, to honor her, to comfort her, and to keep her in sickness and in health, forsaking all others, for as long as you both shall live?"

Zero nodded. "I do."

"Maria. All that, but for this guy?"

She nodded. "I do."

Alan leaned in. "You sure?"

She laughed. "Of course I do."

"Suit yourself. The rings, then."

Maya rose and handed a ring to Maria, while Alan handed off the ring to Zero. The wedding bands were simple, identical but for size, made of gold and each inscribed on the inner side with two words: *Never goodbye.*

"Please place the ring on her finger," Alan told him. "There you go, nicely done. And Maria. Great. Now, repeat after me: I give you this ring as a token and pledge of our constant faith and abiding love."

"I give you this ring," they both said in unison, "as a token and pledge of our constant faith and abiding love."

"Terrific. Done deal." Alan clapped his hands once. "By the power vested in me by the state of Virginia, and by VA-ordained-in-a-day-dotcom, I now pronounce you husband and wife. You know what comes next—you may kiss your bride."

*

Their reception was held in the back room of a posh restaurant called Luna just a few miles from the beach where they said their vows. A table for ten had been set and a server brought them tray after tray of drinks and food while Maya played music from a playlist she had carefully curated just for the event. Zero and Maria had their first dance as husband and wife to the song they had chosen together, "Unchained Melody" by the Righteous Brothers.

And then Zero danced with his daughters, and with Penny and Linda, and Maria danced with her father and Alan and Todd. They danced, and he drank more than Dr. Dillard would have been happy about, but that was far from his mind by then.

At one point in the evening he looked over to see Maria sitting in the corner with her father, both her hands clasping one of his, and though he couldn't hear the words he knew what was being said. David Barren gave a rare expression of genuine surprise and his head turned quickly in the direction of Mischa, and that was how the Director of National Intelligence learned he was a grandfather to a thirteen-year-old girl.

Barren rose, walked right over to her, and extended his hand for a dance.

As the night waned, Zero danced with Linda to "Stand by Me" by Ben E. King, and it was not at all by coincidence that he chose to do so.

"Maria is just absolutely lovely," she told him with a smile.

"She is. I… I can't thank you enough for coming. It means a lot to me."

"She's here too, you know. She'll be with you, always."

Zero nodded. "I know." This had been one of Kate's favorite songs. She frequently sang it while doing dishes, he remembered fondly.

"And she would be happy for you," Linda said. "To see you living. It's been more than four years. You need to live your life; not just for you, but for those girls too." She chuckled. "By God, Sara's face…"

"I know. More and more like her every day."

"Yeah." Linda trailed off and a silence stretched between them as they swayed, enjoying the music, until finally she said, "I have to ask. I've heard your friends call you 'Zero' all night. What's that about?"

He shrugged. "Just a nickname that stuck."

"Doesn't seem like the most flattering one they could have picked."

Zero laughed at that. "You wouldn't think so, no."

For another hour or so they danced, and they drank, and when they called it a night they were all exhausted. The five of them piled into Zero's SUV, Maya driving them home. They invited Linda to stay the night with them before returning to New York but she had already booked herself a hotel room.

When they arrived home they fell asleep in their clothes, Maria almost as soon as her head hit the pillow as she murmured an apology for not consummating their marriage on their wedding night. Zero laughed at that, and pretended he didn't lack the energy himself, and assured her there'd be plenty of time for consummation during their week-long stay in the Bahamas. Or perhaps on tomorrow morning's long flight, he joked. But she was already asleep.

He lay beside her, his wife, exhausted but happy, and as he drifted off he remembered to at least kick off his shoes and marveled at how they had gotten through the day without a hitch, without interruption or a call from the president or some unforeseen disaster.

*But hey,* he thought with a sleepy smile, *tomorrow's another day.*

# CHAPTER TEN

Despite being German-born, Stefan Krauss had perfected many accents over his career. Though, if he could say so himself, it was his American that he was most proud of, near flawless even to native speakers.

"Why yes ma'am," he said into the phone, "three nights, one room, one person. Just me. I know it's last minute, but—well, it's been a tough month, and I just need a bit of a getaway, you know?"

Americans thought they spoke English. Funny—they spoke a creole of English, a pidgin of the actual language. Something that resembled English in a trench coat at a distance.

"Name on the card? Sure, it's Patrick McIlhenney. Yup, I'm gonna go ahead and spell that for you." A laugh. So easy to win someone over with a laugh. The right pitch and timbre earned trust, eased minds.

It had been a little more than six months since Krauss had been left for dead in the frigid waters of the Atlantic. Despite the uphill battle, he was almost fully recovered now; he would never truly be, due to permanent damage from hypothermia and a gunshot wound, but it didn't impede his mobility and he'd been back to his rigorous training regimen for seven weeks.

But he had not been lying idle. He had been planning, searching. They were difficult to find at first: a Palestinian called Al Najjar. An Iraqi who bore the glyph tattoo proving his loyalty to the now-defunct cult of Amun. Two men hiding out in Somalia who claimed to be the last surviving members of the Brotherhood, who had perpetrated an attack on New York City's underwater tunnels.

Despite their differences, all of them shared a few things in common. For starters, the subversive groups to which they had sworn their allegiance were castrated. All of them, unknowing to each other, had been funded at least in part by the businessman and war profiteer who called himself Mr. Shade, now a permanent resident of a CIA black site in Morocco.

All of these men still had access to Shade's funds, despite his incarceration. They had planned on using them to stay hidden forever.

65

And why stay hidden? Because the last thing they shared, each and every one of them, was fear. Fear that the American bogeyman would come for them in the night. Fear that showing their faces to the sun would result in a bullet to the head.

Fear of Agent Zero.

"No ma'am, I won't be needing the flight package," Krauss said into the phone. "Those arrangements are taken care of, thank you. But if you could set me up in something with a view of the sea, I'd be happy to pay a little extra."

The New Zealander, a man called Dutchman, had been indispensable while Krauss was unable to travel. They had met three years prior in Jakarta; one a contract killer still earning his *nom de guerre*, the other a smuggler with an extensive network of contacts.

A few drinks, a few laughs earned the Kiwi's trust. A fistful of money earned his information.

It had taken longer than Krauss would have expected, an entire summer spent collecting the remnants of factions broken like a hull against rocks by Agent Zero. But Dutchman had come through, had earned his fifteen percent of the pot.

The plan was brilliant in its simplicity. Let these ruined men believe they were pulling the strings when all they were doing was writing the check. They didn't have to do anything or even leave their caves; they simply had to wire an amount to the account in the Caymans that Dutchman had established under one of six shell companies he used for his smuggling efforts. Twenty-five million Euros it would cost them to have Krauss kill Agent Zero.

He was going to do it anyway. He just wasn't going to do it for free.

"All right," he told the travel agent on the phone. "You've talked me into it. An upgrade sounds terrific. If I'm gonna do it, might as well do it right." A laugh.

Killing was easy. Manipulation was art.

There was, of course, the small hitch of actually *finding* Agent Zero. No one knew who he really was other than an American CIA agent, and physical descriptions of him—as Krauss himself could attest—were remarkably bland. He was around six foot, with brown hair, average build, somewhere between late thirties and early forties by anyone's best guess.

Congratulations, they had just described twenty million American men.

But someone else kept coming up in the ghost stories told and retold by those who had lived to tell them. A woman at his side, equally deadly. American, blonde, tall, beautiful by all accounts... with remarkable gray eyes.

Now that was something Krauss could use.

Dutchman had a guy from Interpol in his pocket, and a careful peek at their database yielded the profile of a former CIA deputy director named Maria Johansson who fit the bill snug as a glove. They even had a photo on record. But it seemed that Ms. Johansson had stepped down from her position in the CIA and, curiously, had no current occupation listed anywhere that he could discern.

Krauss hadn't expected it to be her real name. But lo and behold—a woman in Virginia had legally changed her name to Maria Johansson the year prior. Since name changes required a court hearing, the records were public—but the information about her before the name change was sealed. Only her new identity was available.

From there the dominoes fell easily. Maria Johansson owned a three-bedroom home in the suburbs of Langley, so Krauss paid a contact of his in the US to drive three hundred and fifty miles to scope the place out and steal some of her junk mail for verification, where he learned that mail to the home came not only to Ms. Johansson, but a man by the name of Reid Lawson.

Reid Lawson was a former adjunct professor of European history, first at Columbia University and then Georgetown, now residing in Langley and seemingly just as unemployed as Johansson. But Georgetown still had a photo of him on their website under the administration profiles.

And—well, imagine Stefan Krauss's surprise when he saw that mild-mannered Reid Lawson had a familiar alter ego. Like Clark Kent without his glasses, that same face, right there on the computer screen smiling back in a suit jacket, that face had shot him and destroyed the railgun and blown up the South Korean boat and left him to die in the middle of the ocean.

It had taken more than five months for all the pieces to come together. To unite all of those who hated him, who wanted him dead, who had been dismantled by him and had the funds to make it happen; to tug at the thread of Zero's identity until Krauss learned, laughably, that he was a seemingly ordinary guy living in a fairly small house with three daughters and a fellow agent.

Of course Krauss could have just flown there. Rented a car. Driven to the address, waited, and put a bullet in the back of Agent Zero's head. But he didn't much like doing business stateside if he could avoid it. There was too much of a paper trail attached to every little thing—as evidenced by the manner in which he'd found Zero in the first place.

Plus there was the niggling doubt, annoying as indigestion but just as persistent, that the information was misleading. He did not want to face him on Zero's own turf regardless, but he did not know what sort of security system would be in place, who else might be there, if he'd be walking into a nest of a dozen CIA agents waiting to take him. He was not about to underestimate Zero or assume he'd get more than one chance. He would have to wait.

But then, serendipity. Dutchman had been discreetly tracking Reid Lawson's credit card activity—not stealing any information, just watching—and it seemed that Mr. Lawson had recently booked a week-long trip to a place called Emerald Bay Resort in the Bahamas.

Perfect. Unknown territory for both of them. No cops around. No one with guns who might decide to try and be a hero. The playing field would be as level as could be—well, for someone who didn't know there was a hit out on them.

"I appreciate the offer, ma'am," Krauss told the phone, "but this is my first time to Emerald Bay and I'd like to scope the place for myself before considering any sort of membership program. Yes, I think that should do it. You've been great. You have a nice day too. Thank you— I *will* enjoy my stay."

# CHAPTER ELEVEN

Maya had set her alarm for six thirty, but she was awake by a quarter after on Monday morning. Despite being exhausted from the wedding her nerves had kept her up half the night. She was awake when she heard her dad and Maria rise, grab their luggage, and quietly leave to catch their five a.m. flight to their honeymoon. She could have gotten another fifteen minutes but instead she rose, knowing she wasn't going to drift off again before the alarm would wake her.

She raided Maria's closet for a cream-colored blouse, navy blue slacks, and a matching blazer. Maria wouldn't mind, she was sure, and besides—she wouldn't be back for a week. She'd never know. Though Maya did make a mental note to go shopping for some more professional clothes. Almost everything she owned was athletic wear or casual.

She applied a modest patina of makeup and tried to put her hair up in a bun, but it wasn't quite long enough for that yet. She settled on pinning it back from her face. She poured some coffee and made toast with strawberry jam, taking her time, keeping cool.

Today was her first official day as a junior agent. As of today, she was officially in the employ of the Central Intelligence Agency. Today she accomplished her goal of becoming the youngest agent in the CIA's history, sooner even than she would ever have guessed, well shy of her twentieth birthday.

"You're going to do great things," she told her reflection in the mirror as she gave herself a once-over. "Great things."

Her phone chimed with an incoming message. It came up as "unknown," which meant it was from Bradlee, and it read: *Report to 1160 Pine Street by 0800.*

Maya read it, and then reread it, her heart sinking all the while. This meant she wouldn't be reporting to the George Bush Center for Intelligence in Langley on her first day. She wouldn't be walking through those doors as a brand-new agent. Her flats would not yet clack over the seal of the CIA embossed in the floor of the bright lobby.

Her mind raced with all sorts of possibilities. Could this be another test? Or was it an operation right out of the gate? Perhaps they had noticed how she excelled and were ready to throw her in the deep end.

So be it; she would swim.

Mischa awoke just as Maya was grabbing the keys to her dad's SUV, which he had left behind for her to use. The girl hadn't washed the makeup from her face the night before and now eyeliner had smeared to her cheek. Maya held back a laugh.

"Morning. I have to go to work, but Sara's here. She'll probably sleep until noon, so remind her to make lunch—"

"To work?" Mischa asked. "Your program is over?"

Maya hadn't even realized she'd said it that way. "Yes. It's over, and they gave me a job."

*To work. My job.* The reality hadn't quite set in yet.

"Okay," Mischa said simply as she went for the orange juice. "We will see you tonight?"

"You will. Bye, kiddo."

*

Twenty-three minutes later Maya pulled up in front of 1160 Pine Street in Washington, D.C. She checked her phone. That was indeed the address Bradlee had sent.

She looked out the window at the strip mall.

"This can't be right," she murmured.

1160 Pine Street was a small storefront called Zephyr Insurance, between a Jewish deli and a pharmacy.

*What is going on?*

She couldn't text Bradlee back to confirm—the message would get rejected—so she did the only thing she could do, which was park in the small lot and head inside.

Zephyr Insurance smelled like disinfectant, just a shade off from the sterilized scent of a hospital. It was a small office space, white walls and blue carpet and a drop ceiling. There were two desks, one empty and the other occupied by a bored-looking African-American woman who was typing on a computer with long red fingernails.

"Um… hi. I'm Maya Lawson?"

"Back there." The woman did not look away from her screen as she pointed to a door at the rear of the office.

"Okay." Maya passed her by and pushed through the door. She didn't know what she should have expected, but what she found was thoroughly unexpected—another bland office space, this one with only one desk, two guest chairs, and two people.

"Close the door, Agent Lawson," Bradlee told her from behind the desk.

*Agent.* A tingle went up her spine at being addressed so, even if she was still thoroughly confused.

"Coleman." She nodded to Trent as she took the seat beside him. He grinned up at her, clearly enjoying her puzzlement. Only compounding it was the fact that he'd shown up in jeans, sneakers, and a hunter-green polo shirt.

"All right then. First of all, welcome." Bradlee leaned back in her chair. Her short silver hair wasn't styled today, and it puffed to one side like a bad case of bed-head. "Secondly, I won't be repeating this address to you again. Remember it. In the future, I'll send only a time, and you will report here. You will be briefed, and you will go. Then you will return here for debriefing. You will tell no one what you do, what you've done, where you've been, or where you're going. You will only report if you are summoned. It won't always be me briefing you, either—"

"I'm sorry." Maya actually raised her hand as if she was in a classroom. Her head was spinning. "What exactly is this place?"

"This? This is a front, Agent Lawson. I don't know if you noticed, but we do not actually sell insurance here. Though your paychecks will come from Zephyr, just so you know. Direct-deposit, every two weeks. You'll be salaried, by the way…"

"What I meant to say," Maya interrupted again, "is why aren't we reporting to Langley?"

"The CIA is not Langley. It's only headquartered there. This is a satellite office; there are dozens like it around the country." Bradlee leaned forward, her chin high as usual, though to Maya it seemed suspiciously like the senior agent was looking down her nose at her. "Did you think you'd be at a corner desk on the third floor on day one? This is paying your dues. I did it. Your father did it. You wanted to be the youngest agent we have, and now you are, but you begin at the bottom like everyone else. Nepotism has no place on my watch—"

"I'm not looking for nepotism," Maya said brusquely, her face flushing with heat. "I'm looking for talent to be recognized."

Bradlee grinned at that. "Then show me talent, Agent."

Maya nodded tightly, though her face was still warm. She wanted to speak her mind but didn't dare. Just like she didn't dare look at Coleman; she could feel his smirk on her.

"Can you at least tell us what this is?" Maya asked.

"Of course. This office is part of a CIA subdivision called Strategic Resource Management, or SRM for short."

"And what is it that we do here?"

"We strategically manage resources," Bradlee said back instantly, in a way that was equally clear she'd rehearsed and enjoyed. "Everything you need to know for your op today will be provided by the briefing package you'll receive en route."

"Where are we going?" Coleman asked.

Maya almost scoffed. *Of course the first question he asks isn't about the incredibly bizarre nature of this entire situation, but where we're headed.*

"Abu Dhabi," Bradlee said simply.

Now Maya *did* scoff. "Sorry? Abu Dhabi? Today?"

The senior agent checked her watch. "The plane leaves in forty-five minutes."

"I... hang on. I can't just up and fly halfway around the world at a moment's notice. I have sisters—"

"Who rely on you for survival? This is the job, Agent Lawson. Bottom rung. When I tell you to jump, you don't ask how high. You understand that I'm already expecting you to give me your best. If you want to get to the next rung, it's through me. Otherwise, you know where the door is."

Maya stared at the floor, unable to meet Bradlee's gaze. This was all wrong. She was supposed to report to Langley. To get a real badge, with her name and title. To have a reason to buy a new wardrobe and look the part. To be able to tell people that she was a CIA agent.

*God. Is that why I did this? For recognition?*

No. It wasn't. How had she lost sight of that? In all her efforts to be the best, top of the class and better, to push herself, she'd forgotten about Jersey.

Maya didn't even know the girl's real name; all she knew was that when she and Sara had been kidnapped and sold to traffickers, Jersey had been with them, one of the other girls stuffed and transported in a stinking cargo container. When that container had opened again, Jersey fought back—and she'd been shot, gunned down in the dirt right in front of her.

It was after that, after her dad found and rescued her, that Maya had decided what she would do with the rest of her life. It had nothing to do with being Agent Zero's daughter. It had nothing to do with clout or glory or braggadocio.

*If I can save even one girl—or anyone—from a fate like that, it'll be worth it.*

"I'm here, ma'am," Maya said at last. "I'm ready."

"Good. Cell phones, please." The senior agent reached over the desk and accepted a phone in each hand. "You'll get them back upon your return. Your families will be informed that you have been called away on business and unavailable. We'll make it sound good."

"What about clothes?" Maya asked. "Shouldn't we pack a bag?"

"We know your size, Lawson. Everything you'll need will be provided. The plane is on runway 13 at Dulles. I suggest you get moving."

"Thank you, ma'am." Coleman rose from his seat, but Maya hesitated. She would do it, of course, but in the moment she felt so completely unprepared that she couldn't quite move.

And in all the hubbub and confusion of the moment, she had neglected to realize that she wasn't just going to Abu Dhabi; she was going to Abu Dhabi with Trent Coleman.

"You coming, partner?" he asked jovially, as if reading her mind.

He was already enjoying this, she could tell.

"I'm driving," she said, and then she stood, nodded once to Bradlee, and followed Trent out of the office and back to the parking lot.

Once they were outside, Coleman let out a long sigh, as if he'd been holding his breath the whole time. "That was crazy, right? I mean I tried to keep it cool, but that was crazy." He laughed, and then he said something else, but Maya barely heard him because she was thinking about how right he was. That this was crazy, and moreover, felt wrong, all wrong to the way that she had thought things would go.

"...You know?" Coleman was saying.

Maya turned, and she pushed him with one hand against the side of the SUV.

"Hey, what gives?" he said, startled.

"I don't like you very much," she told him point-blank.

"No kidding. Kind of gathered that…"

73

"Hush. I don't like you very much, and I'm kind of on edge already. Yes, that was crazy. No, I don't much like it. But if it gets me to where I'm going, I'll do whatever they ask of me. If you screw around and get in my way, I will not hesitate to run you over and leave you behind. Got me?"

Coleman's nostrils flared. "Look, Lawson, I don't know how to tell you this, but… this intensity? It's kind of hot."

She scoffed loudly. "Get in the damn car."

Sara and Mischa would be fine without her. Her dad and Maria were on their honeymoon; they wouldn't know until they got back that she had even left. A part of her now wished that she'd been honest with them about the program, Maybe they could have prepared her better for this.

But would she have even believed them? Or would they have just tried to talk her out of joining the agency at all?

It was too late to know now. She was all-in. She was going to Abu Dhabi. And if the jackass in her passenger seat was any indication, she'd be doing the heavy lifting herself.

# CHAPTER TWELVE

Bill McMahon had no idea where he was.

After the hood had gone over his head, he'd been transferred from the backseat of an SUV to the metal floor of another vehicle. A van, perhaps? Or the covered bed of a truck? He couldn't quite tell. The engine was too loud, rumbling the uncovered floor as they drove seemingly through the entire night, possibly even part of the next day. He lost track of time then. He hadn't wanted to sleep, but his body and mind were equally exhausted, and the rumbling of the engine caused him to nod off. He'd wake again with a jolt, unable to see and panicking before remembering what had happened. That vicious cycle repeated, over and over, at least a half dozen times.

He wasn't even sure he was still in the United States.

Every now and then they stopped—for gas, he assumed—and Bill heard hushed voices outside the vehicle but did not dare to cry out for fear of the Oklahoman commando's warning. And then they were off again.

At long last they stopped a final time, and Bill was startled to find arms pulling on his. Two men carried him between them, actually lifted him up and just carried him rather than having him stumble. He could tell they were going upstairs, and then there was the creak of a door. He was set in a chair. The handcuffs were removed from one of his wrists, and just as Bill was about to thank the good lord that they were coming off, his captors simply looped the chain through the back of the chair and tightened the cuff again around his sore wrist.

Then and only then was the hood removed. The man who tore it from over his head was the Arabic man that Bill had hit with a right cross back in his house. Bonehead, that's what the commando had called him. The man scowled down at Bill but said nothing. He stormed out of the room, slammed the door, and locked it behind him.

The room was small, maybe ten by twelve at best. The old hardwood under his feet was in poor shape, in dire need of a sanding and polish. Wallpaper peeled. An old steam radiator stood in the

75

corner. There was one window and it had a blanket duct-taped over it. Even so, Bill could tell by the tint that it was daytime out.

He craned his neck until it hurt to see behind him. Strange—there was a large sheet of corrugated steel propped against the wall behind him, streaked with rust, at least eight feet tall and almost as wide as the room.

Its presence was as odd as it was unsettling. What was it from? Why was it there?

Bill had no idea how long he sat in that chair, in that empty room. He heard nothing beyond the door or through the window outside. Eventually the blanket duct-taped to the frame lost its tint and grew dark as night came.

The soreness in his wrists became an acute pain. His back and arms ached. He tried to distract himself with thoughts of Gwen, hoping desperately that she hadn't been the first to return to the house, the first to find him missing and the boys dead. He thought of Jim's and Tony's families, whom he'd never met because of security protocol but heard endless stories about. Jim's son was in his senior year at Rutgers; Tony had two daughters in high school. When he was out of here, Bill would visit them personally, share in their grief, and tell them of the heroic stand their fathers had made for him.

He even thought of Bruce and Sadie, those miserable, lovable mutts chasing him down in the glow of taillights.

He would see them again, all of them, no matter what his captors told him. He had to believe that.

After what must have been hours, the locks turned on the other side of the door and it opened. The Oklahoman commando entered with two Arabic men. The commando had a folding tray table under one arm and a plastic grocery bag in his hand. He unfolded the tray table, and then set the items from the bag upon it: a can of soup, a plastic spoon, a single-serving pack of saltines, a bottle of water, and a Sterno can.

"You must be hungry, Bill."

"It's Mr. President to you," he muttered.

The commando laughed. "Still some fire in you? Really? Tough old bastard. I'm Fitz, by the way."

"Fitz Something, or Something Fitz?"

"Just Fitz." The commando, Just Fitz, kneeled in front of him. "Now I'm betting that you would just *kill* for a half hour with those cuffs off. A warm meal, some water. Am I right?"

Bill just stared at him. He noticed that Fitz's eye, the scarred one, drifted slightly of its accord every now and then, the pupil dilating and unfocused. An old injury of some sort.

"But before we do that," Fitz said, "we need to shoot ourselves a little video. Don't worry; you don't need to do nothing but sit there, keep quiet, and look real sad."

A video. They were going to shoot a video to prove they had kidnapped a former president. Likely send it to the media. Bill almost yawned, would have if not for the constant reminder that they planned to kill him anyhow.

"Remember what I said about doing something stupid?" Fitz asked. "Now would be a *real* good time to listen and heed that, because I'm a one-take kind of director." He flashed his lopsided smirk. Then he stood and nodded to one of the two Arabic men, who had a swooping scar running from his eye across his cheek to his ear. "You're up."

The scarred man scowled at Bill, and then positioned himself beside him as Fitz took several steps back and framed them up with an iPhone. "And... go."

The Arabic man spoke in his foreign tongue, his glare directed ahead at the camera phone and his tone harsh, angry, unforgiving. Bill had no idea what he was saying but he knew it was nothing good. He kept his own eyes on a spot on the floor, halfway between his chair and Fitz, unwilling to look up, not willing to show whatever he might be emoting in his own gaze.

Bill couldn't tell what was being said, but then there were a few words he recognized, words in English that were forced from the scarred man's mouth as if he was spitting them out.

"Five. Hundred. *Million*. US."

*We're going to kill you, Bill.* That's what Fitz had told him in the SUV. His captors had no intention of letting him go, and he believed it. But those few English words propelled from the scarred man's mouth meant they would try for a ransom—and if Fitz was being forthcoming, they would take the money and kill him anyway.

The Arabic man was right in the middle of a sentence when Bill looked up, and in as clear a voice as he could muster he said, "The United States does not negotiate with terrorists."

The terrorist in question stopped suddenly, turning to Bill with such avarice in his eyes that he looked intent to kill him right there, handcuffed to a chair, on video.

"Especially not for one man's life," he continued. "No matter who that man is."

The scarred man made a move then, one hand shooting forward and grabbing a handful of white hair at the back of Bill's head. He winced as the Arabic man yanked his head back at an awkward, painful angle.

He said something more to the camera, shook Bill's head once, and then dragged his thumb over his own throat in a symbolic gesture.

Fitz lowered the phone. "Okay. Let him go."

The scarred man said something back that definitely sounded like an argument.

"Come on. Back off." The commando put a hand on the scarred man's shoulder. It wasn't a threatening motion, but could easily become one in an instant. "I won't ask twice."

"Dog," the scarred man muttered angrily, and then he released Bill.

Fitz handed him the phone. "Get this to your pal. Make sure he alters the lighting and removes *any* background noise. I don't want someone hearing a truck go by or something. Let me know when it's ready to upload."

The scarred man took the phone, and with one more hateful glare at Bill, left the room.

Bill's throat ran dry as Fitz knelt in front of him so the two were at eye level. "I asked you very nicely to stay quiet."

The former president shook his head. "You're trying to extort the American government for my life. I won't stay silent. Not if you're going to kill me anyway."

"There are things worse than killing you," Fitz said, his voice low. "Like cutting out your tongue. Or an eye."

Bill's heart rate doubled, but he refused to look away.

Then the commando's lips spread in a wide grin. "Come on, Bill, I'm messin' with you. Truth of the matter is, you just made our little video that much better."

He frowned. "What?"

"See, that video is going to be uploaded to YouTube and social media. Sent out to all the big news channels. They'll probably take it down pretty quick, but by then it'll have been copied a few thousand times. Everyone is going to see it. Of course we know the government's stance on terrorists and ransom. But personally, I think your impassioned little plea is going to help us a great deal. You think the American people are going to see that and go, 'Man, he's right, let's just let them kill him'?" Fitz laughed. "Nah. They'll love you even more for it, and they'll want their government to go to bat for you. Especially when they see that your captors are bearded and brown and talk funny. That's gonna put the government between a rock and a real hard place."

It was probably just the handcuffs, but Bill's fingers felt numb. Fitz was right; him saying anything at all would have the opposite effect as intended. His words were meant for the brain but would strike chords in the heart.

"They won't pay," he murmured.

"We'll see." Fitz stood and stretched. "The money is just icing, Bill. You're still the cake." He reached into a pocket and came out with a small set of handcuff keys. He looked at them for a long moment, and then closed his fist. "But you still didn't listen to me. So I think I'll just come back when you're feeling a little more… pliant."

Fitz strode out of the room without another word, leaving Bill there to wish he had just remained quiet and defiant rather than speaking up against the aggressors.

*

"When?" President Rutledge demanded.

"Not fifteen minutes ago," Tabby told him through the phone. He was aboard Marine One, en route back to the White House—ironically, returning from the same press conference that Bill McMahon should have been speaking at on Rutledge's behalf. Instead it had become almost entirely Rutledge speaking on Bill's behalf, ensuring the press and the American people that everything in their power was being done to locate him and bring him home safely.

And now there was a video. "I want to see it."

"Sir," said Tabby, "that's not advisable. It might be upsetting…"

"Upsetting," he scoffed. "You. Dalton. Bring up the video of President McMahon."

The sandy-haired agent was young, new among them, and his throat flexed nervously at even the shadow of a thought of defying the president. "Yes sir."

A moment later the agent turned his own phone to Rutledge to see. "Tabby, hang on." In it he saw Bill, bound to a chair with his hands behind him. It was some tiny amount of relief—proof of life—but then again he had no idea when this video was made.

Bill sat against some sort of steel structure, partially rusted. Judging by the lighting it looked like he was outdoors. Some old unused military depot? he wondered. A warehouse? A shipyard? It could have been anywhere.

The man standing beside him had a swooping scar on his face that seemed entirely natural above his scowl. He spoke in Arabic for a short while before saying, plain as day: "Five. Hundred. *Million*. US."

At last poor Bill looked up at the camera. "The United States does not negotiate with terrorists." In that moment Rutledge admired the man's strength; in his own predicament he had been too terrified to defy his captors, yet here Bill was staring death in the face and speaking as calmly as if he had been asked the time. "Especially not for one man's life. No matter who that man is."

Then the man with the scar grabbed a fistful of Bill's hair, and Rutledge winced.

"Okay, turn it off." He sighed. "Tabby, are you still there?"

"Yes sir. As I told you…"

"Who are they?"

"They didn't say explicitly, but it wasn't difficult to track down the man in the video. The scar on his face made him very identifiable. He belongs to a group of Iranian 'revolutionists' that have been resisting the Ayatollah's treaty with the US out of fear of westernization and the cleansing of Islamic culture and traditions."

"Preposterous," Rutledge muttered. "And the five hundred million, I assume that's their ransom?"

"Yes sir. And the last thing he says is that if the US government fails to pay, they will kill President McMahon on video and broadcast it."

Rutledge tugged his tie loose around his throat. "By our best estimates, how many people have seen this video?"

"Impossible to say, sir. But it's front-page everywhere. Certainly millions. Tens of millions, around the world."

In just fifteen minutes. *The blessing and curse of an instant-gratification world, having the latest at our fingertips at all times.*

"And?" Rutledge prodded.

"And… and there's not much to say yet, Mr. President," Tabby told him candidly. "National attention is firmly on this situation. Early analysis indicates that many are calling for the government to just pay it and have him returned. But as he said, we don't negotiate—"

"Yes, I heard it too." But he knew that wasn't remotely true; it was much more of a catchphrase than a policy. There were plenty of historical precedents to fly in the face of it, from the Contras to the Taliban and then some. Even the term "terrorist" was a moral quandary, a subjective one—which only meant that Rutledge was going to be under a lot of scrutiny from every side, regardless of what decision was reached.

"Is there any indication or intelligence that suggests where they are?" he asked.

"None, sir."

He didn't want to vocalize the next thought, but it needed to be said. They hadn't heard heads or tails of Bill McMahon for more than twenty-four hours, and now this. It was plenty of time. More than enough time to...

"Tabby. You don't think they were able to get him out of the country, do you?" So far the efforts of the FBI and Secret Service had been focused entirely within their own borders. "You don't think they took him to Iran?"

"We... we simply don't know, sir."

*We simply don't know.* That was the problem, wasn't it? Rutledge had assumed that the worst thing that could happen would be finding Bill's dead body somewhere. But he was wrong; not knowing was the worst part. Watching the situation unfold was the worst part. Knowing that Bill was still out there, alive but under pressure of looming death, that was worse.

"Timetable?" he asked.

"They didn't give one," Tabby said. "They are waiting for an official response from our government."

*From me,* Rutledge realized. They wanted the response to come from him. He felt pressure forming in the front of his skull, an oncoming tension headache. He had no idea what to do and couldn't be told what to do. He could only be advised. The decision itself was firmly on his shoulders.

One thing was certain: this was now about more than just Bill. The peace he had so carefully manufactured between the US and Iran hung in the balance. Even if the Iranian government was on their side, so to speak, that didn't discount the will of its people—or of America's, for that matter. What he and the Ayatollah said publicly mattered little in the face of overwhelming general persuasion.

*We simply don't know.* But if Bill was out of the country, then this would now be a CIA matter. And the one man that Rutledge trusted more than anyone else on the planet to find him was a thousand miles away and unreachable.

# CHAPTER THIRTEEN

Agent Zero had been shot. He'd been stabbed. He'd been blown up. His bones had been broken and healed and broken again. He faced dangers that most men would only ever dream of, often and repeatedly; in fact, he called it "work."

But this… this was a fresh new level of hell.

"Please." He shook his head. "Please don't make me do this."

Maria gripped his arm and squeezed it. "I'm right here. Take all the time you need."

"I don't know if I can," he admitted softly.

"You can. You *have* to."

The resort had no shortage of dining options, but Maria had honed in on the sushi bar. Sure; Zero liked sushi. But when she said "real sushi" he assumed she meant something like the fried shrimp rolls he was partial to, wrapped in rice and seaweed paper and topped with mango.

But this? This was… offensive. The thick pink slice of raw fish swam in a shallow bowl of muddy water, limp and rippled with the still-visible muscle texture of the animal from which it had been cut. "Sashimi," she had called it. And he could not bring himself to put it in his mouth.

"You actually *like* this stuff?"

"I do," she insisted. "And you might too if you'd just try it."

"Really wish I'd known that before I agreed to marry you," he muttered as he maneuvered the chopsticks around the squishy slice. It slipped out from between the sticks on his first try; on the second he pinched harder and it lifted from the bowl, dripping its muddy sauce and looking about as appetizing as a wad of toilet paper in a sewer.

*Here goes.*

He popped it in his mouth and chewed once. That was a mistake; the texture was what he imagined chewing raw chicken was like. He resisted the urge to gag and instead swallowed it whole. That was, he figured, at least one benefit to raw food. It slid easily down his throat.

"Well?" she asked hopefully.

He ignored her and raised a hand politely to the chef behind the sushi bar. "Excuse me? Yes, literally anything cooked, please."

The chef flashed a grin and a nod.

"That's fine." Maria took the bowl and slid it in front of her. "More for me."

He grimaced. "There's a good chance I'm not kissing you tonight."

She leaned over and whispered to him, close enough for her lips to graze his earlobe. "Yes, you will."

It had only been one night and one day so far into their honeymoon and already the trip was absolutely perfect. The first thing they'd done upon arrival to the resort was turn off their phones and lock them in the safe of their suite, agreeing to check them only once per day in case of some unforeseen emergency.

The Emerald Bay Resort was not exactly the most upscale place—it was probably just a small step up from a Sandals, even though he fully admitted he could only make that assessment had he ever actually *been* to a Sandals. But he'd never been all that classy of a guy. He couldn't truly relax at places like that anyway. He'd take a dive bar over a cocktail lounge any day. A light beer over whatever the new craft craze was. And this place, it was perfect.

So far the hardest decision he'd had to make was whether to spend the day lounging poolside or on the beach. Ultimately they'd chosen both; the morning had passed on the beach, casually reading the first third of a book about the Hungarian Civic Revolution of 1848 and catnapping under the sun. And the afternoon they'd spent by the pool, where he learned not only that it was acceptable to drink at one o'clock but also that he was quite fond of a cocktail called a Rum Runner.

Then they'd returned to their suite, where they made love like they were teenagers, got dressed, and headed arm in arm to the sushi bar.

"At least tell me you've had real sake," Maria chided as she poured two small ceramic cups from an eight-inch carafe.

"Of course I have," he scoffed. But then he looked in the cup and frowned. "Wait, why is it cloudy?"

"Oh my god." She laughed at him. "A few thousand years of knowledge in that head, and so many things you haven't done yet."

He toasted. "Plenty of time to do them, and the perfect company in which to." He drained the cup like a shot; it was room temperature, milky and sweet on his throat. "Although… I guess, maybe soon you won't be able to have a lot of stuff like this?"

Maria smiled, but shook her head. "Stuff like what?"

"Raw fish. Alcohol."

*Idiot.* He'd been meaning to broach the subject, had been looking for just the perfect moment—and this wasn't it. The three Rum Runners in him had made it seem like a good idea, but he regretted it immediately.

*Too late now.* He'd opened his big mouth, and had no choice but to forge ahead.

"I mean to say... I've been thinking about it, and, uh... if you wanted to try, I could be open to it. Trying, I mean."

*This is going very poorly.*

Maria blinked at him. "Zero, are you talking about having a baby?"

"Well—yeah."

She laughed at him. "I'm thirty-nine."

"So? Plenty of women have children after forty, especially these days. We would do all the... you know, the tests and everything."

"You're serious?" She scrutinized him carefully, his eyes, his mouth, the way she would during an interrogation when trying to tell if someone was lying to her or not.

"I am."

"We already have three psychos at home—"

"So what's a fourth psycho?" He shrugged.

"I didn't think you wanted that," she said softly.

"I didn't," he admitted. "But I didn't think I'd get married again either. You know, they say a change in perspective is the best illustration of personal growth."

"Who says that?"

"I did. Just now."

She laughed at him again. "Okay. Let's just say we did... try. How would we go about that?"

He stared at her for a moment. "I really shouldn't have to explain that part to you."

"No, you ass, I mean—do we talk to the girls first? Or do we just not tell them until it's for certain? Would we need a bigger place? When would even be a good time to try?"

"Tonight," he blurted out.

Was that the alcohol talking?

No; he felt fine. It was him. He was sure; he was ready for this. He wanted this.

"Tonight," she repeated. "You're ridiculous—"

"Now, in fact." He held out a hand to her. "Come on."

"You must be joking," she said even as she took his hand.

"I'm not." He pulled her to her feet, called out a thanks to the sushi chef, and tugged her toward the door.

"This is crazy," she declared, though her voice was breathless and excited as they hurried down the path that would take them back to their suite.

"Come on, this is the least crazy thing we've done in years." He stopped, thought for a moment, and then kicked off one loafer. "Is walking back on the beach crazy too?"

She was out of her heels in seconds. "Not at all."

They carried their shoes in hand and dug their toes into warm sand and laughed at each other like kids for no reason. It was a gorgeous night, only slightly cloudy overhead but warm, a breeze blowing in off the water as white crests crashed onto the beach in the moonlight.

There were others out there, not many but a few people here and there, mostly couples walking along the beach at night, strolling under the moon just like them, but they paid those people no mind because as far as they were concerned, the beach belonged to them.

Maria ventured down to the surf and gasped a little at the shock of it as it rolled up over her ankles. He laughed at her, and she joined him again, not caring at all that sand was sticking to her wet bare feet.

"*Zero*."

His name came to him as if the ocean had whispered it, barely more than a hiss on the breeze. At first he frowned; the beach and the liquor and the moonlight had slowed his brain. His third Rum Runner had been a double. He turned sluggishly and looked behind them.

A man was there. He was white, though it was too dark for his features to be recognizable. But the silver thing in his hand glinted, and then it came flying up toward him, toward his throat, and he didn't have the reflexes in that moment to stop it or even to get out of the way.

But Maria did. She leapt in front of him and put a hand up to block the oncoming knife. It didn't stop; it completed its arc, high up into the air, as if reaching for the moon.

It took him a moment to realize that she had struck the knife from the assailant's hand. It flew end over end and splashed into the water some yards out.

He tensed, ready to launch himself at the man—

But Maria stumbled.

Zero lurched forward to catch her but his foot sank in the sand and he fell too, fell atop her on his hands and knees, staring down at her, at her wide eyes as her hands flew to the place on her throat that was dark now, dark under the moonlight, staining the sand around her.

"No," he said, though it came out like the ocean's whisper, was drowned out by the crash of a small wave. He put his hand over both of hers and it was instantly slick. "No, no, no..."

She had stopped him, and the knife, and sent it flying into the ocean, but not before it had cut across her...

There were legs nearby, legs in black pants that ended in dark shoes, but Zero ignored them and fumbled with the buttons of his shirt. His fingers didn't work so he tore at the buttons instead and they went popping off, lost in the sand as he wrestled out of his shirt and balled it up in both hands.

The feet were fleeing now, kicking up plumes of sand as they fled, and Zero could have chased him and could have caught him and could have torn him apart, torn off his limbs, turned him inside out, but he couldn't now because he had to press the shirt over the growing dark spot around Maria's hands, and he held it tight as he could with both of his hands, because that would stop it, because that would work, because the knife hadn't cut deep enough and hadn't nicked the artery, it just hadn't, and all the while he didn't realize he was saying, "No, no, no, no, no, no..."

And Maria's mouth went wide and then small, wide and then small like a fish on dry land, like she couldn't get air.

"Stay, please stay, don't go, don't..."

Her fingers clutched his arms like vises even as he felt the strength leave them.

"Help!" he shouted, again and again. "Help! Someone, please help!"

There were voices, and then people, he could feel them nearby and hear them but he didn't look away from her as she stared up at him, her eyes so wide. Then there was a light, impossibly bright and shining on them, a flashlight or a spotlight, and there was shouting and a scream.

And in the sudden bright light he could see it. He'd already known it but now it was real, he could see it, that it was blood. Too much blood.

And her eyes, they were gray, yet they somehow they would dance in the light.

But they didn't any longer.

# CHAPTER FOURTEEN

"Hello? ...Hello? Zero, is that you?"

"Alan, I..."

"Jeez. What time is it?"

"Alan..."

"You sound half a mile away. Why are you whispering? Are you okay?"

"No. Maria..."

" Zero. Did something happen? Tell me what happened."

"Maria... she's dead, Alan."

"...What? What are you talking about? Zero, what are you talking about?"

"She's dead."

"No. No, she's not. What? She's there. You're on your honeymoon. *What?*"

"On the beach. A man, in the dark. Had a knife."

"When? When?"

"Don't know. Maybe... two hours ago."

"Shit. Are you su—? No. Fuck. I'm coming."

"Don't—"

"You sit tight, I'm coming—"

"Alan, no. I need you there."

"Are you hurt?"

"...Yeah."

"Where are you? Where are you hurt?"

"I mean... he didn't get me. He was trying for me. It was meant for me. She pushed me. Jumped in front... oh god."

"Okay. Okay. Okay. Zero, listen to me. I know you're hurting, but please, stop crying for just a second. I'm coming—"

"No. I-I need you there."

"Why? Why?"

"I need you to go to my house. The girls... Jesus. The girls, they deserve to know."

"No. Absolutely not. That should come from you. They should hear it from you."

"I can't, Alan. I can't. It took me... I don't know how long, just to make this call. I can't. It's too hard."

"Fine. Then come home. Come home now."

"The resort is locked down. Cops are here. They're looking for him."

"And then? And then you'll come home?"

"There are arrangements. They'll... they'll fly her body home. Someone should be there. When she gets there."

"Come home, Zero."

"Can't. Locked down..."

"Zero, you come home as soon as you can, do you hear me?"

"Will you take care of her? And our girls? Like I asked?"

"Yeah. I will. Of course I will. But you should be here to do it, and not—"

"You're a good friend, Alan. The best."

"Zero, wait, don't—"

"Goodbye Alan."

*

Alan Reidigger stared at the phone for a long time.

So that was how Maria Johansson exited his life. After fifteen years, all it took was a two-minute phone call for her to be gone. Gone forever.

"Fuck," he said again, and he rubbed his face and smoothed his beard. He turned off the television, where he'd been watching *Die Hard* on TCM, and dialed Strickland.

"Alan? Hey. What's up?"

"Todd. You sitting?"

"Um..."

"Todd, who is it?" Penny's voice in the background. Well—that mystery was solved. But no time to wonder at the moment how the straight-laced Boy Scout had scored the British punk-rock genius.

"Put me on speaker, Todd." This was going to hurt. But so did ripping off a Band-Aid, and there was only one way to do it.

He told them. Todd was stricken silent and Alan gave them time to process, so the only sound for a short while was Penny's sobs.

90

Eventually they quieted, and Alan said: "I know. Trust me, I know. There's nothing I can say, no condolences to offer that will make this any better. It's... goddammit, it sucks. But I need you both listening. Are you listening?"

"Yeah," Todd said.

"Todd—pack a bag. I want you after him. Now, tonight."

"The killer? But we don't know who—"

"No, Todd. I want you after Zero."

"I don't understand."

"I know you don't." Alan sighed. "After Kate's murder, Zero... he went off the deep end. He tore a path across Eastern Europe and then some. They sent me and another agent after him. To kill him. I didn't. We faked it. And there's a lot more to the story that I just can't get into right now. I just need you to find him, detain him, and bring him home."

Todd hesitated. "This sounds like an overreaction. I mean, he's at a resort in Nassau right now, isn't he?"

"He won't be for long."

"I still don't understand—"

I know you don't understand, but I do, so let that be enough," Alan said forcefully. "I would go after him myself, but I'm not as young as I used to be and I made a couple of promises that I have to keep. It would be better if you go. You could do it. You could stop him. Bring him home."

Strickland sighed into the phone. "Yeah. Okay."

"Penny? Are you listening?"

She sniffled. "Yes."

"He has no resources and he won't come to me. He'll come to you. And you'll say no. Do you understand?"

"Yes."

"Good. Thank you. I'm sorry to ruin your night. Todd—bring him home."

"And if I can't?"

"Let's just assume you can."

*Because if not, I'm not sure how we'll stop the CIA from killing him this time around.* Alan had used up his only trick the first time around.

He ended the call, and he thought back to that night on the Hohenzollern Bridge in Germany, where he and Agent Morris had finally found Zero. He had just been standing there, alone, looking out

91

over the Rhine, and to Alan it had very much looked like he was thinking about jumping.

That was the night that Alan had told him about the experimental memory suppressor. It was Reidigger's plan, one that didn't require killing Zero and would allow him to raise his girls and have a job and a home and sink into relative obscurity right under the CIA's noses. It was Reidigger who had stolen the tech for R&D. It was Reidigger who had located Dr. Guyer, the Swiss neurologist in Zurich who agreed to install the chip—at Zero's acquiescence, of course—in exchange for the research it might yield.

And in an ironic twist of the knife, it was Reidigger who had inspired the agency to cease all work on the project and scrap all files on it, out of fear that a double agent had stolen the suppressor and might still be within their ranks.

He took his time putting on his shoes, locating his trucker cap and keys. He would have given anything to switch places with Strickland, to be the one getting on a plane and going after Zero. He would have given anything to have to hunt down and physically subdue his best friend, if it came to that, instead of what he had to do next.

But he'd made a promise. And he would keep it.

# CHAPTER FIFTEEN

Preston McMahon watched the video, and then he watched the video again.

He watched the video in the dark, his tablet screen the only source of light in the small house they had given him on the grounds of Fort Benning, Georgia.

He watched the video, and when it ended, he watched the video again. YouTube had taken it down as a violation of their "community standards," whatever that meant, but there had been no shortage of people and outlets who had copied it by then—himself included.

This time when he watched it, he studied the face of the man speaking. He memorized the swoop of the man's scar, the pattern of grays flecked in his beard. The fact that he punctuated certain words with his right fist. Preston was not fluent in Arabic; he knew only a handful of words and phrases that he'd picked up on tours of duty, just enough to get by with locals. But he knew that the threat of death on the old man if the ransom wasn't paid was no bluff. He knew the silent fury he saw in the man's scowl. *That* he was fluent in.

When the video ended, he watched it again, and this time he studied the old man. He was bound to a chair, his hands behind him. He stared at the floor while the terrorist spoke, but he did not look beaten. He did not look harmed or even all that afraid. That's how the old man was; tough as nails, through and through, not only still kicking at eighty-four but as resilient as ever.

When the old man spoke, he did so with conviction. He meant every word he said, that his own life was not worth giving these men what they wanted.

Preston watched as the terrorist with the scar grabbed a handful of Grandpa Bill's hair and yanked, and his own silent fury built anew with every viewing.

The video ended and he watched it again. This time he studied the backdrop. It was just corrugated steel blemished with streaks of rust. A ship or shipyard, if Preston had to guess—but this was no guessing game and there were no other clues to be had. There was no background noise. Whoever was filming had done so handheld but shown nothing else, not even the floor. There was no swaying or movement that suggested they were on a boat or any sort of vehicle.

The video ended and he watched it again. This time he closed his eyes, and he listened carefully to the sound of the terrorist's voice, his demands, the way in which he said, "Five. Hundred. *Million*. US."

He kept his eyes closed and he listened until he was certain that he could pick that voice out of a crowd if necessary. He watched and studied the face until he was absolutely sure he could find the scarred Arabic man in a football stadium, could pick him out like a *Where's Waldo?* drawing.

Only then did he stop watching, and he started packing.

Preston McMahon had never really liked his name. When most people heard it they assumed he was a recent MBA graduate from a place like Harvard or Wharton whose parents had given him a million dollars to start a tech company so that he could later tell magazines that he was a self-made man.

Truth was, he was named after his grandfather, former President of the United States William Preston McMahon.

They shared a lot, he and Grandpa Bill. In fact, they shared a birthday—Preston had been born at 11:57 p.m. on September 19, and it was a running joke in the family that Grandpa Bill had signed an executive order forcing him out of the womb just in time for them to share the day.

They shared their light hair, or they had before Bill's had turned white. They shared the fact that neither was very tall; Preston had peaked at five-foot-nine, and the tallest Grandpa Bill had ever stood was five-nine and a half.

They shared that they were Mountaineers fans, and would watch games together whenever they could while Preston was growing up.

They shared that they had both gone to the same West Virginia public school district; even though Preston's parents had wanted him to go to private school they had given their son a choice and he had chosen the school that Grandpa Bill had gone to. What he did not realize at the time was that Grandpa Bill had a building named after him at that very school—the William McMahon Athletic Facility—and although McMahon was a fairly common name, it was impossible to escape or hide the fact that the former president was his grandfather.

94

Public school had been tough for a short, stout, smart kid with a connection like that and a name like Preston. He'd gotten picked on a lot. But he didn't regret it, nor did he change his mind about going to private school. Public school in West Virginia had forced him to stand up for himself. It had inspired him to join JROTC in high school, which in turn had inspired him to join the Army instead of heading straight to college.

He'd never forget that night. His mother had cried. His father was sullen. Grandpa Bill had asked him, "Are you sure?" And when Preston said yes, Grandpa Bill shook his hand and said, "You're a braver man than I could ever be."

That was ten years ago now. It had been a very long and busy ten years, and within them Preston McMahon had learned international emergency crisis response, special reconnaissance, and hostage rescue. He had been a part of air assault operations, combat search and rescue, and counterterrorism units.

At twenty-eight years old, Preston McMahon was a member of the 75th Ranger Regiment, the elite combat-deployable special-operations force headquartered at Fort Benning, Georgia.

*Rangers lead the way.*

Preston packed his rucksack with everything he knew he'd need and then everything he thought he might, anything that would fit and served a potential use.

He'd been given one week of emergency leave in light of the circumstances. As if Grandpa Bill was already dead. His first instinct had been to turn it down, but it had been offered by the colonel himself, who told him, "Go be with your family, McMahon. They'll need you more than we do right now."

The colonel was right. They did need him.

His cell phone rang. Preston winced and then answered. "Hi, Mom."

"Hi, sweetheart." Her voice was breathy and hushed. At least it sounded like she'd stopped crying. "Are you heading back yet?"

"No, Ma. I'm not heading back."

"Are you going to drive, or take the bus? Because we can pick you up from the station."

"Mom." He sighed. "Are you listening, Mom? I'm not heading back."

"I don't understand, Preston. Here; talk to Dad."

She was still in shock; her father-in-law had been kidnapped and was being held for ransom for five hundred million dollars under penalty of death. She'd seen the video. She had always been a loving, gentle parent, but not the toughest of them.

"Preston."

"Hi, Dad."

"You coming home?"

"No."

His dad was silent for a moment. "You're going?"

"Yes."

"Can you… do you think you can?"

"Yes sir. I do."

The colonel was right. His family needed him more than the 75th did right now.

Grandpa Bill needed him.

"And he'll be…?" Like Grandpa Bill, William McMahon, Jr. had never served. He was a state prosecutor, an incredible orator with a commanding voice that had on more than one occasion made young Preston pass a small amount of urine when it reached a booming crescendo. But right now that voice cracked slightly. "He'll be…?"

*Alive.*

"Yes, Dad."

"Be safe, son. Love you."

"Love you both." Preston ended the call. He slung his rucksack over a shoulder and strode out into the night to his car. There were a lot of sports cars on base, especially when a unit came back from deployment. These guys, after months abroad, they'd be sitting on more money than they'd ever had in their lives and they'd blow their load on something sleek and shiny with two doors. About two weeks after a unit came home from deployment, half of those sporty sleek cars would be wrecked.

Preston had opted for something more conventional, a reliable four-door sedan that got forty-two to the gallon highway and topped out at one-twenty. In hunter green, his favorite color.

He tossed the backpack in the backseat, and as he navigated his way off base he made a call.

"This is Strickland." He sounded a little harried, out of breath.

"Hi, Staff Sergeant."

"McMahon? Been a while."

"You sound busy, sir," Preston noted.

"About to catch a flight. But I got a minute. And you can drop the 'sir,' I'm not your superior anymore."

"I would, but Todd is a terrible name."

"Sure. *Preston*."

They shared a brief laugh. Very brief; neither seemed particularly spirited.

"I'll shoot straight, Strickland. I need to know if there's anything you can tell me about the hostage situation of my grandfather."

"Oh... oh, man. I'm sorry, McMahon. I completely forgot you were his... Christ. Your family okay?"

"No. Not really."

Strickland sighed through the phone. "I wish there was something I could tell you, but I'm not on it. If the CIA is privy to anything, I haven't been informed. I'm about to head out on an op myself, unrelated, so I won't be available for a briefing even if they had one. I'm sorry."

"It's okay. I figured it was worth a shot. Thanks anyway."

"Look, I'll keep an ear to the ground," Strickland promised, "and if I hear anything, you'll be the first to know."

"Appreciate it. Phone is always on."

"Same. Take care."

Preston ended the call and sighed. He'd hoped that Strickland would have something for him, even if just a crumb, but no. He rolled up to the gate and presented his authorization of leave to the MP there, and then he drove out of Fort Benning and turned to get onto the highway.

Preston McMahon was on his own, but that had never been a problem before. And he had a good idea of where to start.

# CHAPTER SIXTEEN

He had been expecting the knock at the door. It came a bit later than he'd assumed it would, but it came all the same, and he was ready for it.

"Mr. McIlhenney?" The resort staffer was with two white-shirted Bahamian police officers. Their guns were in their holsters but their stern expressions suggested they would use them if necessary.

"Yes?" Krauss said, blinking innocently.

"I don't know if you've heard, sir, but there has been an incident on the property." The staffer was young, pretty, with dozens of skinny braids in her hair and a light blue polo and a skirt. "May we come in and ask you a few questions?"

He frowned. "What sort of incident?"

She flashed him a well-practiced but insincere smile. "Please, sir, we can explain if we may just come in for a moment."

"Um... all right then." He opened the door the rest of the way and allowed the three of them inside his room. It was a simple enough room, a queen-sized bed and nightstands on either side, a television and stand, a small table in the corner with two chairs and a bathroom at the other end. It was facing the sea, as he'd asked, and the upgrade he'd paid for included not only a soaking tub with jets but a shower big enough for two with dual heads.

"Pardon the mess," he said quickly as he scooped up articles of clothing from the bed and chairs. He knocked two empty beer cans into the trash and slid a half-empty bottle of Bahamian rum behind the television, out of sight. None of those had been drunk, of course, but poured down the sink. "I wasn't exactly expecting anyone to come knocking." He laughed nervously and gestured to the pajama pants he wore.

He was not an untidy person by any means but appearances were important. He had been expecting the knock at the door, and he was ready for it.

"These gentlemen have a couple of questions they would like to ask you," said the staffer.

98

"Uh, sure. Fire when ready." He chuckled.

The police did not chuckle, or even crack a smile.

"Where were you," asked the taller of the two, his accent thick, "between nine fifteen and nine thirty p.m. tonight?"

Stefan Krauss frowned. "I'm not entirely sure. What time is it now?"

"It is eleven thirty," the staffer told him.

"Oh. Then I believe I was just getting out of the shower? I honestly haven't looked at the clock in hours." He chuckled again. So easy to win someone over with a laugh—usually. The right pitch and timbre could earn trust and ease minds. But not tonight. Someone had died tonight, and this was no laughing matter.

But Patrick McIlhenney did not know that.

"Before and after that?" the second cop asked. His accent was less pronounced, suggesting he'd either spent some time stateside or had been on the beat for so long in the tourist district of Nassau that it had lost its edges.

"Before that I went for a jog in the gym." The small athletic facility the resort offered was one of the few places on the entire property that had no cameras around—other than the beach.

"Which gym?" the staffer asked.

Krauss pointed with a thumb. "The one that way? Didn't know there was more than one."

"And after?"

"I stayed in. I was here. Had a drink… maybe two." He grinned sheepishly. "But who's counting?"

The taller cop eyed the trashcan where he'd swept the beer cans. "What is your business in Nassau, Mr.…?"

"McIlhenney. I know, it's a mouthful. And my business here isn't business at all. It's pleasure. A vacation."

"Alone?" asked the second cop.

Now Krauss's smile evaporated, and his throat flexed. "Well, if you must know… I had a breakup recently. Pretty bad one. We were engaged. But—water under the bridge, as they say. Would rather not talk about that, if it's all the same to you. Pardon me, but you still haven't told me what this is all about?"

"May we look around your room, sir?" asked the tall cop, ignoring his question.

"By all means. As long as you promise not to judge me by the sad state of the mini fridge."

"Wait outside, please."

Krauss followed the staffer out of his room, where he had a small outdoor sofa and table there, and hooks to sling a hammock if he called the front desk and requested one.

"Ma'am," he said quietly as the cops checked his room. "I'll be honest, this is freaking me out just a bit. Can you at least tell me the *nature* of what happened?"

She smiled her disingenuous customer-service smile and said, "Someone was attacked tonight on the beach, sir. We don't truly believe it was anyone staying at the resort; much more likely that it was a local, perhaps a robbery gone awry, but we're still going room to room, taking every precaution."

"Oh. The person who was attacked—are they all right?"

"Everything is fine," she answered without answering, "and perfectly safe. This is protocol for a situation like this one. A very rare circumstance for which we have a thorough and immediate response."

Krauss flashed her a charlatan smile of his own. "Well. That makes me feel better. Though I still think I'll lock the door tonight."

The police emerged from his room, and they nodded to the staffer. Neither of the officers said another word to him as they retreated down the path that bordered a manicured lawn and palm trees, to the next suite in the row, in search of a killer.

"Thank you, sir," said the young woman. "We would appreciate it if you would stay in tonight."

"I was planning to."

"Have a pleasant night."

"Yeah. You too." Krauss headed back into his room. The police had turned over the things in his suitcase and pulled out all the drawers. He pushed them back in, replaced his clothing, and drew the shades over the large window. He turned on the television and put it on mute, and turned out the light so that the screen's bluish glow was the only thing illuminating the room.

Then he put his head in his hands and sighed. He felt... remorse wasn't quite the right word. Shame; that was what he felt. He was ashamed of what he had done.

His target had been Zero. He'd watched him and the woman, Maria Johansson, from outside the sushi bar. He watched and he waited. He knew that they would be unarmed, unsuspecting, and had had a few drinks. But there were two of them, both highly trained CIA operatives, so the element of surprise and the blade only served to tip the scales slightly in his favor.

He had opted for a knife for obvious reasons. For one, getting a gun into the Bahamas while incognito would have been impossible. Procuring one while there was an unnecessary risk. He could be wandering into a sting operation or purchase a faulty weapon for all he knew. He had no contacts in Nassau.

But a knife, that was simple and personal. There was even a slight elegance to it. He'd stolen the steak knife at breakfast that morning, simply slipped it in his pocket. Back in his room he'd rubbed it on an angle against a rough stone until the serrated teeth were gone, until the blade was smooth and deadly sharp. He'd rinsed the filings down the sink and thrown the rock into the ocean. And then he'd waited.

His target had been Zero, but he missed his target. Not only had he missed his target, but he'd killed a woman. There was no doubt in his mind about that; as soon as he swung the blade, as soon as it had completed its arc and flown from his hand and into the water, he knew she was dead.

Stefan Krauss did not like to kill women. Certainly not for money, and not at all if he could help it. Not unless it was in self-defense, and even then it would have to be absolutely necessary, his life or theirs. Even without the amorality of the action, Johansson was not his target. There was no money, glory, or vengeance in her death.

He was ashamed, and that's what he had been thinking when he fled. He could have stayed and finished the job. When the woman fell, Zero had dropped to the sand with her, ignoring Krauss completely as if he wasn't even there. As if nothing else existed in the whole world.

Krauss had lost his knife, but he could have used his bare hands. Broken his neck or strangled him. But contrary to what anyone might say or think, he was not a monster. He certainly wasn't *afraid* of Zero; that wasn't it. No. To have done so right then would have been... dishonorable wasn't quite the right word.

Unsportsmanlike. Yes, that was it.

Stefan Krauss was not his real name. The real Stefan Krauss was a German footballer who had played for the Dortmund club for one season before dying in an automobile accident. The real Stefan Krauss would likely agree—this Krauss had fouled on the play. He had messed up, and Zero deserved his penalty shot.

At the very least, he deserved to grieve. To be with his daughters. To share in their grief as well.

Nassau had been a bust. As penance, Krauss would stay in his room until he could change his flight. Instead of Germany he would head to the United States. He had not wanted to face Zero on his own turf, but Krauss had used up his own advantage and now felt that he owed Zero some form of one.

But the game was far from over. He was still going to kill Agent Zero.

# CHAPTER SEVENTEEN

"I'm sorry to wake you like this," said the fat man.

Right—"fat" was an unkind word. The man was husky. Ample? Mischa was struggling to come up with a good word for it. Maria had told her that "fat" was not a nice thing to say, even if it was technically accurate.

Mischa had been the one to answer the door when the knock came, a deep and resonant pounding that had roused her from a very satisfying slumber. She had looked through the peephole and saw the man, the friend of Maria and Zero that was called Alan Reidigger, though in public they were supposed to call him Mitch, and she had punched in the six-digit security code and granted him access to their home.

And she had, of course, noticed immediately that something was amiss. Her ability to read body language wasn't even necessary; he wore it in his face. He was sorrowful, in despair over something.

"Hi," he'd said. "Who else is here? Sara? Maya?"

"Sara only. Maya did not return home from her job today."

"What?" Alan Reidigger's brow furrowed in alarm. "What job? Where is she?"

"She is safe," Mischa assured him. "Her job informed us that she was needed elsewhere and would be returning, likely tomorrow. I don't know for certain, but from what I've gathered I believe she may have been training to be an operative of some sort."

The bearded man closed his eyes and let out a sigh so heavy Mischa worried he might actually deflate. "Okay. I don't know how to deal with that right now. Can you wake Sara, please? There's something I have to tell you."

"Yes." Mischa strode to the basement door, pulled it open, and shouted down the stairs. "Sara! Please wake up! Alan Reidigger is here!"

The man huffed, and Mischa frowned. Had she not done precisely as he'd asked?

"What?" came Sara's groggy reply. "Who? Why?"

"Come upstairs, please!" Mischa shouted.

"Jeez. Fine," Sara grumbled as she trudged up the stairs. "It's almost freakin' midnight. Somebody better be dead." Then she stopped suddenly at the sight of Alan Reidigger standing there in their kitchen, as if she hadn't truly believed Mischa. "Alan?"

"I'm sorry to wake you like this," said the fat man, though fat was an unkind word that she was not supposed to say. "But something's happened."

"What's happened?" Mischa prodded.

"Is my dad okay?" Sara said instantly.

"No. I mean, yes," Alan said, fumbling. "He's fine. Physically. Uh…"

"What? What is it?" Sara urged.

"Yeah." His throat flexed under his beard, and then he said: "Maria is dead."

Mischa blinked.

She had not expected that.

*Maria is dead.*

The words rattled around her head like a ricocheting bullet. Now she understood why the man had looked and acted the way he had. It was her understanding that he and Maria had been friends for many years, longer than Mischa had even been alive, while she had not even known Maria for one full year. Still…

*Maria is dead.*

She was no stranger to violence or death; she was well aware that people died all the time, every day, sometimes for barely any reason at all. But Maria had been kind to her, the kindest person she'd ever met. She'd tried her best to make a life for her here. And now…

*Maria is dead.*

She knew what she was supposed to feel in the moment. But did she? What was it that she felt right now? The characters in books she read might have howled in grief, or collapsed to the floor wailing, or perhaps even insisted that Alan was lying. The latter actually made the most sense to her, because Maria was on her honeymoon, on a tropical island, not on a dangerous CIA operation.

"I'm sorry," Alan said. "I'm sorry to be the one to tell you this."

Mischa glanced over at Sara. The older girl was not reacting at all like any characters she'd ever read either. Sara wore a deep frown, her gaze flitting left and right as if she was trying to figure out a complex logic puzzle in her head.

"How?" Mischa asked.

"I'm afraid I don't really know all the details…"

"If you know any, I would like to know them."

"I don't think it's my place to say." Alan stonewalled.

"But it's your place to come here." Sara spoke up at last, not looking up at him, her voice low. "In the middle of the night, to tell us this?"

"Your dad asked me to. He can't leave. He has to deal with the authorities, and he didn't want to do it with a phone call."

"And now you are here," Mischa pointed out, "so you may as well tell us what you know."

"Fine," Alan relented. "I get it; you're not children. You'd think I'd know that by now." He sighed. "Maria was killed by someone who was after… them. They used the honeymoon to their advantage, to strike at a time when neither would expect anything."

"Did they catch this person?" Mischa asked.

Alan shook his head. "No. Not yet, I should say. But they're looking for him."

"How was it done?" she asked.

"Sorry?"

"Did this person use a gun? A knife? A blunt-force weapon?"

"It was a knife." Alan shook his head. "Please. That's all I know."

"And my dad… he'll come back soon?" Sara asked quietly.

"Yes."

He was lying. Mischa knew it instantly. There was so much pain behind his eyes, but in that instant there was deceit as well. Zero would not be coming home as soon as he could, and Mischa knew why. At least she thought she did.

"Okay," said Sara. "Thank you. Thanks for… coming, and telling us."

"I think maybe I should stay," Alan said. "Sleep on the couch. Would that make you feel better?"

Sara shook her head. "Thanks, but not necessary. If we need you, we'll call you."

Alan looked from one of them to the other, and seemed to realize that Sara spoke for both of them. And she did; it was nothing personal against him, but Mischa would feel no safer with him on the sofa than she would with an empty one. His presence would be of little practical value.

"Okay." He nodded at last. "You call me if you change your mind, or if you need anything at all." He retreated then, to the foyer, turning only once as if he wanted to say something more, but there was nothing more to say. And then he was gone.

For a long moment after, the two girls just stood in the kitchen, neither saying anything. Mischa was not sure what to say, if there was anything to say. She did not know if she was supposed to offer condolences or ask if Sara was okay, or perhaps both of those things. Though ultimately she settled on neither of those things.

"Well. I... I think I'm going to go back downstairs," Sara said at last. Her gaze would not meet Mischa's. "Are you... do you need anything?"

"No," Mischa told her.

"Okay." She pulled open the basement door, and then paused. "If you wanted to come down there too... that would be okay."

It was a kind gesture, but as Sara had told Alan, not necessary. "I'm fine. Thank you."

"Okay. I guess I'll... see you in the morning then." She closed the door behind her again.

Mischa headed back to her own room, but rather than trying to sleep again she simply sat on the bed. She stared at the bookshelf that Maria had bought for her, laden with books that she had requested and Maria had obliged. There was the bureau filled with clothes, some of which Maria had bought for her just a few days ago, for school. Atop it was a pink stuffed bear, the purpose of which was still somewhat lost on Mischa, at least in terms of practicality. But she understood that it was an endearing gesture.

*Maria is dead.*

How did she feel?

*I don't know.*

She was sad. Certainly. But she wasn't quite sure how to be sad. She had never really been close to anyone before—even Samara, the former Russian sparrow who had trained her, was more of a mentor than a relation or friend.

But it had been different with Maria. It had been... not quite love. She wasn't sure she knew how to love, not yet. But something close to it. Something that perhaps would have eventually become love, given time. Now it never would.

And what would become of her now? Without Maria here, would she have to leave this place?

She was surprised to find herself angry suddenly, angrier than she'd ever been. She knew that her face did not show it—she was very good at hiding emotions—but she could not keep her hands from shaking. She did not know what to do with this anger, which congealed into energy, energy that needed to come out in some way.

Mischa grabbed the pink stuffed bear, and she held it firmly with one hand and with the other, she tore the head from it. The stitches ripped, and the head loosed from its body with such force that it flew from her grip, bits of stuffing littering the floor in its wake like entrails.

Maria had been taken from her. Her future had been taken from her. Whatever had been changing within her over these past six months was just the start of something that she would never see to the end, not now.

Mischa grabbed the blue backpack that Maria had bought her for school. She stuffed some clothes into it. Her toothbrush. The cell phone Maria had gotten her, and its charger. She put on jeans and her shoes, and she slung the backpack over her shoulders.

In the foyer, she opened the coat closet and reached into the pocket of the well-worn brown leather jacket where Zero kept a loaded, hammerless revolver, and she took that too.

Mischa might have been playing the part of American girl, but she was not one. She was a spy, a soldier, a killer. She still knew things and she still knew people, things and people that could help her at least find out who was responsible for Maria's death, and make sure they suffered a similar fate. Maybe not at her hands, but at least by her facilitation.

Sara would be fine. She was admirably independent, perhaps even better on her own.

Mischa punched in the security code and slipped out of the house. The late August night was cool but comfortable, which she was glad for, because it would take her a long time to get where she needed to go if she had to go on foot.

But it would be worth it if she could find Maria's murderer.

As Maya had said: *If anyone could.*

# CHAPTER EIGHTEEN

*Amun.*

No; they were all dead, hunted to the last man. He crossed it out.

*~~Amun.~~*

*Brotherhood.*

*Fitzpatrick?*

He knew that Fitzpatrick was still alive. But was he active? Would he have been able to move like the man on the beach did, after the injuries he'd sustained?

Zero wasn't sure. This was hopeless. Making a list of those who would want to kill him was little more than a waste of paper. He crumpled the sheet of resort stationery and tossed it. It bounced off the rim of the wastebasket and he left it there.

It was nearly one o'clock in the morning. Almost four hours since Maria had died on the beach, though it felt like minutes, the time passing in a blur. There had been cops, a lot of them, and flashing lights, and men dressed in white took her body away, and they asked him if he wanted to come to the precinct but he couldn't move, not at first.

Everything he had in him had left his body with his tears. He was hollow now, gutted. The tears had dried; the trembling had ceased. He was numb. Just numb.

First Kate. Now Maria. Who would be next? Maya? Sara? Alan, maybe? Was this what his life would be, resigned to lose and lose again every time he thought he'd at last found some sense of happiness?

The police were still out there in the night, searching for the man who had killed his wife. They had tried to find the knife that had been flung into the ocean but to no avail. The resort would remain locked down until morning, but Zero knew that he was far from here, probably already off the island. The Bahamas were an archipelago of hundreds of islets; it would have been very easy for the killer to hop on a boat and be several islands away by now, hidden until he could safely leave the country.

That's what he would have done.

The cops, they had asked him five times if the killer had made any demands. They assumed that it was a criminal, a local who had snuck onto resort property to steal a wallet or some cash. No, Zero told them. No demands. Nothing spoken. Just a man with a knife.

But that wasn't true. He'd heard it, he *knew* he had. His name, spoken in a whisper.

*Zero.*

The killer had known his name.

Now Zero was back in their room, with all of her things that would have to be packed up and shipped back home. Her perfume lingered in the air. Her suitcase was still open, perched on the wooden luggage rack at the foot of the bed.

But he'd already mourned. He'd already given everything he could. There was nothing left in him.

Well—there was one thing.

*Let's just say we did... try,* she had said. *How would we go about that?*

He would start by figuring out who wanted him dead.

Among the most recent was Mr. Shade, the terrorist-funding multimillionaire currently incarcerated at H-6. Could Shade have sent an assassin somehow? Unlikely; Sergeant Flagg ran a tight ship in the Moroccan desert.

The man with the knife was an assassin. That much was certain. He was there only to kill. And while Zero had only caught the briefest of glimpses in the dark, he knew that the man was Caucasian, similar height and build to his own. That was all he saw before the knife glinted.

He'd tangled with assassins before. But Rais was dead. Krauss was dead. Fitzpatrick was... alive, but in what state? He couldn't help it; once he'd gotten the mercenary's name in his head it refused to leave.

He needed to know. The phone was there, on the table; he had pulled it from the safe to call Alan.

He needed to know. It was late, but he took a deep breath and forced himself to make the call. The line rang once. Twice. Half a third.

"Hello?" Penny's voice sounded soft, breathy, unlike he'd ever heard her sound before.

"Did I wake you? I'm sorry."

"No. I was... up."

"Are you in the lab?" he asked.

109

"No. Zero... I'm so sorry."

Ah. So she'd heard. Alan must have called her.

"Yeah," was all he said to that. "Penny, I know it's late, but I need your help. There's a man called Fitzpatrick who used to run a mercenary group called the Division. I don't know his first name but I'm sure the CIA has a file on him thick as a bible. I need you to run down any last-knowns we've got on him—medical history, whereabouts, employment, the works. If we've got a current address, even better. I want to track him down ASAP and find out where he is. Can you do that for me? Tonight?"

She was silent on the other end, silent enough for him to think that perhaps the call had dropped. "Penny?"

"No, Zero. I can't."

He frowned. "Why not?"

"I can't help you," she said in response.

"Can't? Or won't?" He knew what this was. Alan had gotten to her first.

"Come home," she urged. "Be with your family. With us. Make arrangements for her. Do what you need to do—"

"*This* is what I need to do," he said forcefully.

"Not by yourself," she countered. "If you come home, I'll help you. But only if we do it together. Let us help you—and her."

He gritted his teeth. Penny was the last person he would have expected to use Maria to guilt him out of this. "Coming home would waste too much time. I need to be on the trail right now. So—are you going to help me or not?"

"No," she said in a whisper. "I'm not."

He ended the call, reared back, and hurled the phone against the wall. It broke into three pieces, which he stomped further, and then sifted through the parts until he found the SIM card, which he snapped in half and flushed down the toilet.

Maria's phone was still off and locked in the safe, where it would remain. He hastily grabbed up her things without looking at them and stuffed them into her suitcase, which he zipped up and left on the bed. He packed his small carry-on bag with a few changes of clothes, and then stole out into the night, clinging to the shadows of the trees that lined the resort's walkways.

The place was still locked down, but that wouldn't pose much of a problem for him. Getting off the island—that was another story. But he recalled that on the shuttle ride from the airport to the resort they had passed an impressive harbor holding the yachts of the island's super-wealthy, as well as a number of sea planes bobbing in the water.

It would be a slow trip, but if he could find one with a full tank of fuel and outfitted with proper landing gear, it would be hours before anyone noticed it missing. He wasn't the best pilot, had never even flown solo before, but he'd logged some hours on both a simulator and with an instructor. It was like riding a bike, he assumed.

If anyone might know something about this, it would be Shade, who was at H-6—along with no fewer than two dozen others that Zero had put there. Someone had to know something, and it was as good a place as any to start if no one else was going to help him.

It wasn't until he'd scaled the resort's fence and was safely on the other side that he realized he had forgotten his medications, the pills that Dillard had prescribed to him. But he'd come too far to go back for them.

Besides—what good would the pills be? Their purpose was to help him remember.

And right now, forgetting didn't seem like such a bad idea.

# CHAPTER NINETEEN

The city of Abu Dhabi was, in some ways, reminiscent of Manhattan, located as it was on an island, its beautiful skyline set against the backdrop of the Persian Gulf. It was an extremely wealthy city, built on the funds of oil and natural gas reserves, and the second-most populous city in the UAE after Dubai. Its name translated literally to "Father of Gazelles," purportedly because of the large local gazelle population prior to its rapid urbanization.

"Fascinating," said Trent Coleman flatly as Maya shared these facts with him. He stretched in the morning sun. "God, that flight sucked. No wonder we got this assignment. Nobody wants to be on a plane that long."

Maya couldn't help but agree. Her first instinct when they had landed was to reach for her phone to text her dad that she'd landed safely. After a fifteen-hour flight, she'd almost forgotten that she did not have her cell phone, that she was on a covert operation, and that her dad was in the Bahamas on his honeymoon with Maria.

Their briefing package did not make for scintillating reading material either. In it were only two sheets of paper, instructing them to first liaise with a CIA asset for equipment, and then to locate a native Emirati called Ali Saleh, who served on the board of the Emirates National Oil Company, or ENOC for short. There was a photo of Saleh, in a blue suit with a striped tie. He looked to be in his fifties, clean-shaven with deep-set eyes and plump cheeks.

They were to locate Saleh covertly, and then to call the sole number saved in a burner phone they had been provided along with a change of clothes, for further instruction.

That was it. That was everything they'd been provided.

"Feels strange, doesn't it?" Maya asked, craning her neck up at the skyscrapers of downtown Abu Dhabi. They had the taxi from the airport drop them off three blocks from the apartment building in which the asset was located.

"What's strange? That we left on a Monday morning and arrived on a Tuesday morning? Yeah, time zones are weird. The jet lag on the flight back is gonna be murder—"

"No," Maya interrupted. "The lack of details. They flew us halfway around the world and we don't know why we're here."

Coleman just shrugged. "Maybe it's because we're new. They don't want to front-load us with too much info. Or maybe it's so that if we're captured, we don't have any intel to give."

Maya scoffed. "Captured by *who*?"

He shrugged. "I don't know. It wasn't in the briefing."

"You're ridiculous. Let's go." She led the way along the busy avenue, assaulted by the sounds of the city, traffic and car horns and passersby shouting into phones.

"Hey, before we get there," said Coleman, "should we have names?"

"We have names, Coleman."

"No, I mean, like, codenames. Your dad is Agent Zero, isn't he?"

She shook her head. "You *really* need to lay off the spy movies..."

"We don't know this asset guy. Do you really want him knowing your real name?"

She hated that he had a point. "Ugh. Fine. What would you like your 'codename' to be?"

"No, no, you can't pick your own," he told her. "You have to choose mine, and I have to choose yours."

"Sure. Okay." She thought for a moment. "Then you would be... Agent Pita."

"Pita? Like the bread?"

"No. Like the acronym. Pain in the ass."

Trent laughed. "That's good. Real good. But two can play that game. I dub you... Agent Sweetcheeks."

"I *will* hit you." They reached the apartment building, a tower of steel and glass, and were admitted entry by a doorman in gloves and epaulets.

"Let's be serious," said Coleman as they headed for the elevator banks. "How about... Agent Scarlet?"

Maya pressed the up button and frowned. "Scarlet?"

"Yeah. Because you remind me of Hester from *The Scarlet Letter*."

"Trent, I don't know what book you read, but that is *not* a compliment..."

"I'm not explaining this well," he admitted. "She was marked by society, right? But she didn't give a shit what other people thought about her. Like you."

Maya resisted the urge to point out the flaw in his logic because, at its core, it was the most thoughtful she'd ever seen Trent Coleman be. "Okay. Fine. Scarlet it is." The elevator doors opened, and they got in with four other people. Maya pressed the button for the fourteenth floor and they rode up silence.

"Well?" Coleman asked as soon as they'd been deposited on their floor. "What about me?"

"Hmm. I think you would be… Friday. Agent Friday."

He laughed. "Why Friday?"

"Because every Friday in the program, without fail, you would come in and throw your hands up and shout, 'TGIF!'" Maya threw her own hands up in a not-kind mockery of her best Trent Coleman impression.

"I guess I did do that…"

"It was one of the many things I hated about you." She led the way down the carpeted hall, scanning the gold-plated numbers on the doors.

"All right then. Scarlet and Friday. Now I feel like a real spy."

"Good." She paused outside the asset's door. "Put your game face on." She knocked briskly.

A moment later the door opened, only about six inches, and a gaunt face with a patchy beard stared out at her. "What?" he hissed.

Maya glanced over at Coleman briefly. This was not the introduction she had expected. "We were sent to see you," she said simply.

"By who? Who are you? What do you want?" The man was young, no more than thirty, and his voice was thick with an Arabic accent.

"Um…" She wasn't sure how to answer that. It didn't feel right to announce they were from the CIA. Did they have the right place? Had she knocked on the wrong door?

The man opened the door a little wider and stuck out his head, glancing up and down the hall quickly. "You are here for the drugs?"

"What? No! We're here to see someone named Yasser."

"For equipment," Coleman chimed in. "We were sent to you for equipment."

The man's eyes narrowed suspiciously. Then he snorted, and his face broke into a wide grin. "I am sorry," he laughed. "I'm joking with you." His accent was not Arabic at all, but British. "I see new faces, and I can't help myself. You're the agents? Goodness, you look young. Come in, come in."

Maya looked again at Coleman, who just shook his head and grinned as well—probably enjoying a fellow practical joker—while all she could wonder was if she would ever get to work with someone who was half as serious about this as she was.

Yasser's apartment was a small studio, but what it lacked in size it made up for in luxury. The far wall was entirely glass, affording a magnificent view over Abu Dhabi and the gulf beyond. Everything in his place was white, black, or stainless steel, sharp angles all around. Aside from a tiny kitchen and bathroom there was only one main room, a bed separated from an entertaining space by a six-foot-tall, black-paneled divider.

"Wow," said Coleman. "So this is what being an asset gets you, huh? A half-million-dollar luxury apartment in downtown Abu Dhabi?"

"Indeed, my friend." Yasser smiled. "Would you care for some tea?"

"That sounds great—" Trent started to say.

"No," Maya interrupted, "thank you. We're here for equipment and then we'll be on our way."

"Suit yourself." Yasser approached the flat-screen television mounted on the wall. It must have been sixty inches, maybe more. He reached behind it and slid his hand up, then down. Maya heard a click, and the TV swung away like a door to reveal a large steel safe embedded in the wall behind it.

Yasser winked at them, and then covered the keypad with one hand while he punched in a code with the other. The electronic lock slid open, and the thick steel door with it.

"Whoa," Coleman muttered.

In the wall safe, backlit with LED lights, was a small armory. There were a variety of pistols, submachine guns, ammunition, tactical knives, and, if Maya wasn't mistaken, an assortment of grenades.

She had an uneasy feeling in her gut as Yasser pulled out a holstered pistol and handed it to her. "Sig Sauer P229," he told her. "Standard-issue for Secret Service. I know you're most familiar with the Glock 19, but I'm afraid I'm fresh out. Magazine is full, feel free to check for yourself."

Maya felt the weight of the gun in her hand. She slid it from the holster, ejected the magazine, and this time pushed the top round out with a thumb.

It was not made of rubber.

"Do you know why we're here, Yasser?" she dared to ask.

"Nope." He reached back into the safe. "I don't ask, and they don't tell. All they told me was to expect two agents—didn't mention that you'd be practically teenagers—and what to supply you with. So, here you are."

Yasser pulled out a narrow black case of thick plastic and passed it off to Coleman. He took it, laid it carefully on the coffee table, and opened it.

"Collapsible .308 rifle," Yasser explained as Maya and Coleman stared down at it. "Six rounds in there—they said that would be plenty—a suppressor, and a scope with night-vision capability."

Maya's throat ran dry.

"Last thing." Yasser tossed her a ring of keys with an electronic fob. "When you leave, take the elevator one floor below the lobby, to the parking garage. There you'll find a black Mercedes CLA 250. There's a location down by the harbor programmed into the GPS. When you're finished, park the car there and leave the gear in the trunk. I'll come 'round for it. Any questions?"

"No." Maya shrugged out of her jacket and secured the holstered Sig Sauer under her shoulder. She did not want to show what she was thinking. Best to get out of there first. "Let's go, Agent Friday."

Coleman was still staring down at the black components of the collapsible rifle. He snapped out of it and closed the case. "Yeah. Right. Of course... Agent Scarlet."

"Scarlet," Yasser repeated. "That's a pretty name."

"Thanks," she murmured. "For the equipment."

"Godspeed, Agents," Yasser said as he led them to the door.

They took the elevator down to the parking level in silence. Once there, Maya clicked the fob and a car chirped nearby. She got behind the wheel with Coleman beside her, the case on his lap. But she did not start the car just yet.

"What the hell," Coleman muttered.

"I'm going to call." She pulled out the burner phone with only one number programmed into it.

"Wait." Coleman looked uneasy. "At least put it on speaker."

She nodded, hit the call button, and put it on speakerphone. The line did not ring; there was a single click, and a female voice said, "Identify."

"Agents Lawson and Coleman," she said.

"One moment." There was the sound of a keyboard clacking, and then the woman—who was definitely not Agent Bradlee—asked, "Have you located the target?"

*The target.*

Coleman shook his head no.

"Yes," Maya lied.

"You're tracking him currently?"

"Yes," she said again.

"Wait until nightfall," the woman instructed. "Then neutralize."

*Neutralize.*

*To render someone or something harmless by way of opposing force.*

"Christ," Coleman hissed.

She remembered Bradlee's words after the training exercise with James Smythe. *What else would you expect "neutralize" to mean? You can't honestly expect us to put "kill" in a briefing.*

"Sorry, Agent, repeat?" the female operator said.

"What did he do?" Maya asked.

"Excuse me?"

"What did the target do to warrant… neutralizing?" she asked carefully.

"That's classified," the woman said simply. "Neutralize the target, and return immediately." The call ended.

Trent Coleman closed his eyes and sighed into his hand.

Maya's fear was confirmed. The ease with which she had pulled the trigger on James Smythe had gotten them here, sent to the other side of the world to kill someone.

They had been sent here to commit a murder.

# CHAPTER TWENTY

"Sir?"

There were three dainty knocks at the presidential bedroom door—*tock-tock-tock*—followed by: "Sir?"

First Lady Deirdre Rutledge rolled over, let out a sleepy moan, and said, "Darling, I'm fairly certain that's for you."

Jonathan Rutledge had not slept much the night before. He was too worried about Bill McMahon, too concerned about the ransom and the threat of death, of his whereabouts, of delaying the address that he knew he should give. But his advisors, Tabby Halpern included, had suggested he wait the night. An official statement had been issued by the White House saying that the administration was monitoring the situation very closely, had the full support of the Iranian government, and would arrive at the best solution as soon as possible.

They had nothing. They were spinning their wheels, hoping the FBI would find some shred of Bill.

Now it was morning, and Tabby Halpern was knocking gently on the door, *tock-tock-tock*, and calling out: "Sir?"

Rutledge rose with a groan and opened the door. "Good morning, Ms. Halpern."

"Morning, Mr. President." It was not lost on him that she left "good" out of it. "The situation has… developed."

"Should I assume I'll be taking my coffee in the Situation Room?"

"However you're most comfortable, sir."

He glanced down at his maroon silk pajamas. "All right then. Let's go." He closed the bedroom door behind him.

"Sir? Wouldn't you like to get dressed?"

"You said however I'm most comfortable. I don't think it matters what I'm wearing; a suit and tie aren't going to soften the blow of bad news."

"Fair enough, sir."

*

Fifteen minutes later Rutledge sat at the head of the long rectangular table in the John F. Kennedy Conference Room. Rarely was anything positive discussed within these walls, he had long ago realized.

It was seven fifteen in the morning; the assembly today was small. Aside from him and Tabby Halpern, present were Secretary of State Gregory Callahan, FBI Director Arthur Lee, each with an aide or assistant at their side who was unknown to Rutledge, and Vice President Joanna Barkley.

He was especially glad that Joanna was there. He needed someone as level-headed as her at his side. Though only thirty-seven, Joanna was pragmatic, sensible, and had a gift for logic that seemed to border on foresight.

"Okay," he sighed. "Tell me. Has there been any communication from the people holding Bill McMahon?"

"No sir," said Director Lee. "They've, uh, been silent through the night..." Lee cleared his throat, seemingly unable to look directly at Rutledge.

"Never mind the pajamas, Lee. I live here." Rutledge shook his head. "Can someone tell me what's going on?"

As usual, Tabby took the wheel. "Sir, the FBI and Secret Service have not found anything at all yet regarding President McMahon's whereabouts. The general consensus seems to be that he is being held somewhere in Iran."

"Is that opinion, or intelligence?" he asked.

"A bit of both, to be honest," she admitted, and then referred to a report in front of her. "Last night—local time that is, daytime in Iran—sixteen IRGC ships broke ranks and convened northeast of the rest of their fleet. They've refused all orders to return."

Jon Rutledge rubbed his forehead. The Islamic Revolutionary Guard Corps was, for all intents and purposes, Iran's armed forces—however, as he understood it, they were far more aligned with the ideology of a unified Islamic state than loyal to the political affiliation of the country. There had been musings, little more than rumor until now, that there was some dissent in the IRGC over the Ayatollah's recent treaty with the United States.

"So it's mutiny," he asked, though it wasn't really a question.

"It would seem," Tabby agreed. "Though one man's mutiny is another's crusade. And much like our own rules of engagement, the

119

IRGC won't fire on renegade ships without being fired upon first. All they can do is track them, follow them, and attempt to coerce them back."

"And what's this got to do with Bill?"

Arthur Lee spoke up. "The man from the ransom video, the one with the scar, he and his group were last seen just outside of Tehran a little more than a week ago. Intelligence suggests they had been meeting with IRGC officers. In fact, a few of them are former IRGC themselves."

Rutledge nodded. "So you think this group is larger than it would seem, and that they have some of the military behind them. All in the name of what—maintaining Islamic culture? Resisting westernization? They must know that no one has the intention of taking anything from them."

"Feel free to try to explain that to them," Tabby mused. "They believe you're the literal devil."

Rutledge shook his head. "So the running theory is that McMahon was somehow spirited away to Iran, and what—that these IRGC ships are heading to the location? As some kind of backup against a fight that may or may not be coming? That's insane. That would mean…"

He trailed off before he said it, because as insane as it sounded, it seemed like the perfect catalyst for what these people were trying to do.

Civil war. It would mean that either Iran's government broke the peace treaty with the United States, or faced civil war against factions of their own military. It wasn't even farfetched that they'd make martyrs out of themselves for it, too; there was plenty of historical precedence for such things.

These men knew exactly what they were doing. And all they had to do was kidnap one former president.

"What's Iran's official position?" he asked.

"They are… deeply concerned, to say the least," said Greg Callahan. He'd been the Secretary of State for less than a year, but was adept, even invaluable in the brokering of the treaties they'd arranged so far. "They have assured us that they are allocating every available resource to searching for these men. If they are within their own borders, they promise they will find them."

"And we have their cooperation if we were to assist on that?" the president asked.

"We do, sir. The Iranian government wants to maintain the peace however they can."

He nodded. It was time. He felt terrible about it, but Zero had enjoyed two days of vacation so far—it was better than nothing. "I want to put EOT on this. I want them on the ground, in Iran, searching. If they found me in the goddamn Sahara with nothing but a broken truck and a few guns, they can find Bill in an ally country with resources behind them."

No one spoke. No one even wanted to look at him, it seemed.

Except Joanna. She looked him right in the eye, and she told him what everyone else in the room had apparently already heard but didn't want to say.

"Sir. There was an incident last night in Nassau. Maria Johansson was killed."

Rutledge just stared for a moment, because he was sure he had not heard what he thought he had just heard. Killed? An agent was killed?

"What?" he heard himself say. That simply couldn't be. "No," he told them, as if stating a fact. "On... on their honeymoon?"

Barkley closed her eyes and nodded. "The Nassau police report states that a man with a knife approached them late at night on the beach. He didn't say anything to them. He just... acted, and then fled."

*That's not an incident,* he wanted to say. *That's an assassination.*

"Do we have any reason to believe this was linked to Bill McMahon in any way?"

Arthur Lee shook his head. "No sir. They appear to be isolated incidents."

"How is Zero?" Rutledge asked. That poor man, losing his wife on their honeymoon. "Is he okay? Where is he?"

"We don't know, sir," Joanna told him candidly. "Nassau police were called by the resort staff this morning when they found his room empty, but his belongings still there."

This meeting was quickly going from bad to worse to catastrophe. "Was he taken?"

"There were no signs of a struggle. Only a broken cell phone, the SIM missing. The suitcases were packed. Evidence suggests that Agent Zero went AWOL sometime in the night."

Rutledge sighed, and he ran his fingers through his hair, which he had neglected to comb before the meeting, and he tried to process all of this. The Executive Operations Team had started out with five members. Chip Foxworth had been killed back in March. Now, Maria Johansson was dead. Zero was AWOL.

"Agent Todd Strickland is unreachable as well," Barkley told him, as if reading his thoughts. "And Alan Reidigger is looking after Zero's family. Apparently Zero called him after it happened, before he left."

So that was it. EOT was finished, a six-month experiment that ended in failure. The team was gone, done, and with it went their best shot at finding Bill McMahon.

And without finding Bill McMahon, everything he had worked for, peace between nations, could be unraveled. Regardless of the outcome—Iran would either break the treaty, or they would face civil war—other nations would see them as an example of what happened when the US got involved, and when they got involved with the US.

"Tabby, put the call in to CIA Director Shaw," he said at last. "Tell him we want his best guys over there assisting in the search. Allocate every resource we can."

"Yes sir. Anything else?"

"Yes," he said slowly. "I think it's time that we seriously consider paying that ransom."

"Mr. President," said Barkley, "I think that we should seriously consider all other options first. Giving them what they want without any guarantee could be a sign of very bad faith that stands to represent more than just these men, but Iran as a country. It risks incredible divisiveness among the American people—"

"I don't care," he snapped. "Having him end up dead would be worse."

Barkley did not react to his harsh words; she merely stared at him evenly, and then nodded once.

Getting Bill back unharmed was the one thing he had to cling to. If they could do that, maybe they could avert disaster. Maybe. There was no telling—but it was the only step they had that seemed to be in the right direction.

Because now it wasn't just Bill's life on the line, but potentially those of many innocent others… and if they were lost, it would be President Rutledge who would shoulder the blame.

# CHAPTER TWENTY ONE

Zero slapped himself, not gently, and urged himself to stay awake. Ten hours he'd been in the air now, passing through time zones until night turned to daybreak and melted into late afternoon like a sped-up video.

The sea plane he'd stolen from the port at Nassau was small, a white four-seater with a name stenciled down the side in black: *Cassandra.*

*Who the hell names a plane Cassandra?* he'd wondered. He had a lot of time to wonder on the long flight northeast. Like what might have been if last night hadn't happened. What he and Maria might be doing right then, together, instead of one being alone over the Atlantic and one being dead.

There were no more tears, though. The time for that had passed.

There was desert below him now, for which he was only half thankful. On the one hand, it meant that he was drawing very near to his destination. On the other, *Cassandra* was almost out of fuel, running on fumes, and a crash in the desert would not be quite as forgiving as a hard water landing.

He'd torn out the plane's transponder, so they couldn't track him with that, but he was still visible in the sky and on radar. But he had not received any radio calls to identify himself or threats to blow him and *Cassandra* out of the sky. He assumed that was by virtue of where he was, the airspace he was occupying. Anyone watching the skies must have been used to strange planes arriving and departing from the middle of nowhere.

As he flew, he had time to wonder about a lot of things. He wondered what his daughters were doing. How they were feeling. They had each other to lean on right now; they didn't need him to be there to grieve. He couldn't even imagine how any of them would show their grief, couldn't imagine it. They were all so different, all three of them, and different from him as well.

He wondered what Alan was doing, and Penny, and the rest of the team. He replayed those conversations in his head, the one with Alan, parts of which were missing from his memory, and the one with Penny, still fresh enough in his mind to heat his face with anger.

They thought they were helping him by not helping him. As if they knew better than he did what he needed.

He descended to just under a thousand feet as he reached the coordinates, passed by his destination, and circled back to align the plane with the narrow landing—if it could be called that. It was little more than a bumpy dirt road.

Every pilot he'd ever known shared the same saying: "Flying is easy. Landing is hard."

He was about to see for himself how true it was.

Zero dipped the yoke and *Cassandra* descended, the ground coming up faster than he would have been comfortable with. It was tough, without the proper training, to determine just how close or far the ground actually was; it looked to him like he should have touched down by now, but he hadn't, and then the wheels caught roughly on the dirt and he jolted in his seat. The plane bounced back into the air about twenty feet, and then back down again. Only one wheel touched, and the plane dipped precipitously to one side.

Zero gritted his teeth and shifted his weight; if it dipped too far the desert would easily tear the fiberglass wing right off the side. But then the other wheel came down, hard, bouncing him again, and he applied the brake as hard as he was willing.

"Whew," he sighed as the sea plane rolled to a stop. Good thing he'd had the foresight to pick one outfitted with wheels; many of them had only pontoons as landing gear.

He powered down the plane and hopped out. The sun over the Moroccan desert was blazing in a cloudless sky, forming beads of sweat on his forehead in an instant and blinding him for a moment.

His vision cleared again to find him face to face with four Special Forces soldiers, all of them bearded and wearing sunglasses, equipped in full tac gear, with automatic weapons pointed at him.

"You guys really have to wear that stuff all the time?" he asked with a smile. "Must get real sweaty under there."

In that moment, just outside of H-6 in the Moroccan desert, he decided to be Reid Lawson. Reid was easygoing, easy to talk to, genial. Reid Lawson wasn't out to hurt anyone. He wasn't chasing an assassin; he was only pursuing knowledge.

That's what he was there for, after all.

124

The lead soldier grinned. He pushed the sunglasses up to his forehead and let his rifle hang from the strap over his shoulder. "Welcome back, Agent Zero. Been a while." He motioned to the other three, and they lowered their guns.

"Sergeant." Reid shook SFO Sergeant Jack Flagg's gloved hand. Flagg was a former Green Beret, one of many who found civilian life to be less than appetizing, who had been shipped out to the desert to operate the CIA black site designated H-6. Flagg liked to call it the "Special Forces retirement village." Ask any agent and they'd have a different name for it—Hell-Six, the least cozy place on Earth.

Flagg glanced over Zero's shoulder at *Cassandra*. "You came here in *that*?" He chuckled. "Your visits always do brighten up my day."

"You wouldn't happen to have extra fuel lying around, would you?" Reid asked.

"We'll fill 'er up, make sure she's flight-worthy." Flagg nodded to one of his guys, who trotted off immediately. "Walk with me, Zero."

They fell in step and headed toward the fenced-in perimeter of Hell-Six. The grounds had been built to look, from the sky or the ground, like a military forward operating base in the Moroccan desert. The site was one huge square, taking up a few acres, surrounded entirely in chain-link fencing topped with barbed wire. Canvas hung from most of the fence, but was tattered and flapping in the breeze in some places. Beyond the fence were a number of semi-permanent canvas tents and three rows of squat, domed steel structures.

"To what do we owe the pleasure?" Flagg asked as he opened the gate for him.

"I need to visit one of your guests. A recent check-in, goes by Mr. Shade."

"Oh, we all know Mr. Shade. Never seen this place break like a man quite like that before. The things he offers us to let him out..." Flagg laughed. "Just last week he told me there's a sixty-million-dollar yacht in the Mediterranean with my name on it if I let him out the gate. Just out the gate. Like he'd survive a day out there in the desert."

Reid forced a chuckle of his own. "I shouldn't be surprised. Mr. Shade was used to the, uh, 'finer' things in life. Doesn't know any other way than to try to buy people."

*Literally.* One of the many dark deeds that Shade had his claw into, before his incarceration, had been human trafficking.

"Well, let me show you to his suite." Flagg gestured toward the stout rows of steel domes and led the way.

He found it remarkable how easy it was to smile, to banter, to chuckle. As if he hadn't watched Maria's murder just the night before. As if he hadn't cried and struggled and howled. All he had to do was pretend he was someone else—anyone who wasn't Agent Zero.

"Say," Reid asked, "I suppose you guys don't get a lot of news out here, huh?"

"Not really," Flagg admitted. "And when we do, it tends to come late. Why, something interesting happen out there in the real world?"

Reid shrugged. "Nah. Just curious. You have a bottle of water handy? I haven't had anything to drink the whole flight."

"Sure." Flagg shouted to a nearby soldier patrolling around the steel domes. "Hey, Sanchez! Hit me with the top-shelf stuff."

The soldier pulled a bottle of water from a satchel slung over his chest and tossed it in an arc. Flagg caught it and handed it off to Reid. "A bit warm, sorry. Anyway, this is it, Mr. Shade's new home." They came to a stop in the shadow of one of the many nondescript, depressingly dull steel domes, and the sergeant pulled open the thick, creaking door. "You want me to come in there with you?"

"No thanks." Reid flashed him a smile. "I'm good. Won't be but a few minutes."

"All right. Holler if you need anything."

Reid entered the dome and pulled the door shut behind him. It stank inside, like urine and earth. There were no windows and no other way out besides the steel door. At its peak the ceiling was ten feet high and illuminated with a single bare forty-watt bulb hanging from two wires and hooked to a generator. The floor was packed dirt, the desert sand having been scraped away before placement.

The only thing inside the dome, other than the bare bulb overhead, was an iron grate in the floor, about three feet square. From beneath this grate came a rustle of movement.

"Flagg?" whispered a timid voice from below. "Is th-that you, Flagg? Did you... did you think about it, Flagg? Did you?"

Reid ignored the plea and reached for the iron grate. With a grunt of effort, he pulled it open like a trapdoor set in the ground. The grate opened on a small underground room, little more than a hole dug out with an excavator, about eight feet deep with a slanted wooden ladder leading upward.

"Come on," Reid prodded. "Come on up."

Slowly the man climbed out. Last time he had seen Mr. Shade, he was wearing a white tuxedo with his dark hair slicked back. That was five and a half months ago.

The sad shell of a man that climbed out of the hole was rail thin, his cheekbones jutting in his face. His dark hair was tousled, filthy, and turning gray. He wore the unofficial uniform of Hell-Six inmates: a sleeveless brown tunic and brown shorts that were almost comically baggy on his thin legs.

Mr. Shade reached the top of the ladder and grunted as he pulled himself onto the dirt floor of the dome. He stood then, shoulders hunched, eyes cast downward, trembling slightly. At last he looked up, and his eyes widened in surprise.

"Y-you… you're him. Right? Are you him? Agent Zero?"

"Yes."

The man nearly collapsed with the sigh he heaved. "You… you could help me get out. You could get me out! You could tell them, tell them to… they have to listen to you, right? They have to. They *have* to!"

Agent Zero wanted to wrap his hands around the man's thin throat and squeeze. He wanted to break Shade's limbs. He wanted to knock the teeth out of his head and shove his fist in his mouth until he choked to death on it.

But this was not a job for Agent Zero.

"Here," said Reid, holding out the bottle of water. "Drink."

Shade took the bottle graciously and tilted it back. He drank greedily, water running over his lips and darkening the front of the tunic.

"Th-thank you." He was breathless when it was empty, and wiped his lips with the back of his hand. "Now. Please. Tell me what you want. Anything. Money. Cars. I have a yacht in the Mediterranean, if you can help me…"

"Listen to me, Shade," said Reid. "What I want is far more valuable than any of that. I want *information.*"

"Yes. Yes, I have information. Anything."

"Sit. Please." Reid gestured to the dirt floor. He lowered himself first, sitting cross-legged, and Shade sat too with a slight groan. "You remember those people that took the president. The Palestinian faction."

"Yes. Of course."

"And there were others you were funding."

"Yes," Shade whispered. "There were others."

"Okay. This is what I need to know: where would those people go if they needed to hide?"

Shade frowned. "Hide from what?"

Zero came out, just for a moment, as his gaze hardened and he said: "Hide from *me*."

Shade gulped. "I'm afraid I'm not sure."

"Are you sure you're not sure?" Reid glanced into the hole beneath the grate. "Last time I saw you was in a penthouse suite. This doesn't look quite as pleasant."

"Please... I've told them everything. Everything."

"Not everything, Shade. Not this. Where would they go? I need to know. And that is the *only* way you're getting out of here."

"Okay." Shade closed his eyes. He rubbed his temples, gently at first, and then harder, and then actually smacked himself on the sides of the head with both fists. "I don't know!"

Reid sighed. "All right then. I've spent too much time coming here already. Back in the hole..."

"No!" Shade leapt up and backed away quickly, until he hit the opposite side of the dome. "Please, no."

"I need a place, Shade. I need a place, and I need to believe you. Or it's back into the hole..."

"Ankara!" the man cried. He fell to his knees and put both hands over his face. "Ankara. Ankara."

Reid frowned. "In Turkey?"

"Yes. There was... a deed. A deed to a property. It passed my desk... maybe a year and a half ago. They had me put it in the name of one of my companies... so it wouldn't be traced back to them. A safe house. They wanted a safe house."

"The address?"

"I d-don't know... but it would be listed. Yes. It'd be listed, as the Ankara headquarters for, for SMI Limited."

"SMI Limited," Zero repeated. "That's all you know."

"Yes. That's it. I swear it. I swear. Now please." Shade crawled on his knees and actually put his hands around Zero's leg. "Please. Get me out. You said you would. Get me out."

"About that," Zero told him. "I lied. I'm not getting you out."

Shade looked up in a blend of terror and confusion. "What? What? You said... you can't lie!"

"Sure I can. It's fifty percent of my job."

"No!" Shade wailed. He grabbed onto Zero's leg again with both hands.

"Shade, you trafficked teenage girls. You funded terrorist operations that resulted in innocent casualties. You smuggled weapons and armed insurgents. And those are just the ones we know about." Zero leaned over, bending at the waist, so that he was close to Shade's ear when he added, "You're *never* getting out of here. You're going to die in this hole."

"No—"

Zero grabbed him by one thin arm and hefted him up easily. Then he shoved him, hard, and the man tumbled backwards into the pit. He landed with a groan and immediately scrambled for the ladder, but Zero was already swinging the iron grate shut. It clanged into place.

"Get me out!" Shade shouted. "Please, get me out!"

Zero headed for the door, but then paused. "Oh, Shade. One more thing. The cars? The money? The yacht in the Mediterranean? You can stop offering them to people. We found it all. We seized everything. You have nothing left. Anyway, have a good one."

Shade wailed as Zero pushed out through the steel door, back out into the Moroccan late afternoon sun. As soon as the door was closed behind him, Shade's wails were cut off.

The domes were soundproof. Made sense; couldn't have the shouts and cries of three dozen prisoners haunting the camp day and night.

He looked around for Flagg but the sergeant was nowhere to be seen. So Zero headed back the way he'd come, toward the gate. He was heading to Turkey next, it seemed, a much shorter trip than flying to Morocco. He wasn't sure what he would find there, but if Shade thought it was enough information to buy his freedom, Zero would check it out.

*And God have mercy on whoever I find there.*

He exited the gate and stopped suddenly.

Parked right behind the sea plane was another plane, a jet, larger but not very large itself. He knew that plane; he'd been on that plane several times before. It was a sleek Gulfstream G650, a sixty-five-million-dollar jet owned by the CIA.

He hadn't heard it land—because the steel domes were soundproof.

But someone was here.
Someone was here for *him*.

# CHAPTER TWENTY TWO

His first instinct was to turn and go back into H-6, to hide among the canvas tents, but then he spotted Jack Flagg and he knew he'd be given up. Flagg was talking to someone, slightly obscured by the Gulfstream, so Zero walked toward it, not trying to hide or to flee, just walked toward it until he saw the familiar face.

It was Todd Strickland.

He saw Todd say something to Flagg, and then Flagg raised both hands at elbow height and shook his head, and then Todd nodded.

Then Todd spotted him, but Zero didn't stop, he kept walking. Flagg retreated from the plane, coming in Zero's direction, and when he was close enough he said, "Look, whatever's going on between you boys, me and my guys want no part of it."

"Appreciate your time, Sergeant," said Zero, and he kept walking. Flagg closed the gate to H-6 behind him, and then it was just Zero and Strickland, standing on a dusty runway in the desert.

He stopped with only a few feet between them. "Todd."

"Zero. I'm sorry."

"Don't be sorry. You didn't do it. How'd you find me?"

Todd shrugged. "Thought you might come here. Got lucky."

"Sure." He didn't get lucky; it was far more likely that Alan had guessed it and told him to come here. No one could get into Zero's head quite as well as Alan. "You got here fast."

"Yeah, well. Fast jet." Strickland gestured toward *Cassandra*. "You come here in that?"

"I did. Took a while."

"I bet." Strickland chuckled, but it faded quickly. "I'm here to bring you home."

Zero shook his head. "Can't go home."

"Yes, you can. Get on the plane with me. Let's figure this out together."

"I'm already figuring it out. I have to go to Turkey. I could use your help. Let's take the Gulfstream, leave the sea plane. It'll be a lot faster."

131

"Come on, Zero." Strickland took a step closer. "Is this what you think she'd want? You running halfway around the world for—"

"Don't," Zero snapped. "Don't use her to try to guilt me out of this. You don't know what she would have wanted, and now neither do I. This isn't about what she wants anyway. It's about what *I* want, Todd. And I want to kill the man that killed Kate."

Strickland frowned. "Kate?"

*Kate?*

*Did I say Kate?*

"Maria." He shook his head. "I want to kill the man that killed Maria."

"Zero," Todd said carefully, "I don't think you're thinking straight. And that's understandable. We're friends. I came here because I care about you. So let's get on the plane, and go home."

"Counteroffer," Zero suggested. "I take the Gulfstream and go to Turkey. You take the sea plane, and you tell them I overpowered you."

Strickland scoffed. "If I have to tell them you overpowered me, it won't be a lie."

Zero's eyes narrowed. "I need that plane, Todd."

"No. You *want* the plane."

He did not want to fight Todd Strickland. They had once before, almost two and a half years ago now, and he'd won then. Sort of. He was older now, had suffered more injuries, didn't move quite as quickly. He didn't like his odds.

But he needed that plane, and he needed Strickland to get out of his way.

"You armed, Todd?"

"No."

Zero smiled. "You're a good man. But a bad liar." Strickland had a gun, he could tell. He'd brought Zero everything he'd need. "All right. Fine. I'm not going to make you draw on me. Let's go home." He raised his hands, only slightly, the way Flagg had just moments ago when he'd washed his hands of whatever quarrel was going on here. He took a step toward Todd, and just as the former Ranger started to turn to head back to the plane, Zero balled a fist.

He didn't rear back. That would have telegraphed the hit. Instead he twisted his hips and brought the fist straight up from its partially raised position and right across Todd's jaw in a wicked cross.

Todd had a strong jaw. Zero's hand stung, the pain shooting up his wrist and into his arm.

Strickland's head jerked. He fell sideways into the dirt, rolled once, and as he turned onto his back the gun was in his hands, a silver pistol leaping out of its holster and aimed at Zero.

*Predictable.*

Todd would draw. But he wouldn't shoot.

His teeth were gritted and there was fury in his eyes, but Zero was right. He wouldn't pull the trigger on a friend. Zero lurched for the gun, shoving it aside and away from him.

Then he twisted it away.

Strickland howled as it bent his finger, possibly broke it, and Zero wrenched the gun from his grip.

*I'm sorry. But I need this.*

A foot came up, a black boot, and it struck Zero squarely in the chest. He fell backward, the wind knocked from his lungs and the gun from his grip. Strickland staggered to his feet, his jaw bruised and holding his injured hand close to him.

"What the hell is the matter with you?!" he shouted. "I'm trying to help you!"

"If you really wanted to help," Zero wheezed, getting to his own feet, "here's what you can do…"

He faked with his left. Todd moved to block it, but expecting the jab from the right.

That was a fake too. Zero pulled back on the left, and then sent it forward again, cocked like a shotgun, landing at the spot just below Todd's right ear, where his neck met his skull.

It laid him out flat. Todd's eyelids fluttered, his mouth hung open.

"You can lay there a while," Zero panted.

He retrieved the gun from the sand. When he glanced back at H-6, he saw he had a small audience. Flagg and a few of the other Special Forces guys stood near the open gate. They had rifles in hand but at rest, barrels aimed downward, just staring.

Right; Todd Strickland was one of them. Would they do anything about this?

No. They stood their ground but did not advance or make any move.

Zero boarded the Gulfstream, climbing the six steps to the cabin, and then sucked in a breath at the sight of the man seated in the first row of beige leather chairs there.

*The pilot.* He forgot, Strickland didn't know how to fly. Good thing too; he wasn't sure he could fly this thing on his own.

The pilot was wide-eyed, his hands up, as if Zero was hijacking him.

Which, for all intents and purposes, he was.

"Hi." He showed him the gun. "I need to get to Ankara. Disable the transponder, take me there, and I swear on my life that no harm will come to you."

"I know you," said the pilot. "You're Agent Zero."

"That's right."

"I was a friend of Chip Foxworth."

"So was I," Zero told him.

"He spoke very highly of you."

Zero looked down at the carpeted aisle. "He died saving my life."

"What is this?" the pilot asked.

"There's something I need to do. Something that no one else believes in. But it's important. I have no allies. Will you help me?"

Zero put the gun away, tucked it in his pants.

The pilot put his hands down. "Yes."

"Thank you. What's your name?"

"Scott," said the pilot.

"First or last?"

"Last."

"All right then, Captain Scott. Disable the transponder and take me to Ankara. This plane is tagged as a diplomatic envoy; if anyone asks, we had to take an emergency detour without registering a flight path after a death threat over Middle Eastern airspace and we just need to land and lay low for a bit."

Captain Scott frowned. "Will they believe that?"

"Usually."

The pilot went to the cockpit and fired up the engines. Zero buckled into the first row of seats and glanced out the window.

As the Gulfstream about-faced on the runway, he saw Todd Strickland sitting up, rubbing his jaw. Another bridge burned.

First Alan. Then Penny. Then Jack Flagg, and now Strickland.

134

That was fine. He'd burn every bridge he came to if he needed. Nothing was going to get between him and the assassin.

# CHAPTER TWENTY THREE

Sara woke. It was dark. It was always dark in the basement; she liked it that way. But it made it impossible to tell what time of day it was. If she never left the basement she'd lose track of days entirely, she was sure.

Most days, that would be okay.

Today, that would be okay.

She would have liked to think she dreamed it all. That Alan Reidigger had never come, hadn't told them what he did. That Maria and her dad were on their honeymoon right now, at a resort, doing something that she would never, *ever* want to hear about.

But no. Maria was dead.

A man. On the beach. With a knife.

She rolled over and checked her phone. It was ten a.m. Ordinarily she might have groaned and gone back to sleep for another hour or so, but she did feel responsible for Mischa, no matter how independent the girl was. Maya was gone, off somewhere for whatever her new "job" was, and somehow, for the time being, Sara was now the eldest of the house.

It sounded exhausting. But she needed to get up.

"Mischa," she called out when she reached the top of the stairs. No answer. No one in the kitchen, or the living room, or the dining room.

She pushed open the door to Mischa's bedroom. Also empty. The bed was unmade; very atypical for the girl. Sara tried calling her phone, but it went straight to voicemail.

Still she left a message: "Mischa, it's Sara. Where are you? Call or text me as soon as you're able."

No sooner did she end the call than a text came through from Mischa.

It said: *I am fine. Do not follow. Do not worry.*

"Son of a bitch." Sara sat heavily on the girl's bed. Mischa had run off somewhere. Maya was gone. Her dad was, presumably, still in Nassau.

Maria was dead.

A man. On the beach. With a knife.

She thought about Common Bonds. The women that she thought she had helped. Had she? Helped them? What good was that sort of "help" when things like this could still happen?

People got hurt every day; there was no stopping it. All she was trying to do was make sure the right people got hurt and didn't hurt anyone else.

Had she, though?

She thought about the last thing she had said to Maddie.

*You don't want to see anyone get hurt? Must be nice to have that choice. All you have to do is look the other way.*

Sara could not look the other way. She needed to *do* something. She couldn't just sit here, alone, and wait for everyone to get back.

In the basement, she put on jeans and a T-shirt and socks and made sure her phone was charged. In the foyer she put on her shoes and opened the coat closet and dug into the pocket of the brown leather jacket her dad never wore anymore.

Huh. The revolver was gone. He must have moved it.

Didn't matter. She knew he kept a Glock behind the cutlery drawer. There were six guns hidden in the house—that she knew of. Back when she was still getting clean she had distracted herself for an entire day finding all of her dad's "clever" hiding spots—only one of which really turned out to be clever. In the air vent? Under the nightstand? Predictable. Hidden inside the plastic VHS cassette case of *Aladdin*, though? She liked that one.

Sara replied to Mischa's text: *Be safe.*

Then she tried to call Maya, but of course it went straight to voicemail too. What was the point of this family having phones?

Without getting hold of Maya, she had no idea where her dad's car was. She needed wheels.

There was one person. But she didn't like it.

After a few deep breaths, Sara made the call.

"Hello?" Maddie answered on the second ring. A child shouted in the background. A television was on somewhere. It sounded chaotic, while Sara's house was silent.

"Maddie? It's Sara."

"Sara! Hang on." The background sounds faded as Maddie found a quieter place to talk. "I'm glad you called. I didn't like how we left things off."

"Me neither. And we can talk about that. But... there's something else." She took a breath, made her voice shaky, and said, "My little sister ran off."

"What? Oh, god. I didn't even know you had a little sister."

"I do. She's thirteen. My parents are out of town, I was supposed to be watching her, and... I don't know how this happened. And then I remembered your story, about your sister, and—I don't know. I thought you could help."

"Sara," Maddie said somberly, "I think you should contact the police."

"It's only been a few hours. And I think I know where she might be." She knew she should feel horrible doing this, manipulating someone like this. But the truth was, she didn't.

"What can I do?" Maddie asked. "How can I help?"

"Well... I don't have a car."

"I'll come pick you up," Maddie said instantly.

"I think it would be better if I went alone. So she doesn't get freaked out."

There was a moment of silence on the line, the distant sound of children shouting and laughing, and for a second Sara thought she might be busted, or denied.

But then Maddie said, "Okay. We have a pickup that we don't use much. It's old, but it runs well. I'll give you my address, you come here right away for it. Use it as long as you need."

"Thank you," Sara gushed. "Thank you so much."

*I will*, Mischa texted. *Then I will come home.*

*I may not be here*, Sara replied.

She took down the address. Then she made sure all the lights were out. The security system was armed. So was she.

She needed to *do* something. She couldn't just sit here, alone, and wait for everyone to get back.

And once she had the truck, she would head south.

# CHAPTER TWENTY FOUR

*I may not be here,* Sara's text read.

Mischa furrowed her brow at that. Where would Sara go? It couldn't be to find her; she had no way of being tracked. At some point Maria had sneakily gone into Mischa's phone and activated location tracking on her GPS, but it was easy enough to find and disable.

"Here we are," said the driver. Mischa could have walked all this way, but it would have taken a long time to do it, so after the sun rose she had resorted to hitchhiking. A kind elderly man in a Buick had stopped, and much of the ensuing fifty-minute drive had been comprised of him enumerating the dangers of such a young girl hitchhiking alone.

"Are you sure this is the place?" The man frowned.

"It is," she confirmed. "Thank you for the ride. I would offer you money, but I'm afraid I don't have much."

"Absolutely not." The man waved at the offer. "It was my pleasure to help. You be safe now, you hear?"

Mischa climbed out of the car and stood there on the busy sidewalk until the kind old man pulled away. Then she turned her attention to the 300 block of Park Avenue.

Baltimore's Chinatown was quite small compared to most, and primarily dominated by Laundromats and restaurants. It was strange, in fact, to even call it "Chinatown" at all, since the population was just as much Ethiopian immigrants as Chinese.

She could only hope that he was still here.

Mischa hefted her backpack, the revolver zipped securely in the front pouch of it, and headed up the block a short ways, to a Laundromat whose name had changed since she had first heard about this place. She went inside, ignoring the few people seated on long benches and watching their soapy clothes spin around and around, to the rear, through a doorway beyond which was a staircase leading up.

At the top of the stairs was a hall with a door on either side, two apartments. Mischa had never been here, but she knew to knock on the door on the left, and then she reached up with her small hand and covered the peephole.

"Who is it?" a male voice barked in Cantonese.

"A former colleague," Mischa responded in the same tongue. Strange; she had not spoken it in months but she was fluent, and it came back easily.

The man cursed, likely because he could not see out the peephole, and then the door opened just a few inches, the chain lock still on, and she saw his black hair and one suspicious eye look out, and then down, and then open wide at the sight of her.

"Are you Mischa?"

"Yes, Pin. Please let me in."

"I heard you were dead."

"You heard incorrectly. Samara is dead. All the others are dead. I am standing right here."

He did not seem to want to open the door for her. Pin—which was very likely not his real name—was what they called a sleeper, a Chinese agent planted in the US with an identity and a job and everything that made him look legitimate. He lived his day to day as any immigrant might, and he simply waited. If one of his people showed up at his door, he was to let them in, hide them if necessary, feed them or give them a place to rest, treat wounds if they had any, until they were able to move on again.

Back when she and Samara had smuggled the ultrasonic weapon into the United States, Mischa had been made to memorize this address, to know how to access it, what to say, in case she was separated from the group and had nowhere to go.

That seemed like a different life now. But it was all still there, in her head, as if that had not been her at all and she had someone else's memories.

"Open the door, Pin. It is your duty."

He shook his head and his shaggy black hair with it. "No longer. I am disavowed."

Mischa frowned at that. "When?"

"When you and Samara failed. I have not heard a thing from anyone. When I tried to make contact the line was dead. They abandoned me, and probably any others affiliated with you, so that no connection could be made." His one eye visible in the crack of the door narrowed. "Unless… you are finally here to kill me?"

140

She shook her head. "No, Pin. I was not sent to kill you. I too have been... released from service, so to speak."

"Then why are you here?"

"I need information. I have money."

Pin thought for a moment, and then he closed the door on her. The chain lock slid aside and he allowed her in with a sweep of his arm.

She entered the small apartment as he hastily closed the door again, as if it might have been a ruse and Mischa was not alone.

But she was alone, more now than perhaps she'd ever been.

"Tea?" Pin offered.

"No. Thank you." The apartment was shabby, wallpaper peeling in corners, the carpet bubbled from dampness.

"You look well," Pin noted. "Healthy."

"Thank you." But there were small things, things not immediately apparent. Pin's cover was that he worked the Laundromat below him, yet the key ring on the grubby countertop bore the symbol of BMW, a not-inexpensive car. "I was adopted."

"Sorry?" Pin called over the sound of him filling a kettle with water.

She peeked into the open doorway to the small bedroom, which contained a mattress on the floor, a nest of sheets and blankets atop it, a cracked bureau, and a Rolex wristwatch.

"I was adopted," she said again. "By a CIA agent and her family."

Pin laughed behind her. "I was not told you were the type to make jokes."

"I'm not. I tried once, but it did not go over very well." In the corner, near the window, was an old CRT television set, but on the stand beneath it was a sleek gaming console not touched by dust like the rest of the setup was. "The CIA agent that adopted me was murdered last night in Nassau."

Pin set the kettle on the stove and turned on the burner. It clicked three times before blue gas-fueled flames leapt up. Then he turned to her, confused. "What is it that you want from me?"

"As I said. Information. You say you have been disavowed, but you seem to be doing quite well for yourself."

Pin snorted at that. "Look around, girl. This is quite well?"

"I am looking around. And yes. Are you a thief?"

He recoiled as if he'd been slapped. "Of course not."

"Then what?"

"A Laundromat employee. That's all."

"No." Mischa shook her head. "Let me tell you what I think. I think you grew desperate after the abandonment, realizing that your cover was now going to be your life. I think you made a deal, to offer Chinese secrets in exchange for money, and perhaps some form of protection or amnesty. I believe you were probably well paid; you did not spend a fraction of what you were given, simply bought yourself a few nice things and saved the rest so that you could live comfortably somewhere."

Pin scoffed. "This is ridiculous—"

"I believe," Mischa interrupted, "that the only reason you have stayed here this long was fear. Fear that someone would show up at your door one day and reactivate you, and if you were not here they would know and hunt you down. You had to give yourself time, long enough to know for certain that no one would contact you again. That you were completely severed."

This was not a guess. Mischa and Samara had been sent to other places, Switzerland and Brazil and elsewhere, to assassinate similar sleepers who had gotten too comfortable or complacent in their newly established lives. And Pin very much seemed the type.

"Lastly," she said, "I do not think you went to the American government with these secrets. They would not have paid you for them; they would have gotten them out of you, one way or another. No, you went elsewhere. So where did you go, Pin?"

The Chinese man laughed at her. "That's quite an imagination you have, girl." He pulled open the refrigerator. He bent to open the crisper drawer.

Mischa took two quick steps and leapt at him just as he pulled out the gun. Her first blow slammed his head against the top plastic shelf of the refrigerator. As he reeled, her foot came up and kicked the gun from his hand.

He attempted to make a fist, to swing it, and she let him, the blow glancing harmlessly off the side of her head, barely more than a slap. Pin was not a fighter. He did not have the training she did.

She let the blow strike, and then used the moment of advantage to get in closer, to grab two small fistfuls of his shirt and twist at the waist. His legs left the ground and his entire body sailed over hers, crashing to the floor in a remarkable thud that no doubt startled anyone down in the Laundromat beneath them.

Mischa twisted his arm around and back, the tension a centimeter away from the breaking point. Pin cried out in pain and slapped his free hand at the floor.

"Wait, wait!" he pleaded.

"Tell me," she threatened, "or I will break it. To whom did you sell the secrets?"

"It was… it was a guy from New York…"

"What was his name?" she asked calmly.

"I don't remember—aagh!" he cried as Mischa twisted at the wrist. With this sort of tension, one jerk of her arm would break both his elbow and his hand. "Okay, okay! He called himself Mr. Bright!"

Mischa relieved the tension slightly. Mr. Bright was likely not the man's real name, just like Pin. Just like her, presumably; she would never know. "You have the means to contact this Mr. Bright?"

"I do. Yes. I do. But he was just the intermediary. H-he worked for some rich businessman out in Cairo. That's all I know. I swear."

Mischa released the arm and Pin pulled it close to him, his body curling around it. She retrieved the gun from where it had fallen on the floor. It was, of course, Chinese made. A Norinco NP-42 semi-automatic pistol, 8mm rounds. Not the most reliable gun but she'd make do with whatever was available.

"You will contact this Mr. Bright," Mischa told him. "You will do whatever you can to find out who killed the CIA agent in Nassau last night. And I will stay here, holding this gun, while you do." She sat herself on Pin's small sofa. "Your performance and speed will determine whether or not you live to see tonight."

# CHAPTER TWENTY FIVE

Preston McMahon drove through the night, stopping only for gas, to reach Manhattan from Fort Benning, Georgia. He turned on the radio every now and then for company, but then turned it off just as quickly as reports were made. It was everywhere, it seemed, the hostage situation of Bill McMahon, though there was more speculation than fact. Preston did not want to believe what they were saying, that Grandpa Bill was being held in Iran.

He did not want to believe it because that would make his own lead wrong, and he would have wasted an entire night and part of a day. He did not want to believe it because there was little chance he could do anything for his grandfather if it was true. And most importantly, he did not want to believe it because everyone else seemed to believe it—and while everyone was looking that way, the men holding him captive could be anywhere but there.

He hated driving in Manhattan. He'd only had to do it once before in his life and had vowed never again. Yet here he was, battling his way from the Lincoln Tunnel to Midtown, based on a single piece of potentially outdated information.

One of Grandpa Bill's biggest claims to fame during his presidency, perhaps his biggest, was the successful negotiation to release fifty-four hostages, a blend of Americans and Europeans, from a band of radical Iranians in 1984. The hostages were held at gunpoint in a bombed-out elementary school by six young, idealistic men from Tehran. After every other effort was exhausted and the only option the US had left was to send in armed commandos to try and take out the gunmen, Grandpa Bill himself had gotten on the phone. He'd used a secure line, and requested that the twenty-two-minute call not be recorded, so only he and the man he spoke to knew exactly what was said.

But at the end of it, the six men backed down. They threw down their guns and emerged from the school with their hands in the air and allowed the hostages to be rescued.

Some said that the negotiation had won so many hearts and minds that it was singlehandedly responsible for Bill's reelection the following year.

Out of those six men, three had died since then. One was still imprisoned in Iran. The eldest of them, now in his seventies, was convalescing in Egypt. And the sixth, Farrokh Al Bahman, was living in New York City.

Preston had a cousin, Jillian Deep, granddaughter of Bill McMahon, who worked for the NSA. The shred of information she'd given him was so highly classified that not only would she lose her job, it was likely that she'd go to prison and he would get court-martialed if it ever got out she'd shared it.

Strange, to him, that just a single, simple piece of information could be so damning.

Preston parked his car in a garage a handful of blocks from the address—thirty-five dollars a day for parking, insane—and walked the rest of the way. The place he was going was the supposed workplace of one Mohammad Jaffer, a furniture upholsterer who emigrated from Iran in 1993. He was fifty-nine years old, specialized in leather and suede, and was a member of a local squash club.

But all of that was a farce. That piece of information, that simple message that could end both his and Jillian's lives, was this: Farrokh Al Bahman, the sixth man in the 1984 hostage crisis and the one who had spoken with Bill McMahon on the phone, had been granted amnesty by the US government and was now living in Manhattan under the alias Mohammad Jaffer.

To Preston, it made sense to pursue this lead. A radical Iranian who had held Americans hostage more than thirty years ago hides out in plain sight until one day he sees that the US is again sticking its nose in Iranian business, this time with a treaty and sanctions that could threaten to westernize the Islamic country, and said radical decides it's time to come out of retirement and orchestrate the kidnapping of the man who had talked him out of it all those years ago.

Maybe he was reaching. Jillian didn't seem to think so, or she never would have given him the intel. And the more he thought about it, the more it made sense.

Especially since everyone else was looking that way, and no one at all was looking this way.

Preston tried to walk as normally as possible. No easy task; it was August, and even in the northeast it was still warm, which made hiding the tactical vest under his shirt difficult. He'd had to put on a light jacket to obscure it, and it was making him sweat.

He was no stranger to sweating. He was just a stranger to hiding it.

The jacket also helped him hide the two pistols he had holstered under his armpits. A rifle would have been impossible to hide, so he wore jeans while most people still wore shorts or skirts so that he had a pant leg to pull down over the ankle holster that held a Walther PPK.

Preston had an address for Mohammad Jaffer, but it was eleven o'clock in the morning on a Tuesday, so dropping into his place of business seemed like the obvious first step. He was not at all sure what he would find; part of him doubted that Farrokh Al Bahman even knew how to upholster furniture at all. Maybe he would find the address empty. Maybe Farrokh had long since moved on, gone elsewhere.

Maybe, just maybe, he would find Grandpa Bill bound to a chair.

Preston entered the building and rode the elevator up. The upholstery company took up the entire fourth floor. His hand went into his jacket instinctively to reach for a gun, but he thought better of it. Assess the situation first.

The doors opened, and Preston stepped out. The scent of leather hit him first, behind it the waft of chemical cleaner. The floor was cement, the steel rafters in the ceiling open, and between them was—an upholstery company.

A handful of men worked on various pieces of furniture. An armchair here, a sofa there. One man carefully riveted a divan. They glanced up at him as he passed by, and he could not help but notice that all of the men there—five of them, that he could see—were Middle Eastern.

None of them spoke to him or tried to stop him. At last he turned to one, a young man with a wispy beard in a white *kufi* skullcap, and asked, "Where can I find Mohammad Jaffer?"

The young man pointed to the rear of the shop floor. Preston nodded and made his way to the back, where he found an olive-skinned man carefully examining a brown leather loveseat.

The man looked well to be in his late fifties. He was thin, wore owlish silver glasses, and had a slight hook to his nose where it may have been broken and not healed right in his youth. He ran his hands

146

carefully over the loveseat, over its arms, without looking up at Preston.

"Nubuck," he said. "That means top-grain cattle leather. One of the very best materials for a piece like this. It is buffed on the grain side, so the result is so soft it could be velvet." The man's accent was almost entirely gone after so much time spent in the US.

He smiled, and Preston was surprised to see that his eyes were green.

"Come, look at this." He pointed at a spot on the arm that could only be seen by crouching. "This stitch was missed. Thirty years ago, that would be unacceptable. It would be pulled and redone. These days? People like to see that. They'll even pay more for it. It reminds them that it is handmade. Flawed. One of a kind." He chuckled. "Strange how time changes things."

"You are Mohammad Jaffer?" Preston asked.

"I am. Were you referred to me?"

"I was," Preston told him quietly. "By the NSA."

Jaffer's smile vanished. "Perhaps we should speak privately."

Preston nodded, and Jaffer led the way to a small rear office, the desk messy with paperwork covering the computer's keyboard. The former Iranian closed the door and turned but did not sit, so Preston did not either.

"I'm going to make this brief and very much to the point," said Preston. "You are Farrokh Al Bahman. I am the grandson of William McMahon. He was kidnapped two days ago by Iranian radicals. I think you can see how the connection is made. This is your one and *only* chance to come clean, right now, and tell me the truth. Do you know anything about my grandfather's kidnapping? Do you know where he is? Do you know who has him? Did you have anything at all do with it?"

Al Bahman sighed. He took off his glasses, wiped them on his shirt, and put them back on before he spoke. "I had a feeling something like this might happen. I'm not going to say I'm sorry for your loss. I'm not going to tell you that your grandfather is a good man. But I will say that he was very convincing when he needed to be, and that we came to an accord that was mutually beneficial."

"For you," Preston interjected. "Your friends ended up in jail or worse."

147

Al Bahman nodded. "That is true. But the only other way that day would have ended was in my death, and theirs as well, and possibly others', so it seems that more got what they want than didn't."

"You haven't answered my question."

The man stared him right in the eye and said, "No. I did not have anything to do with your grandfather's kidnapping or the hostage situation he is now in."

"You don't know the men responsible?"

"I do not," said Al Bahman.

"Your country is changing. A treaty has been signed. You don't feel some kind of way about that?" Preston prodded. "You're content to sit here and upholster furniture?"

"Look at me. I am quickly becoming an old man. Radical notions are a young man's game." He smiled. "I did not come here by choice, but the United States has been surprisingly good to me. As I said—strange how time changes things."

Preston's nostrils flared. He did not want to believe this man, because that would mean that he had come here for nothing. Yet he had no reason not to.

What had he been expecting? A fight? An immediate admission of guilt? Grandpa Bill, bound to a chair?

"Your guys. They're all Iranian?"

Al Bahman nodded. "Indeed they are. Immigrants who came here seeking a better life. I take them in, teach them the craft. Help them have a chance."

"When did the most recent get here?"

The man shook his head. "I understand you are going through a difficult time, but I cannot have you harassing my employees. They are good people. They have done nothing wrong, and they face enough problems as it is."

A dead end. A frustrating dead end and hours wasted. "All right then. Thanks for your time."

"I'll walk you out." Al Bahman opened the door again and led the way across the shop floor. He pointed at a brown-and-white-spotted piece to the right. "See that? That's spotted cowhide there. Not something we get requested often—a bit gaudy for my tastes—but it certainly looks interesting."

Preston did not look to the right. He kept his head aimed forward but his eyes darted to the left as they passed the young man in the *kufi*.

The young man did not look up at him, but a bead of sweat ran down his temple from the brim of his cap.

"Ah!" said Al Bahman loudly. "And if you are ever in the market for something truly unique, *this* piece over here…"

*He's distracting me.* Preston pretended to look where Al Bahman was pointed, and used his periphery to glance back as far as he could without moving his head, as another Iranian man sewed the back of a sofa with strokes too quick to be considered good craftsmanship.

They reached the elevators and Al Bahman shook his hand. "Strong grip. You carry yourself like a soldier."

Preston nodded. "That's right. Ten years now."

"I bet you've seen much." The man's smile was ingratiating.

"True." He nodded. "Too much."

Something was amiss here, and Preston McMahon was not yet ready to go.

"In fact—do you want to hear a story? It's quick. Craziest thing I've ever seen."

Al Bahman's gaze flitted to the elevator and back. He could not wait for Preston to leave. "Certainly," he said.

"Okay. So one day, me and my unit, we were escorting a supply convoy through Fallujah. Triangle of Death, you know? And things are quiet. Too quiet. I see something up ahead, so I scout it out. It's a dead camel on the side of the road. But something's not quite right about it. I see—pardon my French here, but I see something just peeking out of its ass."

Al Bahman chuckled, but his eyes frowned.

"Now I should have just called it in," Preston continued, "but instead I go over to it. I turn this thing over. It's been dead a while, stiff as a board. And heavy, too. But I manage to get this thing over, and you know what I see? It's been cut, sliced up the belly lengthwise." Here Preston put two fingers to his own belly button and drew a line upward, to his heart. "And then sewn back together. Not well, either. A real hasty hack job. And right away I know what this is, so I start running. And I shout, 'Call EOD!' And that's when it blows. I barely got clear in time."

Preston paused here, and he allowed himself a small chuckle. "You see, they sewed a bomb inside a dead camel, with the radio transmitter *just* barely sticking out its ass. Those Iraqis get creative." His smile vanished. "But even a dead camel isn't quite as creative as sewing bombs into furniture in downtown Manhattan."

He saw it, in that instant that the Iranian man had tried to sew the couch up as he passed. Just the slightest hint of a black box that to anyone else might not have looked like anything. But he'd seen many like it, one of them just barely peeking out of a camel's backside.

Al Bahman did not move, but still he seemed to wither under Preston's piercing gaze. He opened his mouth to speak, maybe to make some excuse, but instead he said just two words in Arabic, and though Preston wasn't fluent he understood them.

"Kill him."

There was movement to his right. Preston dropped to one knee, and in the time it took he had the M9 out of its holster. Automatic gunfire ripped just over his head and he fired in response, once, then twice, and the young man in the *kufi* cap fell.

Preston rolled then, to the relative safety behind a suede sectional. He heard shouts of other men and, over them all, Al Bahman's shriek: "Kill him!"

He quickly shrugged out of his jacket and tossed it straight up into the air. In the instant the jacket attracted shots he yanked out the second M9 and threw himself to the right. The Beretta in his left hand was indiscriminate, cover fire, while with his right he fired three shots and dropped two bodies. He slid behind the spotted cowhide sofa as another deafening rattle echoed over the shop floor.

"Idiot!" Al Bahman shouted. "Not that one! You will kill us all!"

Preston McMahon was hiding behind a bomb.

*Terrific.*

He'd been in worse places; once he had stepped on a land mine and felt it give way under his foot, and had to stand there, his weight on the pressure plate, for four hours while EOD defused it from beneath him. One could say that he and explosives had a relationship that bordered on intimate.

He holstered one of the M9s and flicked open a lockback knife, plunging it into the back of the sofa and tearing at it as Al Bahman shouted commands in Arabic. He caught only one word—"around"—and realized the two men still standing aimed to flank him.

Preston reached into the sliced-open couch and felt around until his hand closed around the device. He held his breath as he pulled it out, five wrapped bricks of C4 daisy-chain-wired to a remote transmitter. It wasn't the ugliest bomb he'd ever seen.

He heard the footsteps growing closer from both sides. Preston reared back, and he scooted the bomb across the floor to his left like a bowling ball. It rolled in front of a pair of legs as a man yelped and leapt back.

Preston grabbed one end of the sofa and upended it, using it as cover against his right side as he fired three shots into the exposed Iranian with a bomb at his feet. Then he turned, moving the upturned sofa with him, until he could see half of the other man, who held an SMG to his shoulder.

Preston fired. The Iranian fired. Blood blossomed on the man's chest and he fell, and the spotted cowhide sofa was ruined.

Farrokh Al Bahman mashed his palm frantically against the elevator button. Preston took careful aim and fired just once. The shot struck Al Bahman's deltoid and spun him as he fell to the floor.

"Farrokh," Preston said as he stood over him. "You lied to me." He didn't have much time. NYPD would respond quickly to the report of shots fired.

"I-I didn't. I told you…" He grimaced. "I didn't have anything to do with the… kidnapping."

"But you're sewing bombs into furniture. Where are these pieces going?"

"All over. Everywhere. An embassy… a governor in Texas… all over."

Preston shook his head, wondering how many similar pieces were already out there. "Farrokh, I don't believe that you were suddenly bolstered by your countrymen and decided to come out of retirement. I'm going to give you one more chance to tell me the truth, or else I'm going to put a bullet in your head. And I get the distinct feeling—"

He heard a grunt and spun. One of the men was still alive, just winged, trying to crawl to an AK-47. Preston fired once more, hitting him in the right temple.

Farrokh sucked in a ragged breath. He'd been right when he said that radical notions were a young man's game. Preston could see in his eyes that it had been a long time since Al Bahman had seen bloodshed like this.

"As I was saying, I get the feeling you're not ready to meet Allah just yet. So." He pressed the barrel to Farrokh's forehead. "Tell me."

"All right. All right," the man gasped. "I… I do know one of them. Their leader. Our families were close. We kept in touch online over the years."

"So you knew what he was about to do?" Preston urged. "Were you involved?"

"No! No. I swear it."

Preston sighed. He didn't have time for this. "Five… four… three… two…"

"Wait!" Farrokh pleaded. "Wait. There was a man. He came to visit me, three weeks ago."

"What man?"

"An American. Former military, I believe. Scars on his face." Al Bahman spoke quickly, half babbling. "He had a reputation, working with people like me. That's what he said. He was trying to make money. I couldn't use him. So I…"

"Referred him to your friend," Preston filled in the blank. "You sent an American mercenary to your Iranian friends? And he helped them?"

"I don't know. I don't know. I know he went to Tehran. That is all."

Sirens wailed, getting closer.

"A name, Farrokh. What was the man's name?"

"Uh… um…" He screwed up his face, trying to remember. "It was F… Fitz! Fitz."

"Fitz?"

"That's all he told me. That's it."

It wasn't quite good enough, but it had to be. He couldn't risk getting arrested and detained now that he'd gotten something. There was no shortage of material to bind Farrokh Al Bahman but he didn't have that kind of time, so he fired one round into the man's kneecap.

Al Bahman howled and clutched his ruined knee with both hands. Emergency personnel would arrive before he bled out. Probably.

Preston grabbed up his jacket, climbed out a window, and hurried down the fire escape. His boots hit the ground as sirens screamed. There were two holes in his jacket, but he pulled it on anyway to hide the Berettas and affected an easy stride, blending in with the people on the street as the police surrounded the building.

When he was two blocks away he pulled out his cell phone and made a call.

"Jillian. It's me. Got something for you. Mohammad Jaffer has been sewing bombs into furniture and some might already be out there.

Any recent clients of his need to evacuate their homes and have bomb squads come check it out. He's alive—for now. His five accomplices are not.

"But I need something too. Got a possible lead, but let's keep it between us. Might be something, might be nothing. I'm looking for someone named Fitz. Could be a nickname, last name, part of a name. American, ex-military, scars on his face. Fact that he's willing to throw in with these types means he's probably been out for a while. Whatever you can dig up, as quick as you can dig it. Thanks Jillian. I owe you one."

He ended the call. Three blocks behind him, SWAT guys in full tac gear were storming the fourth floor of the building he'd just left to find Farrokh Al Bahman and his bomb-upholstering outfit. A little tip from the NSA should make sure that anyone who bought his furniture recently would be safe.

Preston McMahon hadn't eaten since dinner the night before. But he wasn't hungry. He would find this Fitz, and he would find Grandpa Bill. He just hoped it would be in time.

# CHAPTER TWENTY SIX

Captain Scott stayed with the Gulfstream at Ankara Esenboğa Airport while Zero took a taxi into the city. The address was not hard to find; despite SMI Limited being a shell company, it was still registered as a business in Ankara, and therefore required a directory listing online, at least in name, location, and tax classification. Shade was nothing if not thorough, and it gave Zero a small amount of satisfaction to know that it had, in part, been his downfall.

He wondered if Strickland would pursue him. He had mentioned Turkey, and had even left the sea plane behind, the *Maria*, if he really felt the need to keep up the case...

No. That wasn't right. *Cassandra*. The plane was *Cassandra*.

He closed his eyes and rubbed his forehead in the backseat of a cab that smelled like stale food, but that was a mistake. If he kept his eyes shut for any length of time longer than blinking he saw it again. The glint of the knife in the moonlight. The dark growing spot at her throat that he couldn't stop, staining the sand.

*No.*

Instead he looked out the window at Ankara as day turned to evening. It was a beautiful city, a rich blend of history and contemporary architecture. The ruins of Ankara Castle overlooked the city from a rocky hill on the bank of the river, while the lights were just starting to come on in the swooping glass and steel skyline of the Söğütözü, the downtown business district. Just to the north was the Anitkabir, a columned memorial and mausoleum to Mustafa...

*Mustafa...*

The leader of the Turkish War of Independence. His name escaped Zero right now, but it was a small detail, unimportant, little more than a distraction from what he saw when he closed his eyes.

The taxi did not take him to the business district, or to the mausoleum, but rather to the city limits where skyscrapers turned to sprawl before they would eventually give way to suburbs and then forest and farmland. The car stopped in front of a three-story stone building with a flat roof in a district that was part residential and part commercial, one block from a mosque and across from a corner store.

The fare was two hundred thirteen lira. Zero passed thirty dollars over the seat with a muttered apology. "Didn't have time to exchange, sorry."

The driver shrugged and took the money, and Zero got out of the car.

He inspected the building briefly. If anyone inside was looking out they would see him clearly, but he didn't care.

Alongside the building was a stout black gate. He pushed it open and it creaked loudly, but he didn't care much about that either. He was not here to sneak or spy. He was here for information, and had come a long way for it, and was going to get it. One way or another.

Behind the building was a small courtyard, the bricks dirty and mostly broken and pushed up in places by weeds. A wooden door hung in a frame with peeling green paint and Zero pounded a fist on it three times.

A small voice in the back of his head told him this was not the way he did things, and that this seemed like a very good way to get killed, but he ignored it. Like forgetting, getting killed did not seem like the worst thing that could happen, and until it did he would keep going.

He pounded on the door again, and a moment later it was wrenched open from the inside to reveal an angry-looking Arabic man whose beard had grown unruly and shirt had been stained in several places.

"Who…?" he started to ask, but then he took Zero in from head to toe and back, and while Zero wasn't actually sure what he looked like in that moment the confusion on the man's face told him that it wasn't good.

"Zero," he told the Arabic man in English.

That was all it took. The man lurched back, nearly stumbled, and made a dash through the house for the front door. Zero was inside an instant later, in a grimy kitchen that smelled of mildew. There was a table there, the cheap folding kind, with three wooden stools around it. He grabbed one up and hurled it. The stool sailed end over end and smacked the fleeing man in the small of the back with its flat side. A cry caught in his throat as he sprawled to the ground.

The man tried to recover, scrambling to his hands and knees, but Zero had the stool again and broke it over the man's back, forcing him

155

to the floor again. He turned him over and grabbed two fistfuls of his stained shirt.

"Who are you?" he demanded.

The man panted, wide-eyed. "Zero!" he shouted. "Zero!"

And for a moment Zero was confused, because that was *his* name, but the pounding of footfalls above snapped him out of it. The man was shouting a warning, not identifying himself.

He slammed a fist across the man's jaw, stunning him, and vaulted to the stairs, taking them three at a time. They creaked and groaned under his weight as if they might give, but they held, and at the top he sprinted down a corridor to find a second man in his line of sight, in a bedroom, tearing open the drawer of a bureau. He yanked with such force that the drawer pulled free and fell on his toe, and the man cursed as he dropped to his knees and dug through the contents.

By the time his hand closed around the black pistol Zero was already there, in the doorway. The man rose with the gun but Zero leapt in a full-body tackle and tore him to the ground. The gun bounced away somewhere and the man tried to shove him off, but Zero whipped his head forward. The part of his skull at his hairline met the man's nose and it gave easily. His gaze went vacant and his head lolled.

Just for good measure, Zero sent a fist down in a hammer-blow to his abdomen, just above the navel, hard enough that the man's legs jerked in a spasm as the air was forced out of his lungs. He gasped for breath as Zero rose to his feet. He couldn't see the gun; it had fallen somewhere among the mess of strewn clothing, filthy sheets, bare mattresses, and random accoutrements.

He heard the sound of a struggle from another room and abandoned his search for the gun. He threw open a closed door in the hall and winced at the scent of offal in the bathroom. A third man was trying desperately to tug open a window that would not budge. At the sight of Zero he panicked and slammed his elbow through the glass.

Zero resisted the urge to go for his own gun—the shots would be heard and send cops—so he took a quick step back into the hall as the bathroom man plucked up a long, narrow shard of glass from the floor. With a snarl he swung it like a knife, not seeming to mind the blood dripping from the palm and fingers clenched around it.

Zero danced backward as the man swung the glass again and again, aiming for his midsection. He was running out of hallway but the man's swings were sloppy; desperate. He just had to wait until an opportunity to get in closer...

The man swung again, upward, leaving himself exposed for the half-second before the downswing, just enough time for Zero to take a jumping step toward him, arms up as if he was going to hug him. One forearm blocked the fist-enclosed glass from coming back down, while the other pulled down on the sleeve at the elbow. With one smooth motion he folded the man's arm easily, the natural way in which arms folded, and sent the jagged edge into the side of his neck.

The man's mouth fell open, and his fingers trembled around the glass as he attempted to pull it out. Zero released him as he collapsed to the wood floor.

*Two down. But still one alive...*

He rushed back downstairs. The first man, the one he'd broken a stool over, was not where he'd left him. Zero retraced his route and found the man in the small courtyard, staggering in a half-jog. He grabbed him by the back of his collar and hefted him back through the doorway. The man crashed into the cheap folding table and overturned it, sending paper plates stained with the remains of that evening's dinner across the floor.

"Who are you?" Zero demanded.

The man scooted back on his hands and his rear until his back hit the wall. "I am no one."

"Not good enough." Zero glanced around quickly and grabbed a soggy dish towel from the countertop.

"I have no name," the man snarled.

"So you're one of them, then." That group, the Palestinian radicals who had kidnapped President Rutledge back in March, had not given themselves a name, claiming some bizarre ideology of names giving others power. But he knew what it was; it was cowardice, because a name was a way to identify someone. To find them, and to choke the life out of them with a mildewy dish towel.

The man tried to struggle as Zero wrapped it around his throat, but Zero simply kicked him once in the ribs, flipped him over onto his stomach, and put a knee in the man's back. Then he hauled back on the towel with both hands and counted to thirty.

Thirty seconds was not a particularly long time, but for someone who had no air it was half an eternity.

157

The man flailed, his palms slapping the linoleum floor, his head whipping wildly from side to side on his neck as if there would be some way for him to wriggle free. At the count of thirty Zero released the pressure, just enough for the man to take a ragged, gasping breath.

"You were born with a name," Zero said. "What was it?"

"You... you are going to... kill me anyway," the man panted. "I'll tell you... nothing."

"Suit yourself." He hauled back on the dish towel again. This time he counted to thirty-five. The man's face turned almost purple before he relieved the pressure again. "Change of heart?"

"Go... to... hell—*ack!*"

This time Zero did not count. Instead he spoke. "You're right. I *am* going to kill you anyway. Just like I did both your friends upstairs. But before that happens, I can first make you wish you were dead. I've got nowhere else to be in the entire world but right here."

The man's eyes began to roll up in his head. No; he would not let him pass out. He released his grip. The man spat blood.

"Your trachea is damaged. Believe me, this next time will hurt a whole lot worse."

"Al..."

"Al?"

"Nashar." The man's voice was hoarse, difficult to understand.

"Nashar?"

"N-najjar."

"Al Najjar. This is your name? Or it was?"

"Y-yes," the man stammered.

"Good. Now we're getting somewhere. You were part of a group funded by Mr. Shade. Mr. Shade now resides in a hole in the Moroccan desert. Mr. Shade's new home is only marginally less disgusting than this one, frankly. Which seems strange, because Mr. Shade gave you a lot of money. Can you see why I would be confused to find you here, instead of literally anywhere else?"

The man coughed in response.

"A man was sent to kill me," Zero continued. "He failed. But he did kill someone else. Someone that was... with me. And then he fled. I think you hired this man. Maybe on Mr. Shade's behalf. Maybe on your own. Doesn't matter. Who was this man, Al Najjar? Who was the assassin?"

158

"He..." Al Najjar coughed again, and blood ran down his lips. "Failed?"

"I'm here, aren't I? And he's still out there somewhere. Tell me who I'm looking for. Tell me where to find him."

"If he is not dead..." the man croaked, "you will find him... wherever *you* are."

Zero sighed, and he yanked on the ends of the dish towel. He did not count, or speak; he stared at a spot on the wall, a place where the white paint, near-yellow with age and neglect, had peeled away a bit to reveal brown beneath it. Maybe the color the kitchen once was? Or perhaps just grime. Didn't matter. But that small peeled area, no more than a few inches in diameter, was very nearly in the shape of Brazil, he noted. Funny.

"Oops." He released his grip and Al Najjar's head thudded to the floor. Zero turned the man on his side and felt for a pulse. It was there; he wasn't dead. "Hey. Wake up." He slapped at the man's cheek.

Al Najjar coughed weakly.

"I need a name. Or else we're going to go another round."

The man's lips moved, just barely, as he croaked out a word.

"Didn't catch that. Did you say 'house'?" Zero knelt, his ear closer to the man's lips.

"...Krauss."

Zero sat straight up. He stared down at the limp form in front of him. His hands shook slightly, the dish towel gripped tight between them.

"Krauss? Did you say Krauss? Stefan Krauss? Answer me!"

"Krauss," came the whisper.

"No." Krauss was dead. He had been shot and blown up and plunged into the Atlantic Ocean in February. There was no way he could have survived that.

*But you did.*

That was different. Zero had help.

*What if Krauss did too?*

The dish towel fell from his hands. It couldn't be. That would mean that Krauss had survived, and healed from his wounds, but hadn't come after Zero, not yet, not on his own—not until he was hired by these people, the remnants of this group, to assassinate him.

It didn't make sense. There was no connection between Krauss and Shade, or Krauss and the Palestinians. Was there?

159

He shook his head. His mind felt jumbled, sluggish. He dared to close his eyes, to go back to the night on the beach. The glint of a knife. A man—Caucasian. His features lost in the darkness and wan moonlight.

Could it have been Krauss?

In his memory, the face suddenly came clear, as if it had always been there, just waiting. A clean-shaven jaw; sandy hair combed and parted to one side. Features that could have been a hard thirty or a good forty.

He saw Stefan Krauss die. And then he saw Stefan Krauss kill Maria.

Zero was so stunned by the revelation, his mind churning, that he almost didn't see the gun until the shooting started.

# CHAPTER TWENTY SEVEN

The man stumbled. Had he not stumbled, Zero might not have heard him coming, and might have met his end right there in a filthy safehouse near the outskirts of Ankara, Turkey. But the man *did* stumble, on the last step, blood eking from both nostrils of his broken nose and an ugly dark gun in his hand. He raised the pistol and Zero leapt to the cover of the kitchen doorway as he squeezed off several wild shots.

He had killed both men upstairs. Hadn't he? Evidently not, since one of them was now firing at him indiscriminately. He didn't want to use the gun, but had little choice now. He pulled the pistol out of the waistband of his pants, the one he'd taken from Strickland. He couldn't remember what it was called but it hardly mattered now.

The man fired a few more rounds at nothing, as if it would keep Zero at bay. In a way, he was right. In another way, he wasn't. Zero aimed at the thin plaster wall and fired three times. Chunks of plaster flew as the rounds blasted through but he heard no cry of pain. The man with the gun fired a few more rounds back at him, into the wall, and Zero ducked and covered his head as plaster and lathe board rained down over him.

Then there was silence. Zero dared to stand and put his eye to one of the holes he'd made in the wall and saw the man frantically ejecting the magazine to reload.

He stepped into the doorway then, raised the pistol, and put one round into the man's head.

*Now* he was dead, for certain.

So was Al Najjar. He'd taken one of the wild shots to his back, turned on his side as he was, and stared vacantly at nothing, blood still drooling slightly from his lips.

Shame. Not that the man was dead; he was a terrorist and a kidnapper and had facilitated murder, if not committed it himself. Shame that Zero had gotten so little information out of him, and now had more questions than answers.

Was it really Stefan Krauss who had killed Maria?

If so, why had he fled that night?

How had he known that Zero would be there?

Where was he now?

Would he return here? Did Krauss even know where "here" was?

Questions. Just one answer inspired too many questions.

And now he was out of time, too; he heard sirens wailing. Just as he'd feared, the gunshots had brought some unwelcome attention. There was a key ring hanging near the back door; he grabbed it and walked calmly yet quickly out the door, down the pathway, and out the creaking black gate.

He clicked the fob and a car chirped a short distance away. Zero groaned. It was a blue Renault Sandero, a clunky little four-door hatchback that probably topped out at sixty-five. Far from the ideal getaway car, but if he kept it under the speed limit and avoided cops he should be fine.

He slid behind the wheel and turned the engine over. It sputtered a little and came to life, and then he shifted gear and hit the gas. The car chugged twice—not a great sign—but lurched forward.

*You're good. You're clear. Get back to the airport.*

The sirens were close now. Even with the windows closed they screamed so loud that it sounded like they were all around him. But they weren't; they were right in front of him. Two Turkish police cruisers rounded the corner suddenly, white cars with a blue stripe down the side and the word *POLIS* over it. Zero slammed the brakes to avoid hitting them and the back end of the Sandero wobbled. The cops screeched to a halt too, and for a moment they just stared at each other through the windshield.

One of the officers was mouthing something at him, pointing, opening a car door.

*Dammit.*

He yanked it back into gear and slammed the gas. The Sandero was not mighty, but it was small, and it shot the gap between the two cop cars with inches to spare on each side. Zero up-shifted and leaned forward as if that would somehow help the little car move faster.

In the rearview, the two police cars pulled U-turns and pursued. A chase would be no good on these open roads with little traffic. They'd catch up to him in no time.

To his east was the city, its lights twinkling with dusk, beckoning him. He could lose them in the city. He couldn't outrun them, but he

162

could outmaneuver them, get lost and abandon the car as soon as he was clear.

One of the cruisers caught up and came up alongside him, the officer in the passenger seat shouting again. The second cruiser was inching up on his other side.

Zero hit the brakes. He spun the wheel right and made a quick turn as the cruisers jetted forward, slamming their brakes an instant later. The Sandero shot quickly down another street, cut a quick left, and then another right. Horns of passing cars blared at him as he blew stop signs, red octagonal signs just like in the States that instead bore the word *DUR*, a bizarre reminder that he was far from home.

He located the headlights and flicked them on. He toggled the high beams rapidly at a car in front of him and then skirted around it, the Sandero's tires screeching in protest.

Zero looked in the rearview. He'd lost them. He slowed to the speed limit and came to a stop at a traffic light.

The Söğütözü. That was as good a place as any to ditch the car and blend into a crowd. The glimmering business would be busy, full of shoppers and people seeking entertainment or pedestrians on their way to one place or another. He'd be little more than a face in the crowd.

But from there… how was he supposed to find Krauss?

*If he is not dead,* Al Najjar had said, *you will find him wherever* you *are.*

Krauss wasn't finished. He was still after Zero. Had he stayed in Nassau after killing Maria? Had leaving there been a mistake?

He would have to get clear. Find a safe place. And then somehow broadcast his location without alerting the CIA or any other authorities. Draw Krauss in without drawing anyone else.

It sounded impossible.

The light turned green and he eased ahead, driving casually. Blue lights exploded to his left suddenly, flashing, and then a siren wailed.

"Shit." He shifted and pounded the Sandero's accelerator again as a cop car swung out behind him into traffic. Was this the same ones that had been pursuing him earlier? Unlikely.

Then he realized his fatal flaw. He could lose them in the city, or try to—but the city was where all the cops were.

He weaved in and out of traffic. Horns blared; brakes squealed. A red light ahead. Screw it. The car did not even slow. Headlights half-blinded him as he came within a hair's width of being T-boned by a

163

truck. The Sandero shot through the intersection. The sirens were helping; drivers were getting out of their way, and by extension, his way too. Some not fast enough. He swerved right. The tires hit curb and he bounced in his seat. Zero leaned on the horn to alert pedestrians to get the hell out of the way. His side-view mirror clipped someone's hip.

They'd be fine. They should have gotten out of his way. Didn't they understand what he was trying to do? Could they not see what was at stake?

In the rearview there were two cruisers now. They tried to flank him, to get up on one side or the other. He knew what they were going to attempt; a PIT maneuver, or a pit block, gently ramming his bumper and shoving on a diagonal so that the Sandero lost control. And the Sandero *would* lose control, he could feel it. The little car felt like it was barely holding together.

If he was going to lose control, it was going to be on his own terms.

Zero laughed at himself then, at the oxymoron of it, as he tapped the brake just enough to let the police car on his left catch up. Then he yanked the wheel and sent the Sandero into the cruiser.

The hatchback hit the cruiser at about forty-five miles an hour and they both spun, parallel to one another, into the opposing lane of traffic. Brakes squealed. The seatbelt strained against Zero's chest as he gritted his teeth for an impact. The Sandero's tires hit the curb and the little car bounced.

The cruiser kept going, and the rear end of it crashed into a storefront.

Outside the car, people were screaming. There were shouts and bodies running every which way. Smoke billowed from beneath the Sandero's hood. Zero undid the seatbelt and pushed open his door.

The two cops in the cruiser were dazed, blinking and looking around as if they didn't understand what had happened. Their siren had failed but the blue lights were still flashing.

Zero pulled the pistol at his waist and fired two shots into the hood. More screams. More frantic running. The two cops ducked and covered in their seats.

The other cop car had stopped about forty yards from him. There were people, a lot of people, between him and it. He saw the doors fly open and two officers get out. They went for their guns.

Zero aimed carefully. He didn't want to hit anyone. He fired three shots—one, wait, then two-three—and the officers scrambled for the safety of their open doors.

He was well aware that he was shooting at police. But they weren't on his side. They wanted to capture him, maybe even shoot him, and he could not let that happen.

He jogged across the street and fired twice more into the air, as people gave him a wide berth. He was a target out here. But the Söğütözü was only a few blocks away. He could get lost there, in a shopping mall or a department store or perhaps even the subway station. He tucked the gun back in his pants and he ran, a full-on sprint down a side street. From somewhere in the sky came the chugging of a helicopter, but it wasn't close enough. It wouldn't find him before he found cover.

And then he would worry about how to find the assassin that had killed his wife.

But now, he ran.

# CHAPTER TWENTY EIGHT

Stefan Krauss had done exactly what he'd told himself he would not do. It was bold, but it was reckless. Predictable, perhaps, but maybe so insane as to seem not so. He found himself doubting himself at every decision, something he had not done for a long time.

*Is this obsession?* he wondered. If so, it was a foreign feeling, one he did not much care for.

He had flown to the United States using his American alias. He had rented a car from the Enterprise at Dulles under the name of Patrick McIlhenney. He had driven the car here, to the home that was owned by Maria Johansson, now deceased, and by Reid Lawson, also known as Agent Zero, and it was here that Krauss had been parked for the last two and a half hours.

He would never be able to use this alias again. He would have to bury Patrick McIlhenney. Which was a shame; Krauss enjoyed playing the part of an ordinary American imbecile. He found people warmed to the persona easily.

The house itself was as ordinary as his alter ego. One story, simple, with blue shutters and a fenced-in yard. Hard to believe this was the home of Agent Zero. So hard to believe that he did not want to go inside. So he had sat there, in his rented car, and watched. There were no signs of life from outside. No vehicles in the driveway. It did not seem like anyone was home.

It was so... *normal,* just so unremarkable that Krauss did not want to go inside. Except he did want to go inside, some part of him did, because it would afford him a unique window into his quarry. He wanted to see how Agent Zero lived. Because from out here, parked just outside this painfully average place, he could not help but feel that he had pegged the man completely wrong.

What had he expected? A mansion? A posh loft? A fortress? Anything but this, really.

Krauss had made only one stop between the airport and here, to a military surplus store, where he had purchased two knives and a lock-pick set. He would not buy a gun for obvious reasons—he did not have the time and did not want a background check performed on Patrick McIlhenney. Perhaps he could have contacted someone, or had Dutchman do it, and procured a gun. But he had already told himself it would not be a bullet that ended Zero's life, and he planned to stick to that.

Besides, two knives and a lock-pick set did not require identification. It was as easy and trifling as buying a sweater or a bunch of bananas.

At last Krauss got out of the car. He'd waited there long enough and was mostly certain no one was home. He walked up to the front door as casually as if he was going to ring the bell. He even mimed the action, for the sake of any neighbors who might be watching.

Lock-picking was an art that required patience. It was, he had found, not a particularly difficult thing to learn, at least not on a technical level. It was the patience required that made it so hard for many. Krauss slipped the small kit from his pocket and took out two picks, one flat and narrow with teeth on its end like a dull key, and a second with an L-shaped tip. He blocked the locks themselves with his body so that no one would see what he was doing, and he fit the picks into the tumbler.

He did not glance down at what he was doing; he did not crouch and inspect the locks. That would be useless anyway; it was not as if he could see inside them. Instead he navigated by feel alone, and he stood and kept his head up so that to anyone watching it might seem as if he was just patiently waiting for someone to answer the door.

The pick with the jagged edge he raked gently along the pins, back and forth slowly, while the L-shaped pick worked above it, at each individual pin, until one by one they fell into place. It was not fast work, and it was, admittedly, tedious, but at last the pins fell and a quick twist of both picks opened the deadbolt.

Krauss slipped the picks back into his pocket and this time retrieved one of the two knives. One was a folding tactical knife, commonly called a lockback, with a wide and wickedly sharp blade. The second, the one he reached for now, was a stiletto, a long narrow blade that was sharpened on both sides. The knife was a close cousin to the switchblade, but just enough removed to skirt the laws in the state of Virginia that forbade buying, selling, or furnishing that type of knife.

Stefan Krauss licked his dry lips, and then he twisted the doorknob and pushed into the house.

The first thing that struck him was the scent of... what was that, exactly? It was a feminine scent, like perfume, or floral deodorant, maybe even laundry detergent. No, he realized, it was all three and more, the mingled scents of an overpowering female presence in this house.

The second thing that struck him was the beep of the security system from a wall-mounted panel to his right, warning him that if he did not input a code the alarm would sound.

Krauss stepped to it in one stride. He pried the plastic cover from the panel with the tip of the stiletto, tugged one wire loose, and then flattened the blade against two metal leads, connecting them.

It took him only four seconds, and the system stopped beeping. Krauss shook his head as he replaced the cover. He'd expected better from Zero.

He closed and locked the door behind him, and still holding the knife, he made his way slowly down the foyer. It was very clean, white tile beneath his boots. The foyer emptied into a kitchen. In one direction, a living room; in the other, a dining room and a hall. Down the hall was a bathroom, a girl's bedroom, and a master suite.

Krauss stood at the threshold of the largest bedroom. The bed was unmade. There were two closets, one with a full-length mirror affixed to the door. Hers, he was certain, by virtue not only of the mirror but of it being the larger of the two.

He would not enter this room. There was a sanctity to it that he would not disturb. No, sanctity wasn't the right word. Peace? Perhaps.

The woman from the beach, Maria Johansson, she would never step foot in this room again. She would never sleep in that bed, or wear those clothes. This was not remorse or guilt on his part; those words would imply that he had done something wrong, and she had thrown herself in front of his blade. These were just facts.

And then the lock turned in the front door.

Stefan Krauss slipped away from the doorway quickly and returned to the kitchen. He heard someone entering the home, closing the door behind them and locking it again.

There was another door behind him. A closet? He quietly pulled it open to reveal stairs. A basement. In the foyer, he could hear the newcomer jabbing at the security keypad, which would not beep now that Krauss had disarmed it.

168

"Huh?" It was a man's voice, confusion in his tone over the inert keypad.

Krauss positioned himself on the top step leading down to the basement and pulled the door closed behind him, leaving it open just the tiniest sliver, as heavy footfalls thudded on the tile.

A moment later he saw the man. He was burly, large, with a bushy beard and a trucker's cap. He paused in the kitchen, right in view of Stefan Krauss, and he called out.

"Sara? Mischa?" The man moved out of Krauss's view. "Anyone home?"

His grip tightened around the knife. He was not here to kill anyone but Zero, and to do so would be folly. There would be a body, which meant evidence that he was there. His target was Zero; killing this man would ruin yet another chance.

But if the man discovered him, he would have no choice.

The footfalls returned after checking the other rooms. They paused, but Krauss could not see the man through the sliver of open doorway.

"Guess no one's home," the man grunted.

He was right on the other side of the door. Mere inches away.

"Sara?" he called. "You down there?"

The door moved slightly. Krauss held the knife near his waist, the blade ready to launch forward…

A cell phone rang. The door stopped moving, open about four inches. The ringing stopped and the voice said, "Yeah. Todd?"

Krauss flattened himself against the wall, obscured by the shadows as much as possible.

"Jesus," the man said somberly. "Are you all right? Okay. No, you did the right thing."

A pause. And then: "What's in Turkey?"

Krauss could not hear the other person speaking, but he knew what was in Turkey. Specifically, in Ankara.

It seemed as if Agent Zero was hunting his benefactors.

They would talk.

And he would know.

"All right, here's what we do," said the bearded man as he stepped away from the basement door. "Run down the Gulfstream's call sign with every airport in Turkey. Once we find it, have the local PD lock it down. Have Penny keep an eye out for chatter on stolen vehicles. And flag his passport and ID. Reid Lawson—he has no other alias to go by right now. We may still have a few friends in the area; I'll make a couple of calls. But under *no* circumstances do we involve Shaw and the agency, got it? Good. Keep me posted."

The man sighed heavily. "Zero," he murmured. "The hell are you doing." Then he retreated down the foyer, and a few moments later the front door closed after him.

Krauss folded the stiletto and put it in his pocket. He emerged from his hiding place but remained still and silent until he heard the rumbling truck engine fade.

Zero was not even in the country. He had not returned after Nassau. Instead he had somehow ascertained the location of the safehouse in Ankara and was headed there. Or was already there. Or had been and gone.

Regardless of which it was, Al Najjar was certainly a dead man. But before being a dead man, he would talk. Zero would make him talk, and then he would know that Stefan Krauss was not only alive but had killed the woman on the beach.

There was a certain irony to be enjoyed that had Zero simply come home, they might be facing one another now. But Krauss could not enjoy it, found no satisfaction in it, because his target was not here.

But he would be. Eventually Zero would have to come home. His friends did not want to involve their own agency for some reason, which meant they were protecting him from whatever crimes he was committing abroad. If they were able to see to it that Zero returned safely, Krauss would have another chance.

He would just have to find a place to lie low until then.

# CHAPTER TWENTY NINE

Maya rolled her eyes as Trent Coleman groaned yet again and stretched his legs, at least as far as he was able to stretch his legs in the passenger seat of a Mercedes CLA 250.

"If I could just get out for a minute..." he started.

"No," Maya snapped. He'd asked that no fewer than five times already.

"My legs are cramping."

"I don't care." It was long past dark. She was hungry, irritable, and completely over Coleman's complaints. She was miserable, and none of those reasons contributed more to her misery than the simple fact that they were expected to murder a man.

After all the work she had put in, all the strides she had made, everything she had done to get to where she was had been for naught. She had become the CIA's youngest agent, and in return the agency had sent her to the other side of the world to kill a man without any reason or evidence of wrongdoing.

An assassin. That's what they expected her to be. It wasn't right.

They had done everything else they were supposed to do. They had located their target, the native Emirati named Ali Saleh who was a board member of the Emirates National Oil Company. They had staked out the ENOC offices in midtown Abu Dhabi for hours, and eventually saw him emerge. Just as the photo from the briefing, he was plump beneath his tailored suit with round, clean-shaven cheeks and deep-set eyes.

From there Coleman had followed on foot and Maya in the car. They had followed him to a dinner appointment at a posh downtown place, where they waited longer, and then to a nearby shop where he bought a bottle of scotch, and finally they tailed him in the Mercedes along the E20 route, across the Musaffah Bridge to mainland UAE, and into the residential neighborhood of Al Shamkha, a sprawling development of luxury homes and palm trees and a Ferrari dealership.

Saleh's home was nothing short of an estate, with an electronic gate at the end of a long driveway leading to the three-story home itself, the front façade spotlighted and bright. The Mercedes was parked a short distance away and across the street, in the shadow of a stout palm but with line of sight of the driveway and front of the home.

They had done everything they were supposed to do except the one thing, the final thing. They had retrieved their equipment, located the target, tailed him, and waited past nightfall.

Now all they had to do was kill him.

But they had been sitting in the Mercedes, in the dark, parked outside of Ali Saleh's house for the better part of three hours.

"Can I ask you something?" Coleman broke the silence yet again. "Just one thing?"

Maya closed her eyes and tried to summon the silent strength to deal with Trent Coleman. "Fine. One thing."

He twisted in his seat to face her. "Look, this sucks, right? I get it. I don't want to kill anyone unless I have to. But... back in D.C., you shot James Smythe without thinking twice. If those bullets weren't rubber, he'd be dead. So... I guess what I'm asking is, what's different now?"

The lie came easily. "I knew what Smythe's offense was."

Coleman scoffed. "So you were willing to kill him for smuggling some documents to the Croatian mob? I'm not buying it. Come to think of it, is there really a Croatian mob? We didn't even know what was supposed to be in that briefcase..."

"Just drop it, Coleman."

"And you put two in his chest like it was nothing—"

"I said drop it, Trent," she growled.

"I don't think the CIA would just have us murder some guy. There must be a reason, right? This Saleh guy could have a basement full of children, or be planning to bomb an embassy or something!"

It was the girl," she blurted out.

Coleman blinked at her. "The girl?"

"The one in Smythe's room. In his bed." Maya shook her head. "Bradlee said that everyone else failed the test but us. That's because everyone else, when they burst into that room, they saw that Smythe was up to more than just smuggling documents, and they wanted to know what. Like they'd... I don't know, catch a bigger fish or turn over some new rock. But... but that's not why I did it." She wrapped her hands around the steering wheel and squeezed. "I saw that girl, and she looked way too young, and I assumed she'd been trafficked, because why else would this young girl be in a room with a sleazy guy like

172

that… I assumed things about him, and then I executed him on that assumption." She chuckled bitterly. "Or I would have, if those bullets were real."

Coleman was quiet for a long moment. "So, I guess you've got a soft spot for trafficking victims then?"

She scoffed. What a ridiculous thing to say. Who didn't? Who wouldn't? Except… to someone like him, it was just something you heard about, in the news or on TV. It wasn't real, at least not the way that it was real to her. He hadn't lived it. He couldn't understand the way that she did, the way that she had lived it.

Maya stared at the emblem in the center of the steering wheel. They were partners, or they were supposed to be. Maybe he couldn't understand, but he at least deserved to know.

She told him, "I *was* a trafficking victim."

"Oh." Coleman leaned back in his seat and blew out a breath. "Christ. I didn't know that, Lawson."

"Few do."

"I…" He shook his head. "Sorry."

"I got into this to be a protector. Not a killer."

"Yeah," he agreed. "Me too."

They sat like that for a long time, neither speaking, just staring ahead. They could sit there all night as far as she was concerned; she was not going to kill Ali Saleh for no reason.

"So I know this isn't the best time," said Coleman. "But I *really* gotta pee."

Maya scoffed. "Seriously?"

"We've been sitting here for hours! The cramping and boredom is one thing, but I don't think I can hold it much longer. I seriously might piss myself. It'll take like thirty seconds."

"For god's sake… fine. Go. Hurry up, and don't be seen."

"Thanks." He pushed open the door and was gone in a flash.

Maya sighed, and then she realized she was still gripping the steering wheel, and that her knuckles had turned white. She peeled them away and flexed her fingers.

On the floor of the passenger seat was the black case, inside of which was the collapsible .308 rifle. The sight of it made her angry all over again. She was not going to sit here all night and pretend to deliberate when she'd already made her decision. When Trent returned, they would make the call to the number in the burner phone, and they would tell whoever answered that they weren't doing it. They would not kill this man. They would especially not be storming an entire estate with only two people, a rifle, and a single pistol…

*The pistol.*

The Sig Sauer that Yasser had given them. She'd had it, earlier in the day, but when they split up and Trent had followed Saleh on foot she'd passed it off to him, just in case.

He still had it.

Trent Coleman might have gone to pee. Or, he might have gone to kill the man himself, to spare her from it.

"Son of a bitch," she hissed as she shoved her door open and hurried out of the car. Where had he gone? She couldn't hear a thing aside from chirping crickets.

Maya stole across the street, keeping low and out of the glow of streetlamps. She skirted carefully around the gated entrance to Saleh's driveway for fear of cameras. The western edge of the property was enclosed by a perfectly manicured hedge wall, about six feet high. Impossible to jump, branches too thin to climb. But not so thick that one couldn't push through it.

She half-jogged along the hedge wall in the darkness. "Coleman?" she hissed in a half-whisper. "Coleman, you idiot! Where are you?"

"Lawson." The voice came to her, not far, and she crouched further, peering around. "Over here." She found him then, or at least half of him, as the front half was in the hedge. "Think I'm stuck."

Maya grunted in frustration, grabbed Coleman by the back of his belt, and hauled backward. He came free of the hedge and fell onto his back.

She stood over him with her hand out. "Give me the gun."

"No," he told her. "I'm going to do this, and we can go home—"

"Until the next time they send us to kill someone? I don't think so. Give me the gun, Trent. I'm not messing around."

He rose to his feet and brushed himself off. "I'm not giving it to you. You shouldn't have to do this."

"You shouldn't either!" she argued.

"Neither of you are going to do it."

Maya spun at the new voice, her hand instinctively going into her jacket for a gun that wasn't there. Coleman whirled as well, pulling the Sig Sauer, though he nearly fumbled it in his grip.

"Who's there?" he demanded.

The stranger stepped forward. He was a tall African-American man in a black shirt, black jacket, black pants. His hands were clasped in front of him; he was unarmed.

He had shaved his head since Maya had last seen him.

"Coleman." Her voice was shaky as she said with new urgency, "*Give* me the gun."

Standing before her was a man who had saved her life twice. A man she honestly thought she would never see again. A man that her father had called a friend. So had Maria, and Alan Reidigger.

This was the man who had murdered her mother, Katherine Lawson, on the street outside the museum where she worked in New York.

"Give me the gun, Trent." She did not take her eyes off of Agent John Watson, or former agent, she had assumed, since he had seemingly vanished more than two years prior. She did not take her eyes off of him but she held her hand out. "Give it to me."

"Maya," said Watson. He held his hands up then, as if surrendering. "Please. Let me explain."

The sound of her name on his tongue snapped something inside her. Gun or no gun, this man was going to die. She threw herself forward, and with it a fist aimed for his face. He ducked it by an inch but she already had a knee coming up on trajectory with his groin. Watson twisted his hips so that her knee struck his thigh instead—he grunted with the impact—but it allowed him to get in close, close enough that she could smell his aftershave, close enough that he could bring one arm around to her opposite shoulder. With her legs in too close, almost right against his, he yanked backward and she was off her feet then, in a throw over his hip, and she landed in the grass like a hefted sack.

"Stop, please," he told her. "We'll make too much noise."

Noise? She didn't care about noise. She cared about watching the light leave his eyes.

She leapt to her feet, fists balled, ready to charge again, when the heel of a boot came up, too fast, and struck her in the chest. She fell again, the air knocked from her lungs.

Maya had dreamed of this moment, of facing John Watson and using everything she had learned against him.

It wasn't enough. He was better than her. Faster. Stronger.

"Stop!" Coleman ordered. "Or I'll shoot!" He pointed the Sig Sauer at Watson.

"Agent Coleman, stand down. My name is Agent Watson."

He frowned. "Agent? What?" He glanced from him to Maya, who tried to tell him to shoot, but breath failed her at the moment, let alone words, and in the instant his gaze was off Watson the older agent reached for the gun and twisted it out of Coleman's hands easily.

*Idiot.* Maya climbed to her feet, ready for another round even as Trent Coleman put his hands in the air.

"Wait," Watson told her. He held the gun he took from Trent but did not point it at her. "I know you want to hurt me. I understand if you want to kill me. But I have information you need to hear, and you can only hear it if I'm able to speak."

Maya narrowed her eyes. She did not want to hear anything he had to say.

"Maya... do you know this guy?" Coleman asked, finally coming up to speed.

"I do." Her breathing was still ragged but her voice returned enough to say, "He killed my mother."

Coleman just stared, and in that stare he seemed to be reevaluating every decision that had brought him here.

"Please listen," Watson insisted. "I've been following you two since you arrived."

"What? Why?" Maya demanded.

"I imagine everyone thought I fled," he told her. "And I did, in a way. I was reassigned to SRM. Strategic Resource Management, the same subdivision you were recruited into." He shook his head. "This isn't the place for you, Maya, and I tried to tell them that."

"You... you've been watching me?" she said in disbelief. The man who murdered her mother in cold blood had been behind the scenes this whole time? She did not want to believe that.

"SRM is where I started, and where I ended up," he told her. "It's where your dad started too. 'Dark agents,' we call each other. It's a fast-track to field agent— but what we do is not glamorous..."

"You kill people."

"We remove obstacles," Watson corrected. "Consider it 'course correction,' but on an international scale."

It took everything in Maya's power to not attack him again. With Coleman's help, they could probably take him down, but her "partner" just stood there like a deer in headlights and muttered, "What sort of obstacles?"

"Obstacles like this man, Ali Saleh. You've been out here a long time; I understand that you don't want to kill him without knowing what he's done."

Maya's nostrils flared in self-defiance, but she couldn't help herself. "What's he done?"

"I'll give you the short version. The polar icecaps in the Arctic Circle are melting, opening new waterways that previously did not exist. Many countries will by vying for control. Saleh is orchestrating a plan for his company, ENOC, to be among the first to drill new territory in the Arctic, but to do so, he's made back-room deals with private militias to help them gain and maintain certain waterways—the same waterways that are being eyed up by China, Canada, Norway, and the United States, among others. The difference is that Saleh is employing more... nefarious methods. Methods that will most likely end in bloodshed."

Maya blinked at the sudden influx of information, trying to make sense of it. "You're suggesting that Saleh needs to be killed to... avoid a fight in the Arctic?"

"Potential war," Watson corrected. "We're talking about a *lot* of oil, which means a *lot* of money. The type of money that any developed country might start shooting over. Saleh is planning to shoot first."

"But that's..." No; what he was suggesting was not only impossible, but deplorable. "That's impossible to predict. You're murdering people on conjecture. No way could you know for sure what would come of it. Besides, if what you were saying was true, there wouldn't be any war at all, would there? There wouldn't have been a 9/11. The president wouldn't have been kidnapped. You could have just, killed a handful of people and avoided it all."

Watson nodded slowly. "True, it's impossible to predict everything. But I like to think that the world might be a lot worse off if we didn't do what we do."

Maya scoffed and looked away. For the moment she'd forgotten that she was in a rich neighborhood in Abu Dhabi, thousands of miles from home, outside the estate of a man that her government had deemed it necessary to kill for the sake of possibly saving lives because—because what, a computer model told them so? A team of analysts? A fortune teller with a crystal ball?

"You don't belong here, Maya," Watson said. "I tried to tell them that. But you passed their tests, and they insisted."

"And if I refuse now?"

"I'll see to it that you're transferred. You're too valuable to just let go." He chuckled slightly and added, "Which, I may add, I can only do if                          I'm                          alive."

In her mind she saw a pair of scales: on one side, Watson's satisfying death at her hands; on the other, maintaining her goal, her career, and her dream. It was of little surprise to her that they were even.

He studied her face and seemed to see the deliberation there, because he offered, "You could always try to kill me again later. But right now you're needed elsewhere."

"Why?" she asked carefully. "Where?"

"Maya, I'm sorry I have to be the one to tell you this." Watson actually sounded genuine at that. And then he told her: "Maria is dead."

"What?" The words came so candidly from his mouth—and why shouldn't they, he was a killer—but that only made their sting all the sharper.

*Maria is dead?*

"That... that can't be." She shook her head. "They... they're on their honeymoon..." This was another test. A trick. A ruse. To see how she reacted. She could feel it. It *had* to be.

"I'm sorry. It happened about twenty-one hours ago, in Nassau. An assassin followed them on the beach at night. He fled afterwards." He shook his head. "It took everything I had not to reveal myself sooner to tell you."

Maya felt numb. She studied his face for a sign, any indication that he was lying, but saw none. "If you're telling the truth," she said, though she could hardly muster more than a whisper, "then where's my dad? Did he go home?"

"I think we both know he didn't," Watson said sadly. "He left Nassau on a stolen plane. He assaulted Agent Strickland in Morocco. Intelligence suggests he was last in Ankara. There were three bodies found, and local police were shot at during the getaway."

Maya closed her eyes. Maria was dead, and her dad was on a tear across Europe that could get him killed. The strange thing was, he was doing exactly what she would expect him to do in that situation.

"Where is he now?" Maya demanded.

"Not sure, at the moment. But I've been kept informed..."

"In case he becomes an obstacle that needs to be removed?"

He nodded once. "Yes. But I'm not going to do that. Any information I get, I'll pass on to you. Go to him. Take the car back to the jet. As soon as I know something, you'll know. The agency wants him dead if necessary, but—I think you could stop him better than I could, Maya."

John Watson never really smiled, but his expression now was as close to one as he'd ever come, and it only made Maya's anger rise anew.

"Don't look at me like that. This doesn't make us friends, and given another chance, I'd still kill you."

"Rightfully so."

"What about Ali Saleh?" she asked.

"I'll take care of him," Watson said. "Didn't think you would anyway. In fact... glad you didn't. It changes a person."

She looked past him to Trent Coleman, who was awkwardly following the exchange between the two. "And him?"

"I'll make sure he gets home safely. Go find your dad. Get him home too. And then, if you still want to kill me, you can come find me."

Strange, that a part of her didn't just want to leave Trent Coleman there. But she had to. Assuming Watson wasn't lying—and she didn't believe that he was—Maria was dead, and her dad was in a very dark place.

"I will," she promised. "You going to be okay, Coleman?"

He shook his head a little. "I... I barely have any idea what's going on right now."

He'd be fine. Maya turned, and she took a few steps, but then she thought of something else and paused, glancing over her shoulder.

"My mother. Was she one of those obstacles that needed removing?"

"Yes," he said bluntly. "In a manner of speaking. She was a name and a photo, just like you got today. I didn't know who she was until after. And back then, I didn't ask."

"Because you wouldn't have done it if you knew?"

"I didn't say that."

Maya nodded, and tore her gaze from her mother's murderer. Another day, another time, she would find him again, and she would kill him. But today, letting him live could mean saving her dad's life.

# CHAPTER THIRTY

Jonathan Rutledge paced the terrace overlooking the White House Rose Garden. He'd removed his tie and his jacket, but that hadn't been enough to overcome the stifled sensation he felt. Being out of doors would do the trick, he'd thought, but now as he paced he realized that nothing could help him.

Nothing short of getting Bill McMahon back alive.

More than a hundred years ago this area, just outside the Oval Office and the West Wing, had been stables for horses and coaches. It was the wife of Woodrow Wilson who had first established it as the Rose Garden, in 1913. Since then it had gone through a few redesigns, most notably in the sixties during the JFK administration, hence many people referring to it as the Kennedy Rose Garden (even if much of the planting had actually been done by Jackie O.).

Rutledge had planted seeds. They had just begun to sprout, too, in places like Saudi Arabia and Iran, Palestine and Israel. But now they were withering and dying before his eyes.

Iran was not handling this situation well. In their government's desperation to maintain peace both abroad and within their borders, they had ordered full-scale manhunts for the captors of Bill McMahon that so far had yielded three hundred forty-three arrests. Anyone affiliated even loosely with the scarred man in the video and his cohorts had been rounded up and interrogated fiercely.

Such Gestapo tactics had not, historically, sat well, and they weren't sitting particularly well with the world now.

The IRGC ships that had broken rank in the gulf were still on the move ever north, ignoring threats and warnings and now being pursued by the rest of Iran's navy, despite the central government making no comment or statement on the matter as if it wasn't even happening and they were not on the brink of civil war.

Shaw's CIA teams that had been dispatched had been equally fruitless, and in fact stymied by the overzealous nature of the Iranian government.

180

Rutledge's own cabinet was fighting him every step of the way, against agreeing to pay the ransom on Bill's head. Their indecisiveness was leading their own people to believe that the United States didn't care much for what happened to President William McMahon, and at the same time insisting that Iran's inability to find the culprits must mean they didn't actually want peace with America.

Such black-and-white notions were ridiculous to him, but they were the way of the world. People tended to believe that if one thing was true, it must mean another was false, or vice versa. A logical fallacy that was far too easy and convenient for most *not* to believe in. Like those who, in recent months, had said such things as, "If he's so focused on peace in the Middle East, he must not care about homelessness here in America."

Or starving children.

Or the veterans.

Or the unemployed.

Jonathan Rutledge felt impotent. He felt boxed in. The Oval Office had felt stifling, talking heads suggesting what they say, what they do, what their position should be.

He had never wanted this job, until he did, and then he did until he didn't.

If every day was a battle against himself, how was he supposed to lead a nation?

"Jon."

He winced, convinced it was Tabitha Halpern, come to alert him of some new development, new crisis, new stance or new plan.

But no. It was Joanna who stepped out onto the terrace. She waved behind her to indicate that the Secret Service agents could give them some space, and she joined him as he paused in his pacing and faced the Rose Garden.

"Beautiful," she noted.

"Never ceases to impress me." He turned to her. "Joanna, tell me what to do."

"No," she told him directly. "We built this together, you and I. Let's fix it together. What do you know is right? Not just for Bill, but for the most people possible?"

He took a breath. "We agree to pay the ransom. But only if they tell us the location where Bill is being held. We pay them. We get Bill back. And then we hunt them down, every single one involved, and imprison them for the rest of their lives. We make examples out of them, and then we help Iran with their renegade situation in the Gulf."

She nodded once. "All right. Then let's do that."

"It's not that simple," he argued.

"It is. And given recent developments, it seems the most logical course of action. You are the president; you can sign an executive order to pay the ransom if need be. Some people won't like it, of course. Some people won't like it if you wear a red tie, or dye your hair. Some don't like it that you even attempted this in the first place. But I'm on your side, and I agree that this will help the most people that it can."

His vice president paused for a moment, and then she added, "Though I will admit that I didn't like it much when you dyed your hair."

He chuckled, but it ended in a deep sigh. "How do you do it? How can you just... break everything down so easily like that?"

"I try to keep emotion out of it as much as possible," she admitted.

"Is it really that simple?"

"No," she told him, as he felt her gentle hand on his shoulder. "It's the hardest thing in the world."

*

Fitzpatrick paced the rear porch of the old house overlooking a veritable dust bowl of a backyard. He'd removed his tac vest and traded his boots for flip-flops, but that hadn't been enough to overcome the stifled feeling inside the place. It had no A/C, and even though it was nearly September it was still very warm in this part of the country. Being outside would do the trick, he'd thought, but now as he paced he realized it was just as goddamn hot out here as it was in there. It seemed that nothing could help him.

Nothing short of getting five hundred million USD.

More than fifteen years ago this place had been someone's home. Then it had been foreclosed on. It sat vacant for a while, no one wanting to put the money into renovating such an outdated building. Then the housing crisis occurred in 2008, and this old house was on the verge of being condemned. That was when a certain someone swept in and snatched it up. A certain someone who was looking for cheap places to use to lie low. A certain someone had gotten it for thirty-five

182

thousand, a cash offer with zero caveats, just an as-is purchase with no questions asked.

Funny, though, he'd never used it before. Had never needed to. And as long as someone owned it, it stood standing, wouldn't be condemned. So it had sat, waiting until someone from the Division might need a place to squat for a little while, to let the heat cool down. But then the Division was no more. And still the house sat, loyal as a dog waiting for its master, refusing to fall over or collapse.

"Dog. American dog."

Fitzpatrick winced at the nickname that Scar Man had given him, which frankly wasn't entirely unfair since he had dubbed him Scar Man first, and there were worse things one could be called than "dog."

"Yeah?"

Scar Man stood behind the screen door. "You should not be outside. Someone might see."

"No, friend, *you* should not be outside. No one is looking for me."

Scar Man huffed, and then said, "They have responded."

"Well, about damn time." Fitz pulled off his ball cap, wiped sweat from his brow, and replaced his hat before heading back inside. The wallpaper in this room was peeling badly, yellowed with age, the floral pattern that was probably once vibrant now browned and withered.

There were four others in the room besides him and Scar, the small crew he had brought over from Tehran to carry out the plan, who consisted of the Tall Man, the Scrawny One, Drab, and Bonehead, the latter of whom came off as tough but stupid, leading Fitz to believe he must have quite a thick skull.

"What did they say?" he asked.

The Scrawny One turned a tablet toward him, but Fitz waved it off.

"I don't care about any statement about morality or diplomacy or whatever-the-shit. Just tell me what he said."

"They will pay the ransom," said the Tall Man, the self-proclaimed leader of the bunch whose bomb-making compadre in New York had referred Fitz to. "But they want the location of the former president."

Fitzpatrick could hardly contain his glee. He clapped his hands once, and followed it up with an exuberant, "Hot damn! If that ain't perfect." He turned to Scar Man. "Your IRGC pals in the Persian Gulf still on the move?"

Scar Man nodded.

183

"Call 'em up, tell them the plan won't work unless they halt." Scar Man had done an excellent job stirring up some dissent among a few IRGC higher-ups who were less than excited about the treaty and sanctions. "We've got another video to shoot." Fitz headed toward the stairs.

"Wait," demanded Scar. "They will not pay if we do not give them the location. How do we ensure that we receive the money?"

"Oh, we'll give them the coordinates," Fitz told him. "Half upfront, half after the transfer goes through. By the time they realize what's there, my friend in New York will have moved that money through so many companies and accounts it'll take them weeks to unravel it."

"I think you should tell us who your friend is," Scar challenged. "We are trusting you with far too much."

Fitz sighed. What was the harm? It wasn't like the guy used his real name. "Sure thing, Scar. My guy is a fellow named Mr. Bright. Used to be one-half of a terrorist-investing partnership until his business associate got busted. He likes your type because they make him money, and you can trust him because there's a lot *more* money to be made if Iran goes to war. Is that good enough for you?"

Scar thought about it for a moment, staring Fitz down, but at last he said, "For now."

"For now. Sure." Fitz chuckled. "Get camera-ready, Scar. You're my star."

Fitzpatrick jogged up the stairs, a bounce in his step. The plan was exceedingly simple, so much so that it almost astounded him that it wasn't transparent. The US government was going to give them five hundred million dollars for the return of Bill McMahon. In response, they would give the US government the coordinates of the halted IRGC ships in the Persian Gulf. The Fifth Fleet would be called in; he had no doubts about that. They would not, in fact, find Bill McMahon, and whatever happened after that would happen. Best-case scenario, the overzealous IRGC renegades would resist and fire first. Rules of engagement dictated that the Americans would fire back. The rest of the IRGC would watch the Americans sink their pals. And Iran would have to choose between a civil war with their own military, or turning their back on the United States.

By the time all that happened, Fitz would be much richer and long gone.

He could have probably screwed Scar and Tall Man and his cronies out of their fair share, but he was not a greedy man—and if he was being honest, he didn't really trust himself with that much more than the ten percent he was getting. He didn't want to draw undue attention in his new life.

At the top of the stairs, Fitz went to the second door on the right and unlocked it to find Bill McMahon in his chair, handcuffed, his chin touching his chest and his eyes closed.

"Psst. Bill. Hey, Bill."

The former president looked up slowly. His eyes were red-rimmed and bleary from lack of more than fifteen minutes of sleep at a time.

"How are you, buddy?"

"We're not buddies," Bill said, his voice thick and slow. "You're a monster, and a traitor."

"A traitor? Yes. A monster?" Fitz circled the chair to inspect Bill's wrists. They had stopped bleeding, but they were raw and red, dark in places with dried blood. "How about I take these off for a few minutes and we can bandage these wrists up?"

"Don't want your help," Bill muttered.

"Maybe not. I know you're a tough old buzzard. But I bet you'd like some water. Maybe stretch your legs for a few. There's just... *one* tiny thing I need from you first. We're going to do another video. And I need you to look as pathetic as—well, as pathetic as you do now." He patted Bill McMahon on the shoulder. "It'll just take a few minutes, I promise."

He wasn't a monster. He was just pragmatic, and maybe just a little bit cynical.

Of course, he had this thought at the same time that he reminded himself they would still have to kill Bill McMahon before it was over. For one, it would be the ultimate humiliation to the US after all of this. It would make Iran look extremely guilty of having the world look one way while they pulled something off behind everyone's back. All the American people would cling to is that Iranians had killed him. And finally, Bill might still be aware of the final piece of the puzzle. Fitz wasn't sure—Bill hadn't said anything, and he wasn't about to ask.

*Say, Bill, do you know where we are?*

After they'd taken him from his home, they'd driven all night, exchanging vehicles a few times, in the hopes that he would believe he could be anywhere. And he *could* be anywhere. But in reality, he was

185

in a former Division safehouse in Virginia, not two hours from his ranch in Six Springs, West Virginia—and less than ninety minutes from Washington, D.C.

Fitz and his new friends were instigating a war right under everyone's noses, and by the time anyone figured it out Bill would be dead, and he would be gone.

# CHAPTER THIRTY ONE

Zero crossed the border from Turkey to Greece by bus. He figured it was the second-least likely way anyone would assume he'd travel—the most likely being to steal a car, which he didn't dare do, and the least likely being by ferry. Which was exactly why he'd gone to the ferry terminal and bought a ticket using his credit card. He'd even used the ATM there, and then he'd traveled north a short ways up the coast to a bus depot and paid for a ticket in cash.

The only alias he had at his disposal was his real identity, Reid Lawson. And Reid Lawson's passport would get stamped in Greece. He was certain that Penny was tracking his passport, if not the CIA, and could only hope that the ferry fake-out worked.

The bus ride was uncomfortable, cramped, but he was glad for it. It kept his heavy eyelids from closing. It kept the recurring nightmare he'd lived from invading his thoughts. He fought sleeplessness, aided by being in a center seat shoulder-to-shoulder with strangers, and instead he planned.

His first notion was to keep traveling west, across the Mediterranean, all the way to Israel. He could seek out Talia Mendel there, the Mossad agent who had helped him several times in the past. They understood each other, he and Talia. While everyone else had turned their backs on him, she would not. At least he didn't think so.

But Israel was a long way off and would take too long to get to. He didn't dare travel by plane, at least not legally. And then he remembered something else: the apartment in Rome.

For years his team had maintained a safehouse in Italy, a small apartment overlooking a courtyard in which sat a fairly famous fountain, the Fontana delle…

*Fontana delle…*

Turtle Fountain. In English it was called the Turtle Fountain. No one alive knew about the apartment other than him and Alan; they'd hidden the recurring expense under damages done on an op and paid on it for a decade.

Maria had known about it. But she wasn't alive anymore to know. Just thinking about going there made his heart ache; it was there at that apartment that they had reunited after two years of being apart, after the suppressor was torn from his head and his memories had just begun to return. He hadn't even known who she was, not at first. But he could remember it now, the moment he had pushed open the door to the apartment in Rome and she had come around the corner, a teacup in one hand...

*She had light, creamy skin and blonde, tousled hair pulled back into a loose ponytail. It was still early; she was in pajama pants and a tank top, as if she had just woken up.*

*But her face told a different story. Her slate-gray eyes were wide in shock and her mouth agape as she stared directly at him.*

*A teacup slipped from her grasp and shattered on the floor.*

*"I don't... I just..." she stammered, at a loss for words. "Is it really you?"*

*"Yeah. It's me."*

*"God. You look like hell." She let out a short laugh. "I just can't believe this!" She moved to take a step forward, but he held up both hands. She froze, an eyebrow raised.*

*He pointed down at the floor. "Glass." Her feet were bare on the tiled floor.*

*She looked down quizzically, as if only now noticing that a cup had broken, and then she leapt deftly over the shards toward him. Before he could even get his hand out of his pocket, she flung her arms around him and pulled him close, burying her head in his neck.*

*"God, I can't believe it! You're alive! Why didn't you reach out, try to contact me? Jesus, you're alive!"*

Zero woke with a start and a sharp breath. At least he thought he woke; had he fallen asleep? Had he dreamed it, or remembered it?

The bus slowed to a stop. A light rain fell outside as they arrived in Thessaloniki. The ferry had been heading to Larissa, a ways south along the Greek coast. From here he would travel west, find passage across the Ionian Sea that gapped Greece and Italy, pay someone off or stow away so that the authorities still believed he was in Greece. Then make his way to Rome.

There he would find a way to draw Krauss in.

And then he would wait.

188

Zero disembarked and made his way to the bus terminal. He wanted to be on the move quickly, but he was in desperate need of coffee, or soda, or even caffeine pills at this rate—anything to keep him alert. Inside the terminal he spotted a café and made a beeline for it, the scent of roasted coffee beans making his mouth water.

A man in a suit fell in step with him, at his elbow, too close to be a fellow traveler.

"Agent Zero," the man said. He had an accent—Italian, if he wasn't mistaken.

"Sorry?" He feigned ignorance. His ferry scheme had apparently not worked as well as he'd thought. Or there were people waiting in Larissa as well.

"Please come with us," the man told him, and before Zero could ask who "us" was, a second man in a dark suit fell in stride at his other side.

They weren't CIA. They weren't Greek. That could only mean…

"Interpol," he guessed aloud as he slowed his pace. Ah—Alan must have called in a favor with their old friend Vicente Baraf, former Interpol agent who was now a section chief.

They'd gotten to Baraf too. He wondered if they'd spoken with Mendel. He had abandoned his temporary friend, Captain Scott, in Ankara. Did he have anyone, a single ally left in the world?

Zero spotted a third man in his periphery, suited and standing with his hands clasped, not far from the nearest exit to the bus terminal. How many? If three were showing themselves there were likely at least four.

He stopped, and the two men flanking him stopped as well.

"We just want to speak with you," said the man on his left.

"Sure. Let's speak then."

"Are you armed, sir?"

"I am." He gestured to the bag hanging off of one shoulder. "It's in there."

"Would you keep your hands where I can see them, please?" The Interpol agent's tone was hushed; clearly he did not want to make a scene.

"Are you going to cuff me?" Zero asked.

"We'd rather not," he admitted. "I don't see why this can't be a peaceful exchange. If you would just follow us outside—"

"Because I'm going to resist."

The agent's expression went blank. "Sir…?"

"Did you not hear me?" Zero asked, his voice growing louder. "I'm going to resist. In fact, I wouldn't bother with the cuffs if I was you. You should take out your gun. I assume you're armed?"

He glanced over his shoulder at the second agent, who opened his mouth to speak, but no words came.

"Um... yes, we are armed, sir. But we were told you would be cooperative—"

"You were told wrong," Zero said point-blank. "You should take out your guns."

Neither man moved. There wasn't exactly a protocol for an armed suspect giving ample opportunity for them to prepare themselves. But he had, and they had not taken it.

"Suit yourselves."

He twisted and an elbow shot back, into the face of the agent behind him. It connected firmly with an orbital bone, and also cocked Zero's arm at a near-perfect parallel to strike forward with a fist. The second agent tried to move out of the way, but not fast enough, and caught the blow across his nose.

Zero mule-kicked backward, a solid hit to the abdomen, and then lunged forward. His arms snaked into the agent's suit jacket as if he was embracing him. He twisted and kicked back his left leg into a wide stance, throwing the agent to the ground, while his right hand came out of the jacket with a Beretta.

The third agent, the one who had stood near the entrance, was running toward him and pulling loose his own pistol from its holster. Zero fired twice at him...

*Nonlethal!* a voice shrieked in his head.

Both shots sailed right over the agent's head, missing by less than a foot, but close enough to send him skittering for cover. Travelers screamed and ran every which way in the terminal, clearing the wide floor quickly, making an easier target of him but also easier for him to see...

Movement, to his right; another agent, this one already gun in hand, aiming. Zero fired twice more—

*Nonlethal!*

One shot hit the agent in the shoulder and spun him to the ground with a yelp. Zero let out a grunt of frustration; he hadn't meant to hit the man at all and would certainly have to answer for that later.

He dashed for the exit as a shot rang out behind him, and then another. Chips of tile exploded from the floor; a glass door shattered. Zero slid, like a runner sliding into home, clear under a bench and to the other side. He used the bench back as cover and returned fire, three shots, then four. A cry of pain, but not a mortal wound.

These men were against him too. Everyone was against him. The world was against him. All for what? For wanting to bring Kate's murderer to justice?

He fired twice more, wild shots that hit nothing living, and then he leapt up and burst into a sprint for the door. Zero leapt through the shot-out glass and then he was outside, dashing down concrete steps. He still had a gun in his hand, and people could see it, clearly, as they screamed and shouted, pointed at him, ran for cover.

Sirens shrieked. They weren't far off. And he was sure there were others out here, waiting for him. He paused, catching his breath for one second, looking for anyone who might be coming for him, taking aim at him...

"Stop!"

He spun, gun raised. Finger on the trigger.

"Dad, stop!"

For half a second, Zero aimed the Beretta at his daughter, and then he dropped the gun as if it was white-hot. It clattered to the concrete between them as he stared in shock.

"What? No." He rubbed his eyes, certain that Maya was not standing in front of him, unarmed but with one hand up, palm toward him, her gaze stern and more than a little sorrowful. That would be impossible. She couldn't be there; this was a trick, his mind betraying him again.

He rubbed his eyes and the vision flashed behind his eyelids, of being on the beach at night and the knife and the dark spot that wouldn't stop growing.

He blinked spots away and he looked again, and Maya was still there, closer now, having taken a few steps toward him. She waved someone off to his left; the Interpol agents had caught up, and their guns were on him, but they stayed where they were and he didn't even bother to look their way. He chose to focus on her, his daughter, her face that looked so, so much like his own, so that if they shot him where he stood at least she would be the last thing he saw.

"Dad," she said, breathless. "What are you doing?"

191

"Maya..."

"You have to stop this."

"No. No, I can't. I can't just stop. I have to find him."

She took another step toward him. "Find who?"

"Him. The one that killed Maria. Rais."

Maya shook her head. "No. No, Dad. Rais is dead, you killed him in Dubrovnik."

"Not Rais..."

*Dammit.* His mind was a disaster. Maria was right; Rais was dead. It was someone else who had killed Maya. Maria. Not Rais.

"Krauss," he managed. "It was Krauss. Need to find him..."

He'd killed her on the street in New York City, with an injection of a toxin called TTX.

*No. Wait.*

"You're coming home," she told him. "You're coming home now, with me. There's only one alternative and it's no choice at all."

Like forgetting, getting killed did not seem like the worst thing that could happen, and until it did he had to keep going.

"No, you don't," Maya said firmly.

Had he said that aloud?

He wasn't even sure how she was really here, how this was possible.

"I was given special permission," she explained, "to bring you in personally. By our... mutual employer."

*Mutual...?*

"Oh." Her secret program. Her return to D.C. The long days gone from dawn to dusk. Maya was working for them, for the CIA. She'd done it.

But... why hadn't she told him?

"We can talk about that later." She was closer now, close enough to reach out and take one of his hands in both of hers. "You haven't been taking your medication, have you?"

He shook his head. No.

"You're dealing with a massive trauma. You haven't slept. I bet you haven't eaten and you're probably dehydrated. Dad..." A thin, sad smile lit on her lips. "You're a mess. Please, let me take you home."

*Home.*

He realized, finally, what he'd been doing wrong all this time.

*You will find him wherever you are.*

All this time he'd been on the move, seeking out the man who killed Maria, never stopping long enough to realize that the most likely place for Krauss to come for him was where anyone would assume he would be.

Home.

Had he endangered his family by leaving them unprotected? Had Krauss gone to the most likely place that anyone would think to come for him?

"The girls. Are the girls okay?"

"The girls are fine," Maya told him. "Alan is looking after them. Come with me; you'll see for yourself."

"I'm… I'm a mess." Her face blurred as his eyes stung with tears. "I think I might need help," he said, barely above a whisper.

"Let me help you. Come with me. We'll get on a plane. They've shipped your stuff home from Nassau; your pills will be there. And… Maria, she'll be there too. Let's take care of her, yeah?" A tear ran down Maya's cheek, and he reached for it, wiped it away with a thumb.

She never cried. Maya never cried in front of anyone.

"Yeah." He was wrong. The entire world wasn't against him. There was at least one person on his side, right here, holding his hand in hers.

There were others. He knew that. Some part of him knew that. Penny had told him no. Strickland had tried to bring him home. Alan had done what he could. They did what they thought was right, and he did what he thought was right, and maybe none of them were right or wrong because that's not how the world worked.

His daughter took him by the hand and led him away from there, to a waiting car, which took them to a plane, which would carry them back to the US, to home, to his family.

And he let her, because it was the right thing to do.

# CHAPTER THIRTY TWO

At some point on I-95, between Savannah and the border to Florida, Sara had an epiphany.

The engine of Maddie's borrowed truck rumbled loudly, loud enough to be concerning, as if smoke might start spewing from beneath the hood at any moment, as if it might break down at any moment and leave her stranded on the side of the highway. But it held for the entirety of the trip, a trip that should have been eleven hours, twelve with traffic, but ended up being fourteen with the frequent stops. The truck was a gas-guzzler.

But Sara didn't mind. She was in no rush. She stuck to I-95 southbound and after a while the rumbling of the truck's engine just became another sound, the way people grew accustomed to the sound of blood rushing in their own ears, almost comforting even, the way the gentle snoring of someone sleeping beside you could be. She had turned her phone off, and she didn't turn on the radio, or talk to anyone at the gas stations she stopped at. She just kept driving.

She just hoped that Maddie wasn't keeping tabs on the odometer.

Sara had told her that her younger sister was missing. That part was true; Mischa was gone. Sara had told her that she would go looking for her younger sister. That part was not true; she had no idea where Mischa was and no way to locate her other than texting and asking, and she doubted she'd get a straight answer.

Mischa would be fine. She was smart, capable, and independent.

Sara was capable and independent too. But maybe not quite as smart as she thought.

That's where the epiphany came in. Even the name of it escaped her, or it had for a bit. She didn't have Maya's brain or Mischa's voracious appetite for knowledge or her dad's ability to recall endless facts about history. She kept thinking "euphony" for some reason.

*This is a euphony. No, wait, that's not right.*

*Timpani? No. That's a music thing.*

At last it came to her—*epiphany!*—and she had a word for the realization she'd made.

When she'd first heard about Maria's death, when Alan had come in the middle of the night to tell them what had happened, she'd felt... how had she felt? Not helpless. That wasn't quite right. Helpless meant she couldn't do anything without help, and that wasn't true.

Incapable? No... she'd proven otherwise more than once.

Ineffective. That was it. That was how she felt. Ineffective, and inadequate.

People got hurt every day; there was no stopping it. All she had been trying to do was make sure the right people got hurt and didn't hurt anyone else. But those people, the ones she was hurting, they had already done their share of hurting. And they wouldn't stop just because they were hurt. People like that would never just stop.

She knew that, because she was a person like that. She'd been hurt, and she'd done her share of hurting, and she wasn't going to stop either. How was she any better than them? Because her motives were virtuous? How could she guarantee that the people she hurt never hurt anyone again? She couldn't. Not really.

Unless...

It was long after dark by the time she reached Jacksonville, and she stopped once more to refuel, and then drove on to a not-great neighborhood on the east side of town. She slowed down a bit as she passed a beige storefront in a small strip mall, its façade dark after closing, though the two words painted on the inside of the window in large white strokes were still visible: SWIFT THRIFT, where she used to work.

Sara kept driving, and soon she passed a brown, ramshackle two-story house on a tightly packed street. There were lights on inside but the blinds were closed. She thought about her former roommate and friend Camilla, who had completed rehab in Virginia and gone god-knows-where, because Sara wasn't the greatest at keeping up with people, and she wondered if Tommy and Jo still lived there. But she didn't stop.

It was here she'd lived for nearly a year after emancipating herself from her dad. This wasn't where it had started for her; it had started long before that, with her mother's murder and her father's lies, with being taken from her home and pushed into the clutches of traffickers and sent halfway around the world and leaping from a moving train.

It hadn't started here, but this was where she had come to escape it. This was where she'd tried to run, and turned to drugs to forget and to feel better, and for a while it worked. But ultimately even drugs had been ineffective. Inadequate.

She kept driving, surprised that she remembered the way so easily, and soon she parked on a street outside a rowhouse with grimy siding and a broken washing machine on the front porch.

Sara had briefly been a runner for a local dealer named Ike—*her* dealer, in fact—who had brought her on in exchange for his goods and because she looked innocent and wasn't likely to be stopped or harassed by the cops. It had kept her hooked, for a while, until the day she stole the package she was supposed to deliver and OD'd in a stolen car parked by the beach.

She had barely any memory of that day anymore, and they never really talked about it, but it was her dad who found her somehow, who had tracked her down and found her there alone and dying, and he saved her life and brought her back north with him.

How many times? How many times had she been helpless, and he had swept in and saved her? How many times had she needed what she was trying to give to these other women—some semblance of safety? Too often.

She would not be helpless anymore.

Sara got out of the truck, stretched her legs. She heard voices through open windows but there was almost no one out on the street at this time of night.

It hadn't started here, but Rais, the man who had taken her and her sister, he was dead. The traffickers he had passed them on to were either dead or in custody. There was no going back for them, no one to go back for, so it may as well have started here.

Sara walked past the broken washing machine on the front porch and she knocked on the front door. Inside a dog started barking, deep and throaty woofs from the thick-necked Rottweiler that she knew was fairly friendly unless you made a threatening move toward his owner.

"Shut up, already!" a voice shouted at the dog, a male voice, and then the door swung open, the inside door, leaving the thin screen door with the tear in it between them.

The guy was tall, muscular, tattooed, wearing a black tank top and a flat-brimmed cap. He looked almost the same as she remembered, and had to remind herself that it wasn't all that long ago she'd last seen him, no matter how long ago it felt like.

Ike squinted for a moment, and then his eyes widened in recognition, and then narrowed again in anger, all in the span of three seconds.

"You," he hissed. The dog barked again behind him. "Shut up!" he snapped at it. "You must be out of your damn mind, showing up here after what you did to me."

Sara said nothing.

"And now you're here on my porch after, what, a year? You looking to score or something?" He scoffed. "No way I'm selling to you. I got half a mind to slap a bitch. You best get out of here before I do."

Still Sara said nothing. She didn't move, didn't blink. Just stared.

"What are you, deaf *and* stupid?" Ike shoved open the screen door, and now there was nothing between them, nothing to stop him from hurting her if he wanted to. "Swear to god, little girl, don't think I won't..."

Ike raised an arm as if he were about to backhand her.

Sara raised an arm too, holding the Glock level with his chest.

"Shit," he said softly.

She fired once. It was shockingly loud, explosive even, but she liked the way the gun jumped in her hand. It felt powerful.

Ike's mouth fell open and he looked down at the hole in his black tank top.

The dog barked. Someone inside screamed. A woman, by the sound of it.

She fired again. A third time. Four, five, six. With each shot Ike's body jerked and he took another involuntary step back, but Sara didn't move. The dog barked, but he'd retreated to a corner, terrified by the deafening blasts. She could see the bottom of the stairs, where a dark-haired Latina woman cowered, covering her head with her hands.

Finally Ike fell, already dead before he hit the floor.

Sara turned and strode quickly back to the truck. There were other noises now, confused voices through open windows and shouts of alarm, so she started the truck's rumbling engine and she floored it down the street, away from there, headed back north.

# CHAPTER THIRTY THREE

She told him everything, Maya did. It was a long flight; they had time. She told him about the CIA's "junior agent" program, which had turned out to be a dark agent program, and she told him about the test with James Smythe. She told him about the op to Abu Dhabi and Ali Saleh. She told him about encountering Watson and how he had helped, as much as she didn't want his help, to find him.

She told him everything, and it sounded so improbable that he wouldn't have believed a word if it hadn't been for the look in her eye as she told it.

She asked him, "Is that really how you started out?"

And he remembered a Bosnian boy, stooping for a shiny pebble in the road. He remembered a businessman leaving a hotel, a bulky cell phone to his ear. He remembered how they had been in his crosshairs, and he said, "Yes."

He added, "Watson is right. It's not for you."

"I don't want him to be right. I want him to be dead."

Zero understood. He drank water and he ate some saltine crackers from a plastic packet. At some point over the Atlantic Maya handed him a pill and said, "Take this, it'll help you relax."

When he fell asleep, it was deep and dreamless. There was no beach, no glint of a knife, no dark stain. No voices beckoned to him from anywhere beyond. It was just dark.

When he woke, it was daytime and the plane was no longer moving and neither of those things seemed right. He groaned and sat up, his head swimming. Out the window were tarmac and cars and men in suits. He'd slept through the landing somehow.

A sedative. Maya had given him a sedative.

"Dad." She was there, at his elbow, clutching it gently and looking him in the eye. "Are you awake? Are you listening?"

"Maya. Where are we?"

"We're at Joint Base Andrews. Are you listening?"

"Yeah. I'm listening. What's going on?"

"Here." With her free hand she passed him three pills, familiar ones, and then a bottle of water. "Your medication. I had them bring it here. Take it."

He did as she told him, and then asked again, "What's going on?"

Maya sighed. "In a moment we're going to get off the plane, and those men outside are going to have to take you into custody."

"What?" He tried to stand but his knees were weak and Maya's grip on his elbow suddenly tightened.

"Hey. Calm down. You said you were listening."

"I am… but Maya, we have to go…" He still had to find Krauss. He still had to finish this.

"Dad, you killed three men that haven't yet been identified. You shot at the police, and you wounded two Interpol agents. I promise you we'll figure this out, but first you have to go with them. You can't fight this."

He could. He wanted to. But he knew that's not what Maya was saying.

"We're going to get all this sorted out," she promised. "I'll take care of the girls until then. But right now, please do this for us."

Zero shook his head. "But what if he's here? What if he finds you? I can't go through that…"

*Again. I can't go through that again.*

"He won't. Look." Maya pointed through the window. Out on the tarmac he saw two familiar faces: Todd Strickland and Alan Reidigger stood near an SUV, the younger leaning against it and the older with his thick arms folded, watching the plane. "They're here. They're going to keep an eye on us too. We'll be safe."

His throat felt dry and he reached for the water bottle again. He'd given up. He had a plan and he conceded. Now there was no choice.

"I'll walk out there with you," Maya told him. She stood and held out a hand to him.

He took it. She pulled him to his feet, and together they made their way toward the front of the jet and the exit. Outside the weather was warm, the sun was bright enough to make him squint.

At the bottom step two men in black suits flanked him. "Agent Zero, we're going to need you to come with us, sir."

He looked from one to the other. They weren't CIA, and didn't seem like FBI. "Secret Service?" he guessed. "Why?"

199

"As a member of the Executive Operations Team, your… indiscretions fall under investigation by our agency," the man rattled off.

*Indiscretions.* He'd been careful not to use the word "crimes."

Even as a prisoner he was receiving preferential treatment by not being handed over to Director Shaw or the Bureau.

"Will handcuffs be necessary, sir?" the other agent asked him bluntly.

"No," Zero told them. "They won't. I'll come."

The agents each took him by an elbow and led him away. Behind him, Maya stood on the bottom step and watched. He passed by Alan wordlessly, and he looked away as he noticed that Todd's hand was in a splint where Zero had broken his finger.

"I'm sorry," he managed hoarsely, as the two agents put him in the back of the black SUV.

*

Maya watched as one of the Secret Service agents forced her dad's head down to clear the frame and gently pushed him into the backseat, while the other closed the door on him. Then she couldn't see him anymore, dark tinted as the window was, and a few moments later the SUV rolled away.

Only when it was out of sight did she approach the two men still on the tarmac. "Where do you think they'll take him?"

"Not sure," Alan Reidigger grunted.

"For what it's worth," she told them, "I'm sorry for the trouble he's caused."

Alan shook his head. "It's just the way he copes."

Todd Strickland looked at the splint on his finger. "It'll heal."

"No," Maya said forcefully. "We can't make excuses for this. We all lost someone, not just him." She felt for her dad, she truly did, but he couldn't expect to do things like that and not face repercussions.

"Did you tell him?" Alan asked. "About the girls?"

"No. He doesn't need that right now, on top of everything else." Alan had gone to the house to find it empty, both Sara and Mischa gone. Neither were answering their phones and, it seemed, had turned them off. It could be that they had gone somewhere together, to deal with this in their own way. Or…

*No.* She didn't want to think about that.

"That's next on the to-do list," she said. "I'll go after Mischa if you think you can locate Sara."

"Been trying," Alan admitted. "Without her phone on, and now that she doesn't have a tracker anymore, it's slow going."

"She said something a few weeks ago about a support group at the local community center," Maya noted. "Maybe check in with them?"

Alan nodded. "Will do. You think you can find Mischa?"

"I do." At least she had an idea about that.

"Not sure if it means anything," Reidigger said, "but I heard a report out of Baltimore late last night. Police responded to shots fired and found a Chinese Laundromat employee wounded in his apartment. Took two shots, one to the leg and one to the gut. He'll live—but his statement claimed it was a 'little blonde girl' who broke in and stole his Rolex."

Maya frowned. *Chinese?* Was Mischa still in contact with people from her former life? If it was her, what was she sniffing out?

"Maria's stuff," she asked. "Was it shipped back?"

"Yeah." Alan gestured to his pickup, parked nearby. "I have it."

"I'll need it," Maya told him, though she didn't elaborate on why.

"You don't think…" Todd started, but he trailed off as if he didn't want to say it aloud. "You don't think he came here, do you?"

Maya shook her head. "No. I don't." She didn't *want* to think about that; her sisters were fine somewhere. She had to believe that. Besides… he'd have to be crazy to come here and mess with *this* family after what he did.

# CHAPTER THIRTY FOUR

"I got to say, sir," said the Secret Service agent behind the wheel, "it's kind of an honor."

"What is?"

"Well... you're Agent Zero. I mean, we've all heard of you. Heard stories, anyway. Is it true, what you did back in March?"

Zero shrugged and looked out the window. "Depends on what they say I did. Where are you taking me?"

"A secure location," the passenger-side agent replied. He looked young, younger than Zero anyway, thick-necked with a strong jaw line, but a tiny bald spot stared back at Zero, barely more than the size of a quarter.

*A secure location.* A jail cell was a secure location. A bunker was a secure location. A hole in the ground could be a secure location.

"Can I ask you something, sir?" said the driver.

"What's your name?" Zero asked.

"It's Reynolds." Reynolds couldn't have been more than thirty, if that, and his gaze flitted between the road and the rearview, bright eyes flashing in the mirror every time he snuck a glance back at Zero.

"Sure. Ask away, Agent Reynolds."

Reynolds glanced at him again in the mirror. "What happened out there?"

Zero frowned. "You don't know?"

He shook his head. "No, sir. We were just told to come pick you up, and where to bring you."

"I see." Zero thought for a moment and then told him, "My partner was killed. I went after the man who killed her." It wasn't the whole truth, but it didn't need to be.

The two agents in the front seat exchanged a glance, and though they said nothing Zero could tell each was gauging whether they'd do the same for theirs.

"So you guys haven't heard anything?" Zero asked. "About Nassau, or Turkey...?"

Reynolds shook his head. "No sir, we haven't."

"Not that we would," said the agent in the passenger seat. "The news is pretty much monopolized by the kidnapping."

"What kidnapping?"

The passenger agent twisted in his seat. "You haven't heard? How long have you been out of the country?"

"Uh… four days." *I think?* He'd lost track.

"Huh. Well, hate to be the one to tell you, but President William McMahon was kidnapped by Iranian hostiles."

Zero blinked. "Bill?"

It had been a long time, a very long time since he'd thought about Bill McMahon.

"You know him?" asked Reynolds.

"I do. I mean… I did." The memory was distant, but it was there. Fifteen years ago, Zero had done his time with SRM and was a rookie field agent with the CIA. At the same time, William McMahon was acting as interim ambassador to South Korea in the wake of the former ambassador suffering a heart attack when a group of North Korean insurgents posing as the crew of a cargo ship had kidnapped him.

It was Zero's first covert op, being part of the four-man team sent to rescue him. He wasn't even Agent Zero yet; that name would come later, thanks to Alan Reidigger. Back then Agent Steele was his only alias, and by the time he had located Bill McMahon, Agent Steele was the only agent on his team still standing; the others had been gunned down during the daring raid on the cargo ship. Zero found Bill, but they were trapped on the boat with armed insurgents. They had locked themselves behind a bulkhead and defended their position for eight hours before help arrived.

And help did arrive, eventually. It would have taken far too long for the CIA to send a response team, so they activated an asset they had nearby. A brand-new asset, in fact; a private group, called…

*The Division.*

The now-defunct mercenary group led by Fitzpatrick.

There he was again, rearing his lopsided smirk in Zero's memory.

"Do they know where he is?" he asked.

"They do now," Reynolds told him. "President Rutledge agreed to a huge ransom, five hundred mil, for the coordinates to McMahon's location. Turns out he's on an Iranian ship in the Persian Gulf."

"They're sending a battalion from the Fifth Fleet to retrieve him as we speak," the other agent added. "With any luck, we'll avoid war over this."

"I'm not sure the people will just accept that, though," said Reynolds dubiously. "Those videos were pretty unpleasant."

"Video? Can I see it?" Zero asked.

"Sure." The passenger agent brought it up on his phone and passed it back to him.

Zero watched it, not bothering to turn the sound on but rather studying the face of William McMahon. He looked… "well" wasn't the right word. He was, after all, a hostage handcuffed to a chair. Healthy—he looked healthy.

Fifteen years ago, he and Bill had spent eight hours behind a locked bulkhead while insurgents tried to break their way inside. Poor Bill, he suffered terribly from seasickness, so much so that he had vomited to the point of dehydration.

Wherever this video was taken, it wasn't on a boat in the Persian Gulf.

*But why would they say it was?*

That part was easy—to break down relations between the US and Iran. Someone wanted a war. Tell the US government that Bill was on an IRGC ship. Send the Fifth Fleet after him. The IRGC claims they don't have him. The US demands they come aboard to see for themselves. And when tensions run high enough, the shooting starts.

"Where was Bill taken from?" he asked.

"His home in West Virginia," Reynolds said somberly. "Bastards killed two of our own that were protecting him."

"May they rest in peace," the other agent murmured.

"And how long before the video was released?" Zero pressed.

"Uh… sixteen hours later?" Reynolds guessed. "Maybe eighteen?"

Certainly enough time to get Bill to Iran. But it didn't quite add up.

*How would you do it?* he asked himself. *If you wanted to incite a war, would you be in the place where the war was about to happen?*

Of course he wouldn't. Just like the Palestinians hadn't, or the Brotherhood, or Amun. Just like Mr. Shade operating out of Egypt, or the French virologist who wanted to unleash smallpox on the United States.

No one stayed at ground zero unless they were willing to die, and no one asked for five hundred million if they were planning to die.

"And this ransom... they asked for it in US dollars?"

"They did," Reynolds confirmed. "Why, you got a hunch back there or something?"

"Maybe," he murmured.

He'd seen this tactic before. When Deputy Director Riker had the Division in her pocket, she had sent mercenaries after him and his team.

*I'm getting paid a whole lot of money to babysit you for the next couple of hours. So we're just going to sit tight for a while.*

Those words had come from the leader of the Division, Fitzpatrick, only a few minutes before Talia Mendel had hit him with a car. His plan had been to keep Zero and his team from stopping the bombing of the Midtown Tunnel, and then pinning stolen CIA equipment on him.

Fitzpatrick was... alive, but in what state? He couldn't help it; once he'd gotten the mercenary's name in his head it refused to leave.

"What are you thinking, sir?" Reynolds asked again.

"I'm thinking," Zero said slowly, "that we need to stop the car."

Reynolds chuckled. "Yeah? Why's that?"

"I need to borrow it." He still had the agent's cell phone in his hand; he slipped it into his pocket.

"And go where?" asked the second agent.

"Not sure quite yet. But I have an idea, and I need to follow up on it," Zero told them. "I'd invite you along, but I don't want you to get into any sort of trouble."

*Or get in my way.*

"So you can just tell them I overpowered you."

Agent Reynolds scoffed. "No offense, sir, but if we tell them you overpowered us, it'll be the truth."

Zero sighed, and wished he could tell them how well that had worked out the last time someone had said that to him, as he quietly undid the clasp on his belt. "At least slow down then. I don't want you guys to get hurt. Not too badly, anyway."

The passenger agent twisted again in his seat, this time a stern expression on his face. "If you're looking to give us any sort of trouble, I'm going to have to break the cuffs out."

"You might as well," Zero told him. "I'll need them in a minute." Then he whipped the belt around Reynolds's neck, and the SUV swerved.

# CHAPTER THIRTY FIVE

Maya knew there were cameras, but she didn't care. She knew that the CIA logged every swipe of a keycard, but she didn't care about that either. She knew that there was probably a heavy penalty for using the ID card of a deceased agent, but some things were more important than a job, and family was certainly one of them.

At least she was finally in Langley. She was still wearing the professional attire she'd been wearing before leaving for Abu Dhabi, her hair pinned back in a way that framed her face well and made her look a few years older, so no one stopped her when she entered the building. No one said anything when she swiped Maria's card at the guard station; they didn't even bother to double-check it, as long as the security light turned green.

No one stopped her on her way to the elevators, where she swiped the card again, in the semi-hidden slot that Alan had told her about, and she punched in a four-digit code on the floor buttons that would take her down, farther down than Langley was supposed to go.

The doors opened on an empty, white-walled corridor with concrete floors. Her footfalls echoed as she made her way quickly to a steel door and swiped the card again, the one that had been with Maria's things that had been shipped back from Nassau—only a bit strange, she thought, that Maria had brought her CIA credentials with her to the Bahamas, but she supposed Maria had always been ready for anything, even being called away from her own honeymoon for work.

The door opened, and Maya sucked in a breath.

The CIA research and development lab was entirely underground yet big as an airplane hangar. The walls were painted bright white, and halogen bulbs hung high overhead in a way that almost simulated daylight. Storage the likes of which she'd only ever seen in vast warehouses was arranged in the shape of a huge H, containing all manner of objects, some of which Maya recognized—drones, weapons, robotics—and others that had her baffled.

She stepped lightly, or as lightly as she could in a place where the slightest sound reverberated like a cave, across the floor. From somewhere beyond the high shelves and amid workstations were voices, and she caught the occasional glimpse of a white lab coat scurrying this way or that, but she didn't call out to anyone or try to make her presence known. Instead she treaded carefully along until she spotted a head of mousy brown hair, a bright orange T-shirt over corduroys, with hoop earrings big enough to put a fist through.

Dr. Penelope León was a lot of things, but a conservative dresser was not one.

"Penny," she said when she was close enough to be heard without shouting.

Penny glanced up, then back down, and did a double-take, her eyes wide. "Maya? Maya!" She dropped the clipboard in her hand and scurried over to her, clogs clacking against the floor. "What in the bloody hell are you doing down here? How did you even get here?"

She flashed Maria's keycard in response.

"Good grief." Penny shook her head. "You *are* your father's daughter, you know that? I'm going to have to clear the logs now. Blank the cameras." She groaned in frustration. "Would a phone call not have sufficed?"

"No," Maya told her plainly. "This had to be in person." *Because I don't think you'd be honest with me otherwise.* "Mischa is missing, and I need to find her."

Penny frowned. "Have you tried tracking her phone?"

"She turned it off, along with location sharing."

"Then I'm not sure I can help you, Maya. I'm very sorry—"

"After my sister and I were taken," Maya interrupted, "my dad had us chipped. These little subcutaneous trackers, small as a grain of rice, right here." She patted her upper arm. "He told us it was a tetanus shot. We've had them removed since. But Alan reminded me of them, just this afternoon. And then I remembered a couple months ago, Maria took Mischa to get a flu shot. And I remember thinking, what a strange time to do it, in the middle of summer. Sure enough, that night she had a Band-Aid on her arm." Maya patted her upper arm again. "Right there. Now… it could have been a flu shot. Or maybe she had Mischa chipped."

Penny's throat flexed, and Maya knew right away that she was right.

"If she did," said the doctor, "what makes you think I had anything to do with it?"

"Because," Maya replied, "I can't think of anyone else she would have trusted to do it. Not only that, but I think it was a secret between you. I bet not even my dad knows it. Maria didn't want to come off as paranoid or untrusting. But she was also afraid something might happen to her, like what happened to us."

Penny looked at the floor.

"Please," Maya implored. "If I'm right, and you know where she is, tell me. She might be in danger."

"Well, that's the trouble," Penny admitted. "You *are* right, but I *don't* know where she is." To Maya's puzzled expression she said, "Just... come with me a moment."

Penny led her across the lab floor, past researchers and assistants and workstations, to a hard-shelled laptop that she awoke with a tap on the space bar. She navigated to a secure server and typed in a serial number as she said, "Maria didn't want to abuse the chip. It was a worst-case scenario contingency. So she had me install it, and she set access with a four-letter keyword. I'm afraid she was the only one that knew it, Maya."

Over her shoulder Maya could see that the prompt was asking for a password.

"Only four letters?" she asked, doing the math in her head.

"Yes," Penny said. "With repetition, that means every letter has twenty-six available options, which means there would be four hundred fifty-six thousand, nine hundred seventy-six possible combinations."

"You could hack that easily," Maya argued.

"You're right," Penny admitted. "I could. But... I made a promise that I wouldn't."

Maya scoffed in frustration. "You're kidding. Mischa is missing! If Maria was standing here right now—"

"She's not," Penny countered. "And if she was, she would put in the password. That was our agreement."

"Fine," Maya relented. She thought for a moment. "Did your promise say anything about it needing to be her?"

Penny frowned at that, puzzled.

"Can I try?"

Penny's eyes went skyward, considering it, and then she stepped aside. "I suppose you could."

Maya put her fingers to the keys and thought for a moment.

*A four-letter word that Maria would choose as a password.*

Her first guess was obvious: Z-E-R-O.

INVALID PASSWORD, the screen told her.

Fine. Mischa's name didn't fit. Maria's name didn't fit. Her real name had been Clara, and that didn't fit. Her agent handle had been Marigold; that didn't fit. Her favorite color was green. Mischa's was...

P-I-N-K.

INVALID PASSWORD.

Maya blew out an annoyed breath. Just for the hell of it, she tried her own name.

M-A-Y-A.

INVALID PASSWORD.

S-A-R-A.

INVALID PASSWORD.

*Dammit.* Every incorrect guess was more time wasted, more time that Penny could have tried to hack the system, or more time that Maya could have been out there, actually looking for Mischa instead of guessing randomly at a password.

A-L-A-N.

INVALID PASSWORD.

T-O-D-D.

INVALID PASSWORD.

"Shit," she hissed.

"I doubt that's it either," Penny said. Then: "Sorry. This is no time for jokes."

"If you have any suggestions, I'm all ears," Maya muttered.

"I... I don't. Truth be told, I didn't know her all that well," Penny admitted. "Not half as well as I would've liked, in hindsight."

"Yeah." Maya knew the feeling. Sure, she and Maria had talked plenty. They had done the "getting to know you" thing, and Maya had even borrowed her clothes when they realized they were roughly the same size. But now that Maria was gone, she didn't feel like she really *knew* her. Not like her dad did; he and Maria had a long history together, as he told it, one that spanned more than a decade. There were things about him that only she had known, that may very well have died with her...

"Oh," Maya said in a whisper. Of course; it was so obvious when she thought about it.

The first time she had ever met Maria was before she knew that her dad was a CIA agent. Maria had accidentally called him by a different

209

name, the name that she knew him by, a name that had confused Maya at the time.

K-E-N-T.

The screen blinked, and a map loaded. Maya breathed a sigh of relief. Maybe she knew Maria a little better than she'd thought.

She leaned in to see where the small blinking red dot was located.

"The Hilton Grand," she murmured. Mischa was just outside the Hilton Grand in downtown D.C.—the very same hotel where Maya had shot fake-Smythe with two rubber bullets to the chest.

*What the hell is she doing there?*

"I have to go," Maya said. "Thank you for your help, Penny."

"Wait! Before you go. I have something for you. Just in case there's trouble. Come with me, quick." Penny led her away, toward an antechamber off the central lab. "By the way... who's Kent?"

# CHAPTER THIRTY SIX

Zero pressed further on the gas and the speedometer reached ninety as he barreled down the highway toward the next exit. He wasn't concerned about speed limits or traffic laws; he just wanted to get as far away from where he'd left the two Secret Service agents as quickly as he could. They were on the side of the road, one cuffed and the other bound with his belt, and mostly intact—their egos were likely more bruised than their bodies. He had relieved them both of phones and firearms, but it was only a matter of time before they were freed or found, and then he could be easily tracked.

He used the agent's phone to dial a number he knew by heart. The line rang once, twice, as he said, "Come on, come on, pick up..."

"This is Dr. León." Penny's voice sounded very professional when she didn't know who was calling.

"It's me. It's Zero."

"Zero! Jeez, I was just talking to your daughter like two minutes ago..."

"What? Which daughter? Why?"

"Never mind. Just a social call," she said quickly. "Wait—aren't you supposed to be with the Secret Service? In custody? Todd told me..." She trailed off as the realization hit her. "Oh, Zero. Tell me you didn't."

"I didn't!" he protested. "Okay, I *did*, but for good reason—"

"I'm not going to help you," she said sternly. "I already told you that."

He grunted in frustration. "This isn't about that, Penny. This is about the president, Bill McMahon." He reached the exit and guided the SUV to the off-ramp. "I have a hunch that I need to follow up."

"A hunch? Zero, President McMahon is being held on a ship in the Persian Gulf."

"Has anyone confirmed that?" he demanded. "Has there been a visual?"

"Well... no," she admitted. "But the government has paid the ransom and the captors gave the coordinates. Our ships are en route to retrieve him. Why would they...?" She trailed off again, this time for a longer moment.

"Oh," was all she said.

He was glad Penny was brilliant; he really didn't want to have to explain it. "Exactly. Listen, please. I have a hunch but I need to confirm it. I can't go to anyone with this but you because—well, because they'll come for *me*. Will you help me?"

"What do you need?" she asked hesitantly.

"There's a man named Fitzpatrick who used to run a mercenary group called the Division," Zero explained quickly. "I don't know his first name, but I'm sure the CIA has a file on him thick as a bible—"

"You asked me this before," Penny interrupted. "About this same man, in connection to Maria's death."

"I..." Did he? Yes, that's right. That first night, in the hotel at Emerald Bay, he had called Penny and asked for her help to track down Fitzpatrick. Already that night felt like a month ago.

But Fitzpatrick wasn't the assassin. Krauss was. Zero had been wrong about the right person. Or right about the wrong person. He wasn't sure which.

"I know I did," he said, "and I couldn't get him out of my head. Maybe this is why. Either way, I have personal reason to believe he may be involved; this has his MO all over it. His group, the Division, was shut down a couple of years ago by the CIA. Any assets that belonged to them were absorbed. I need you to run down deeds that were formerly owned by the Division that are now CIA property."

"Hang on, hang on. You're not only suggesting that McMahon wasn't taken out of the country—but that he's being held in a *CIA* safehouse?"

"Yes." Fitzpatrick was a pain in the ass, but he wasn't stupid. "Because, if I'm being honest, that's what I would do." After all, he'd been planning on using the apartment in Rome to draw out Krauss. His own plan hadn't been all that far off from this one.

"Well, you're right about one thing. We can't go to anyone with this; you'd be committed." Penny blew out a breath. "All right. I'll help you. Should I send the info to this number?"

"No. I'll call you back from a different number." He ended the call and steered the SUV into the parking lot of a convenience store, adjacent to a fast-food burger joint. He left both agents' phones in the car—he could be tracked with them, not to mention the Secret Service–

owned vehicle—but took both pistols, tucked into the back of his pants, adjusting the hem of his shirt to make sure it covered them.

Then he hurried inside and bought the first pay-as-you-go phone he saw, a slider for $24.99 with fifty minutes of prepaid airtime on it. He dropped thirty bucks on the counter and told the clerk to keep the change.

Outside he tore open the package with his teeth and dialed the activation number. Once active he called Penny back. "This phone. Thanks." And promptly hung up.

Zero had to leave the SUV behind. He could have looked around, chosen carefully, hotwired something, but that would take time. He spotted a middle-aged man coming out of the burger joint with a bag of food and a large soft drink.

*Sorry, pal, but it is not your lucky day.*

Zero pulled one of the Sig Sauers out as he approached. He didn't point it at the man but he made sure he saw it—and he did, evident by the widening of his eyes and the uncertain step backward, away from the gray sedan he was standing next to.

"Sir, I'm going to need to borrow your vehicle."

"Wh-what?" the man stammered.

"I need your car. Give me the keys, please. It's a matter of life or death."

"Oh god, please don't kill me!"

"Not *your* death. Just… hand over the keys."

The nervous man fumbled his soft drink and it fell, the lid bursting off and soda splashing over the parking lot as he reached out a shaky hand and gave Zero the keys.

"Thank you. You'll get it back in one piece. Probably." He slid behind the wheel and left the bewildered man standing there with his bag.

He had just put some distance between himself and the burger place when the burner rang.

"I've got three addresses," Penny told him, "all formerly Division-owned, now CIA property. One is in Oklahoma. The other two are in Virginia, both in a fifty-mile radius."

Zero thought for a moment. "Out of those two, have either been used by the agency since the acquisition?"

"Um…" He heard keys clacking, and then she told him, "Yes. One of them is being used as storage."

"Okay, then give me the address of the other. And make anonymous calls to local PD on the other two."

"Maybe… maybe we should send backup to all three," Penny suggested.

"No. If I'm right, cops or Feds or Secret Service will show up in full force. They'll bring SWAT and bullhorns, and they'll attempt negotiations…"

"Oh, you mean the way these things are normally done?" Penny said sarcastically.

"Yes. And also the way that would give those men plenty of time to put a bullet in Bill's head."

Penny said nothing to that, so he added, "Text me the address," and ended the call. It came a moment later, and he headed back out onto the highway toward his destination. He kept to the speed limit and resisted the urge to stomp the accelerator; he was in a stolen car, after all, and didn't want to attract any more attention than he already warranted.

A few minutes later he passed a familiar exit. If he took it, it would lead him home.

Home, to where Stefan Krauss might be waiting for him.

He found himself pulling at the steering wheel, veering toward the exit.

Maybe Penny was right. Maybe they should let someone else go after Bill McMahon.

And if Krauss was there…

A deep horn blast jolted him from his thoughts. He swerved back into the lane, narrowly avoiding a collision with a tractor trailer he hadn't even checked for. The exit passed, and Zero's heart pounded in his chest.

Now was not the time for that. Krauss could wait for another day. Or he could try to strike at Zero from the shadows. Come what may, Zero was going to see this through.

He pushed the thoughts from his head and turned on the radio.

"…Anonymous source inside the White House tells us that negotiations are rapidly deteriorating in the Persian Gulf," a female newscaster reported, "as the US Navy attempts to recover President William McMahon. His captors claim that McMahon is aboard one of sixteen Iranian vessels that broke away from the rest of the fleet in the Persian Gulf, but the Iranians are claiming no knowledge of the former president's whereabouts. In a televised statement, the Ayatollah of Iran ardently requested that the US ignore the rules of engagement should the Iranian ships fire first—a move that some believe is a plea to avoid war, while others, like Senator Breckenridge of Michigan, are calling it a blatant bid to humiliate and discredit the United States and our ongoing attempts at world peace—"

Zero turned off the radio. He thought he'd have more time, but this was it. Things were coming to a head quickly. He stomped on the gas and the car lurched to eighty, then eighty-five, ninety.

He needed to get to his destination before any shots were fired. Before something happened that couldn't be taken back. Before the *most* important shot was fired—the one that would end Bill McMahon's life. Because, he realized, there was no way these men would be true to their word. Regardless of the ransom, Bill would not live to see nightfall without intervention. They couldn't leave him alive and he knew it.

*Because if I were them, that's what I would do.*

# CHAPTER THIRTY SEVEN

"Yes sir," said Fitzpatrick into the phone. He knew he was grinning like the cat that ate the canary, but he didn't much care.

He was about to be *rich*.

"No, no, sir—thank *you*." He ended the call and turned to his temporary Iranian comrades. "It's done. The transfer was made, and as we speak, Mr. Bright is funneling the money."

"Funneling how?" asked Scar Man, his eyes narrowed suspiciously—which Fitz was starting to think was just how his face looked.

"You know. Funneling. They, uh, split it up, run it through a bunch of other companies, and, uh…" He threw his hands up. "Hell, if I knew how it worked we wouldn't be paying him to do it, now would we? All I know is that when it comes out the other side, y'all are four hundred mil richer, and I'll have my fifty."

"Four hundred?" Scar Man challenged.

"Yes. Ten percent to me, ten percent to Bright leaves you with four hundred. Simple math, *amigo*."

The man with the fishhook scar shook his head. "It should be four hundred and five. You get ten percent of what is left."

"No," Fitz growled, "it's ten percent of the total. I told you that upfront. Don't screw me over five million."

*This freakin' guy.* At some point between planning in Iran and now, Scar Man had grown a pair of balls, and established himself as de facto leader of the Arabic-speaking group. Not even the Tall Man challenged him, and here Scar was bristling like a dog vying for alpha.

He seemed to have forgotten that Fitz was the American dog.

But they were almost at the finish line. He wouldn't start a fight now, nor let one start.

"Look." He held up his hands, placating. "When all is said and done here, you're going to walk away with a whole lot of dough, okay? And it's all gonna be nice and clean. As far as anyone will be able to tell, some big oil corporation is paying you beaucoup bucks for crude-producing property in east Iran. You couldn't ask for a better deal."

216

Scar Man stared him down for a long moment, and then at last nodded. "Fine. Then there is just the one last thing."

"Yeah," Fitz agreed. "Just the one last thing."

"You will do it?"

He nodded. "I will." It was his plan, after all. It only seemed fitting that he be the one to put a quick and painless end to Bill McMahon.

"Then do it, and let us be away from here," said Scar Man plainly.

"Now hang on, let's not be too hasty. We should at least wait until the fireworks start." As they spoke, the Fifth Fleet battalion was facing off against the IRGC, demanding Americans be allowed aboard to search their vessels for Bill McMahon.

They just needed someone to fire a shot.

"Why wait?" Scar asked.

"Because," Fitz told him slowly, "two reasons. First, he could still be an asset if things don't go quite the way we want. We could shoot another video, claim he's been taken elsewhere. Secondly, we don't want his body found until *after* an act of war is made, by one side or the other. Otherwise would defeat the whole purpose. *Comprende?*"

"I see," said Scar Man. "You don't want to do it."

Fitz rolled his eyes. *What is* with *this guy?*

"Fine. You want me to do it? I'll do it. Take your guys, get clear of here. I'll finish him off, and then I'll split, and we never have to see each other again—"

"No," Scar hissed. "I want to see."

"You want to... see?"

*Sick bastard.*

"Yes," Scar confirmed. "You and I, we will go. Right now."

None of the others moved or said a word. "Christ. All right, Scar. But then we're going to skedaddle quick, all of us, because I'm not having my soon-to-be-awesome future ruined because local PD responds faster than usual to shots fired."

"That will not a problem," said Scar. He nodded to Bonehead, who reached into a satchel at his waist and produced two objects: the first, a black Walther PPK, and the second, a suppressor barrel.

"Well, ain't you guys full of surprises." Fitz took both and screwed on the suppressor. "All right, Old Bill," he murmured. "Time to take you out to pasture."

He and Scar headed for the stairs.

Zero parked the car a block from the address. He put the burner on silent and brought it with him, along with the two pistols, tucked in the back of his pants. He got out of the car and he walked casually down the cracked sidewalk, and he wondered if he was making a terrible mistake.

Of course he was. He'd already been in deep water, taken into custody for what he'd done. Then he'd gone and assaulted two Secret Service agents and stolen a car. *Two* cars, in fact. He had a solid hunch about the kidnapped president and he hadn't shared it with anyone but Penny. He was alone in a dying neighborhood of dilapidated homes that looked as if they'd been neglected for decades and if he failed here, or if he died here, if there was even a difference between those, what an ignominious yet oddly fitting end that would be.

Getting killed did not seem like the worst thing that could happen, and until it did he would keep going.

*Why does it always have to be you?* Maria had asked him that once, just before he ran off in the direction of some certain danger. He heard her now, her voice in his head.

He couldn't remember what his answer had been. The truth was, he didn't know. What was he chasing? What was he running toward?

Zero shook his head. This wasn't the time to ponder those questions. All he knew was that if she had been there with him, she'd be running toward it alongside him.

The house was the tallest on the block, three stories, the wooden front porch sagging and paint peeling from the shutters. He checked his periphery and saw no one, no cars on the road and no people on the street, and he quickly stole alongside the tall brick house.

He crouched low enough to stay beneath the windows and duck-walked along the side. At the second window he dared to stand just enough to take a peek, but the shade was drawn.

At the rear of the house was another porch and a small backyard that was little more than a dirt patch, and a screen door. He heard voices behind it and crept closer, listening. He made out only a few phrases—"Get rid of that," one said, and then, "Leave no trace."

The voices were speaking Arabic. And it sounded as if they were preparing to leave.

That clinched it. Whether Bill McMahon was here or not, these men did not belong in an unused CIA safehouse. So far he'd been half-right. But he couldn't very well burst in, guns out; any indication of his presence too soon might cause these men to panic and end poor Bill.

Zero returned to the side of the house, where there were the fewest windows, just two on the first floor and two on the second. The mortar was chipped; the bricks were cracked and crumbling, and he could see a path upward using crevices as handholds. He reached and pulled himself up, his boots getting traction against the rough façade.

He did his best to keep his grunts to a minimum as he reached again, pulled up, reached, pulled up. His fingers ached terribly but he kept going, reached—a section of brick pulled loose and fell, and he held his breath as it clattered to the concrete below him. He clung there and waited, but no one came, so he reached and pulled himself up again, until the second-floor window was only a few feet to his right.

Zero sidled to it and peered inside. The room was small, empty, and dark, with peeling wallpaper and void of furniture. He clung to the windowsill with one hand, his toes curled in his boots as if it would somehow help him stick to the wall, and pushed up on the window with a flat palm on the glass.

At first it didn't budge and he cursed silently that it was locked. He pushed again, and it moved a half an inch. He wriggled his fingers under it and hefted it upward.

The window squeaked as it opened and Zero gritted his teeth. This would be the worst time for someone to notice him, clinging to a dirty sill fifteen feet in the air while forcing open a window. But still no one came, and when the window was open just wide enough he shimmied his way inside.

The room smelled musty as an attic, and dust particles hung in the air, floating into his nose. He shook off the urge to sneeze and carefully made his way to the open door to get an idea of the layout.

Zero peered into the hallway.

An astonished young man blinked back, not two feet from him. He was tall, scrawny, wide-eyed, and his mouth fell open to shout a warning.

Zero lurched forward and rammed two knuckles into the young man's throat. A choking sound escaped him, but no shout. He grabbed the front of the man's shirt and pulled him out of the hall, into the empty room.

The young man flailed, his lanky limbs slapping harmlessly against Zero. He got an arm around the Iranian's neck, and with a quick jerk he broke it. The man went limp in Zero's arms. He let him slump to the floor, and then padded back out to the hall.

*One down... how many to go?*

There were no fewer than six rooms off the second-floor hall, the doors all closed. Zero took a cautious step forward. He heard something then—murmurs, words he couldn't make out. Where were they coming from? He put his ear to a door. Not that one. Further along, close to the stairs.

He heard the voice clearly, speaking in English on the other side of the closed door.

"...real sorry about this, Bill."

*Fitzpatrick.*

He was sure of it.

"I'm gonna at least take the handcuffs off, so you can die on your feet like a man."

Bill wasn't dead yet.

It sounded like he was about to be.

Zero pulled a Sig Sauer from his waistband and put a hand on the knob.

There were heavy footfalls on the stairs. Someone stomping up them.

"What is taking you so long?" a voice barked in Arabic. A moment later a man came into view, a dark-skinned Arabic man who was... admittedly, unremarkable-looking.

He stopped in his tracks, staring at Zero. Zero pointed the gun at him.

*No. Don't shoot him.* Even one shot would alert Fitzpatrick behind the door.

"Intruder!" the man shouted. "Intr—"

Zero flipped the pistol around, gripping the barrel, and before the man could get a second word out he swung it in an upward arc. The grip connected under the man's chin—his teeth clacked together loudly—and he fell backward, tumbling down the stairs.

It might as well have been a gunshot, for all the noise it made.

He had no choice now. Zero flipped the gun back around, and he barged into the room.

# CHAPTER THIRTY EIGHT

"Son of a bitch," said Fitzpatrick.

Zero held the gun level, aimed at the mercenary's head.

Fitzpatrick held a Walther PPK with a suppressor barrel to Bill McMahon's head.

There was another man in the room, with a swooping scar across his cheek to his ear—the man from the video. He was unarmed and stood against the wall, his back to it, confused and glancing quickly between the two armed men.

It was shot here, the video. He saw the chair, a pair of cuffs on the seat. A length of rusting corrugated steel against the wall behind it, serving as a backdrop.

He was right. Bill McMahon had been here the whole time.

Fitzpatrick held the former president around the neck, in front of him, with the gun aimed at his right temple. He was only a few inches taller than Bill; not enough to get a clean shot.

For what he had been through, Bill looked all right. He had bags under his eyes, and the color had drained from his face. His wrists were raw and red, but otherwise he appeared unharmed—aside from having a gun to his head.

"Of course it's you." The mercenary chuckled bitterly. "It's always you."

"What are you waiting for?" the man with the scar said in accented English. "Do it!"

But Fitzpatrick didn't move. His finger was on the trigger but he didn't dare squeeze it, and Zero knew why.

Fitzpatrick wanted to live, and the second he put a bullet in Bill, Zero would put several in him.

"Do it!" the man shouted again.

"Shut up," Fitzpatrick snapped at him. He didn't take his eyes off of Zero. "So what do we do now, Zero? I shoot him, you shoot me. You try to shoot me, maybe hit ol' Bill here, or maybe don't get it off fast enough and I shoot him anyway."

Zero heard feet pounding on the stairs. Angry shouts. More of them. At least two. He reached back with a foot, without looking, and kicked the door closed. He put his back to it, knowing men would try to barge in any second.

"Tell your guys to stand down," Zero said, "or things will get ugly real fast." He pulled out the second pistol and aimed it at the man with the scar.

The Arabic man scoffed. "I am not afraid to die."

"Stand down!" Fitzpatrick shouted.

The voices on the other side of the door hushed.

"Stay where you are," he called out to them. "He's armed. Don't come in here."

"They do not take orders from you!" the scarred man spat. "We had an agreement! You promised to end his life, now end it!"

"Listen here, Scar." Fitzpatrick stared at Zero. "I'm not dying here, not today, especially not at the hands of this asshole, and *super* especially not in this disgusting house with the likes of you!"

"Coward!" the scarred man cried. In his periphery, Zero saw a glint of steel as the Iranian pulled out a knife.

*Don't...*

He saw the look in Bill McMahon's eye. An almost imperceptible nod of his head.

*Don't...*

The man with the scar raised the knife over his head and let loose a guttural cry.

He ran at Zero.

The door smacked into him from behind as the men on the other side shoved it open.

He had no choice. He had to act.

Zero mule-kicked backward, feeling the door connect with a body before it slammed shut again. At the same time he ducked low, narrowly avoiding the swipe of the curved knife arcing where his throat was a moment ago. He spun away from the scarred man as the silenced PPK chirped twice.

He looked up in alarm, for half a second, to see Bill grappling with Fitzpatrick. The Walther was aimed at the ceiling as bits of plaster rained down on them.

The scarred man whirled and slashed out with the knife again. Zero leapt to the side—not fast enough. The blade slid across his arm.

He had no choice. He had to act, and there was little point in keeping silent anymore.

Zero raised the Sig Sauer in his right hand and fired once, between the scarred man's eyes. The round was deafening in the small room, and for an instant, no one moved—except the man with the scar, whose brain and skull spattered the door as he fell backward.

Three more shots rang out as holes blasted through the door. Splinters of wood stung Zero's face as he ducked and covered his head. The men on the other side didn't seem to care who lived or died anymore; anyone in that room was a potential target.

Fitzpatrick yanked the Walther away from Bill, but the former president was still on his feet, grabbing at him again. The old man had some fire in him, and neither seemed to care much about the men shooting through the door. All that mattered was the gun between them, and Zero couldn't get a clean shot.

He dropped both pistols and ran at Fitz, wrapping both arms around the mercenary and twisting his hips. He threw Fitzpatrick to the floor and the PPK skittered out of his grip.

"Bill, get clear!" he shouted. The old man retreated to a corner, crouching as more shots came through the door. Zero grabbed at the sheet of corrugated steel, and before Fitzpatrick could get back on his feet, Zero hefted it away from the wall and sent it crashing down atop the mercenary.

To his surprise, there was a door there. Hidden behind the sheet of steel that Zero had assumed was just a backdrop, and perhaps was meant to be, there was a door. He grabbed at the handle and yanked; it was heavier than it looked, painted to look like wood but made of iron.

"Bill!"

The old man covered his head and dashed for the heavy door even as the men outside the room continued blasting into it. Zero shoved him in and then followed, yanking it closed again behind him as bullets pounded it from the other side.

There was a crossbar there, on the inside of the door, on a lever. Zero threw it into place, locking them in. He put his hands on his knees and panted. The shooting stopped on the other side.

"Are you hit?"

Bill caught his breath as he shook his head. "No. Are you?"

"No." Zero checked the cut on his arm. It was wide and bleeding but superficial.

223

"Well," said the former president, glancing around. "How does the old saying go? Out of the frying pan…"

"And into the fire." Zero looked around too. The room was small, empty except for a single wooden chair, with the thick iron door and its heavy bolt and a light fixture overhead that had lost its dome and had only one bulb. There were no windows, no other points of egress.

This was a makeshift panic room, or likely had passed as one at the time this house was built.

They were trapped.

# CHAPTER THIRTY NINE

Zero put his ear to the door and listened to the argument on the other side. The voices were muffled, but if he held his breath he could just barely make out what they were saying.

"We must leave at once!" an accented voice shouted.

"No!" That was Fitzpatrick, who had seemingly been extricated from beneath the corrugated steel. "Not yet! It's not done! Do you know who's behind that door? It's not just McMahon. That's Agent Zero."

There was a brief exchange that he couldn't quite hear, the voices hushed, and then Fitzpatrick shouted again: "You! Get on the police scanner, see if the shots were reported. And you—get me something to open that door with. We've gotta have something. A saw, a goddamn axe... a torch? Yeah, a torch'll do it. I'm gonna get this son of a bitch. Cut him out of there like cracking open a lobster." A fist pounded on the iron door. "You hear me, Zero? You got no guns. I'm coming for you!"

There was a cold fury to his tone. This was no longer about money. This was personal.

Fitzpatrick was right; he had no guns, but he did still have the burner phone. He pulled it from his pocket and hit the call button to dial Penny.

No service. He had no reception in this tiny room. It was a dead spot in the house, perhaps by design.

Zero rubbed his forehead. They had no way out. And if no one had reported the gunshots, it would just be a matter of time before Fitzpatrick got inside.

"Hey." Bill McMahon took him by the shoulder and gestured toward the chair. "Why don't you sit, son?"

"I'm fine. You should sit."

"I've done my fair share of sitting these past few days, believe you me." Bill chuckled. "Don't lose heart, kiddo. We're not dead yet."

This time Zero chuckled. Not just at being forty and called kiddo by a man more than twice his age, but at Bill's resilience. This man had spent the better part of three days handcuffed, probably starved, possibly worse, and yet he kept his chin up higher than Zero could muster at the moment.

"You did good out there," Bill told him.

"*You* did good out there. Not many people would be able to act with a gun to their head."

"Eh," said Bill, "like I tried to tell 'em. Not my first time. You look well, by the way."

Zero grinned. "You remember me?"

"Course I do, son. You don't vomit on someone's shoes without remembering them." He gestured toward the iron door. "Kind of just like old times, except the boat and the seasickness."

"And this time we don't have any weapons."

Bill shrugged. "We got this chair."

Zero nodded slowly. That was true; they did have the chair. He flipped it over, examined it, and then snapped one of the legs off. The end broke unevenly, leaving a jagged stake in his hand.

It wasn't much, but it was something, and something was better than nothing.

"Say," said Bill, "where are we?"

"Virginia. Little run-down neighborhood just east of Stafford."

The former president scoffed. "No kidding. Sneaky bastards."

Zero heard a hiss, and then a low roar from the other side of the door.

"You hear that, Zero?" Fitzpatrick sneered loudly. "Acetylene torch. I'm gonna cut through this door in no time. Hope you're ready."

No one had called the police. Which meant that Penny would not see any report that indicated he was in trouble. She wouldn't be able to get through on the burner. Would she send someone? Or would she wait?

Did it matter, if Fitzpatrick was just going to cut through the door in the next few minutes anyway? Help wouldn't arrive that quickly.

"Hey. Tell me about yourself," Bill said behind him. "About your life."

"Now?"

"Yes, now. No time like the present. Let me think—you were married. I remember that. And you had a little one. No... two of them. Just a few years old."

226

Despite their situation, Zero laughed, astounded at the old man's memory. "That's right. Two girls. Practically adults now. And I was married. She, uh… she passed away."

"I'm so sorry to hear that, Reid."

Zero blinked away the threat of tears. Bill was genuinely sorry to hear that—and he knew him by his name, his real name. He remembered those eight hours on the cargo ship. He'd told him then, he'd told Bill his real name, and Bill had remembered it.

He knew what Bill was doing, and he was glad for it, because in that moment, forgetting *did* seem like the worst thing, and so did getting killed, and until either happened he would keep going.

The torch hissed on the other side of the door. He couldn't see sparks or feel heat, but he was certain that Fitzpatrick was slowly slicing through the hinges on the other side.

"What about you?" he asked.

Bill smiled. "Still married. Gwen is… she's a whirlwind, that one, even at seventy-nine years young. Got a couple of good dogs. I'm a great-grandpa. Life has been kind to me."

"Until now," Zero murmured.

Bill shrugged. "You're here, aren't you? That man could have put a bullet in my skull and that would've been that. But somehow you found me—*again*—and here we are. Like I said, we're not dead yet."

Zero couldn't help but be awed by him. Eighty-four, facing imminent death, and a smile on his face. Seemingly unruffled in the face of it all. A born leader, Bill McMahon was.

"Bill?"

"Yeah, Reid?"

"Two things. First—call me Zero."

"Sure thing."

"Second." He tightened his grip around the pointed chair leg. "What do you say we get out of here?"

Bill hefted the rest of the chair, holding it in front of him like a lion tamer. "Right behind you, Zero."

The torch hissed.

The door shifted in its frame. Zero could see a sliver of waning daylight around its edges. If it wasn't for the crossbar locking it in place, it would have fallen by now, and it was only a matter of time before Fitz cut through that too.

Zero reached for it, one hand on the crossbar, ready to throw it. To try to get the drop on Fitzpatrick, who was undoubtedly armed.

He held his breath, his muscles tensed.

That was when gunfire erupted from somewhere in the house.

# CHAPTER FORTY

"The hell is that?" he heard Fitzpatrick bellow. "Take care of it, now!"

Someone was there. Someone was shooting.

He didn't know who. But someone was there.

That was all he needed to know.

Zero heaved the crossbar up, and as soon as it was clear he shoved his body weight into the iron door. It gave easily. He hadn't expected it to give so easily. The door fell out of its frame, and Zero fell with it.

It thudded to the floor in a stupendous crash with Zero atop it. Fitzpatrick was on the other side, and he shuffled back quickly to avoid being crushed by it. He dropped the acetylene torch, still burning, and he screamed as it seared his thigh.

There was more shooting below them, more than one gun. It sounded like a whole team had come. Penny had sent the cavalry; she must have. But he couldn't let that distract him. Zero scrambled on his hands and knees, wooden stake in his hand, as Fitzpatrick reached for the PPK on the floor.

He'd brought a chair leg to a gun fight.

Bill McMahon came from behind him then, and he swung the three-legged wooden chair harder than Zero would have assumed possible for a man of his age. It broke into a dozen pieces over Fitzpatrick's head, and Bill reached for the gun.

But Fitzpatrick was as stubborn as he was tough. He was up again in an instant, bleeding, roaring as he kicked the gun away and slammed a fist across Bill McMahon's chin. Bill went down, and Zero leapt to his feet as Fitzpatrick pulled a black-handled Ka-Bar from his belt.

More shots blasted below them as Zero circled, waiting for Fitzpatrick to make his move.

The silver blade in his hand glinted as he raised it up, and then it came down, toward his throat, and in the moment Zero could think only of the beach. Of Maria. Of the moonlight and the knife, and the dark spot that wouldn't stop growing no matter how much he tried.

`He tried to move out of the way, he wanted to, but it felt like his legs had turned to jelly.

Bill was there then, on his feet, leaping in front of him, putting up a hand as if it would stop an oncoming knife.

*No.*

Zero reached out and caught Bill by the collar and yanked the old man back, right off his feet.

The blade hit his shoulder and pierced it, shirt and skin and muscle, finally hitting bone, buried deep as Zero's mouth stretched in a silent howl of pain. Fitzpatrick's face was close, inches from his own, teeth gritted and eyes wild. He could see every line, every tiny scar spider-webbing out from the mercenary's injured eye. Fitzpatrick grunted and his hand trembled as he tried to push the knife further, deeper into the shoulder, and it was all Zero could do but let him.

From between Fitzpatrick's gritted teeth there was blood. His lip trembled, and his hand fell away from the hilt of the Ka-Bar.

Zero looked down. In his hand was the jagged chair leg, or some of it, the last five inches or so, and the rest of it was buried in Fitzpatrick's chest, impaling him. Blood ran warm over Zero's hand. Slowly his fingers unwrapped from around the wood, shaky, no feeling left in them.

"Son of a... bitch." Fitzpatrick collapsed to the floor, the chair leg jutting from his chest.

Zero fell to his knees, breathing hard.

"Jesus, Mary, and Joseph," Bill murmured. The former president was there, at his shoulder, inspecting the knife wound.

"Doesn't look like it hit anything vital," said Bill. "Zero, I'm afraid you'll live."

And Zero chuckled, though it hurt to do it, and despite everything, because a part of him was afraid of that too. That he would live, and he'd have to deal with everything, all of it.

Then he noticed how silent the house was now.

"Shooting stopped." He grunted as he climbed to his feet, and retrieved the PPK from the floor. "Move slow and stay behind me."

Zero stepped over the scarred man's body and cleared the hallway carefully, seeing no sign of movement. He made his way to the top of the stairs and looked down.

At the bottom was a body. The man he'd kicked down the steps earlier. But the fall hadn't killed him; bullets had. Two to the chest and one to the head.

"Stay here," he whispered to Bill, and he left the former president at the top of the stairs as he made his way down slowly. There was no way to pad his footfalls on the bare wooden steps or to stop them from creaking loudly.

At the bottom he cleared left first, and then right, but he should have cleared right first because he came face to face with the barrel of an M9 pistol.

"CIA," he said quickly.

"US Army." The man beyond the barrel was young, fairly short, five-nine at best, with a square jaw and features that... well, if he didn't know any better, he'd say he looked like a young William McMahon.

"We clear?" he asked.

The man nodded. "Clear."

Zero slowly lowered the gun.

So did the stranger. Then he frowned. "You have a knife in your shoulder."

"Yeah. I noticed."

"Well, I'll be damned." Bill McMahon came down the stairs, past Zero, and wrapped the young man in a hug. "Zero—I'd like you to meet my grandson. Preston McMahon."

"Grandson?" Zero blinked. "How the hell did you find this place?"

"Was going to ask you the same question," Preston admitted. "Though I'm glad you found it first. Seems I was just a little late."

"No," Zero told him. Past Preston were three more bodies, none moving, and Zero realized that what he thought was an entire team was just this one young soldier. "I'd say you were right on time."

He pulled the burner phone from his pocket and was glad to see three bars of reception. He made the call.

"Zero? Jesus, I've been trying to reach you, I sent Todd your way, he should be there any mo—"

"Penny," he interrupted, "I need you to get through to the White House, right away. Tell President Rutledge to call off the Fifth Fleet immediately. Iran and the IRGC had nothing to do with the kidnapping. And tell him there's someone here that he would very much like to speak with."

231

Zero passed the phone to Bill, and then he made his way to the front door and out onto the sagging wooden porch. The sun was setting. Sirens wailed in the distance, no doubt coming his way.

He put the gun down and he sat. With his right hand he reached across to his left shoulder, clenched his teeth, and pulled the knife out with a grunt. The wound burned; it would need stitches.

Zero dropped the bloody knife, and he couldn't help it. His mind went back to the beach, and the knife, and the dark spot...

*No.* He shut his eyes and forced the scene out of his head. That's not how she would want to be remembered. On the beach, yes—but not on that beach. On a small stretch of private beach, hidden away by a copse of pine trees, in a simple white gown, her hair flowing wild around her shoulders and smiling radiantly, knowing she'd never looked lovelier.

That's how she'd want to be remembered. That's how he would remember her.

His shoulder burned, and there'd be hell to pay, probably. But he smiled anyway.

# CHAPTER FORTY ONE

Mischa knocked on the door to room 414 of the Hilton Grand in downtown Washington, D.C., and then she took a step back.

The man answered, and looked down at her quizzically. He was sandy-haired, clean-shaven, somewhere between thirty and forty, if she had to guess. He wore denim jeans and a white T-shirt and plain black sneakers, and he kept one hand obscured behind the frame of the door.

"*Sind Sie* Stefan Krauss?"

Are you Stefan Krauss?

She spoke in idiomatic German, conversational. He was, after all, a native speaker.

He smiled thinly at her. "*Wer sind Sie?*" Who are you?

"*Bist du allein?*" she asked. Are you alone?

The man glanced down, noticing her empty hands, and then craned his neck through the open doorway and looked left and right.

"*Du?*"

"Yes," she told him in English. "I came alone."

"I too am alone. Who are you?"

"My name is Mischa Johansson. You killed my..."

What was the right term?

"You killed my adopted mother in Nassau."

"I see," said Stefan Krauss. "And what? Is Zero using you as some kind of bait?"

Mischa shook her head. "No. As I said, I came alone. I'm here to kill you."

Krauss smiled at that. "You are a child."

"I am aware."

He shook his head. "What sort of joke is this?"

"It's no joke. I found you. I came to kill you. I have a gun." The revolver was tucked in her pants at the small of her back. "But I would rather not use it in a busy hotel." She gestured to the hand still hidden behind the door frame. "Do you have a gun?"

Krauss chuckled. "No. Just a knife." He showed it to her, a long narrow stiletto blade in his fist. "I would rather not use it on a girl, unless she gives me no choice."

"I won't," she promised. "Give you any other choice."

The man sighed. "This is… not what I expected."

"No. You expected Agent Zero. That's why you made it easy to find you, if one knew where to look."

"Indeed," he admitted.

"But he is not here," she said. "As far as I know, he is not even in the country. I am here."

"I see that." Krauss stroked his chin. "And you think you can kill me?"

"I do."

"All right." He glanced over his shoulder at the small hotel room. "But not here."

"Then where?"

He thought for a moment. "There is a small courtyard, with trees, behind the hotel. I imagine there will not be many people there at night. We'll go there."

She nodded. "All right."

Krauss folded the stiletto and tossed it lightly to the bed, and then he joined Mischa in the hall. "Come. You have my word I won't make a move unless you do."

"Fair." She walked alongside him down the corridor. To anyone else it might have seemed strange, but this was far preferable to fighting in such cramped quarters as a hotel room, possibly having other guests or security get in their way or try to break it up.

"Let me ask you a question, Mischa Johansson," said the assassin. "You have a gun. Why did you not use it and shoot me as soon as you identified me? I understand this is a busy hotel, but you are just a girl. It is unlikely anyone would suspect you."

"I admit," Mischa told him, "I have used that to my advantage in the past."

"Then why not?"

How to word it? "In Nassau, you killed Maria on the beach. She was not your target."

"No," he said softly. "She was not. She got in the way. She gave her life for his."

"And in return, you let Zero live," she said. "Why?"

234

"To give him a fair chance to kill me," Krauss said. "Because it was... sportsmanlike." He grinned down at her. "Ah. I see. No honor among thieves, but it would seem there is among killers. Yes?"

"It would seem," she agreed. They reached the elevators and he pressed the down button.

"How did you learn my name?" he asked. "Did Zero see me that night?"

"I don't know what he knows or thinks," Mischa told him. "I know your name because a former acquaintance of mine did business with your employer, who gave you up."

Krauss chuckled at that. "I have no employer." The elevator doors opened, the car empty, and they stepped inside. "I am... how would you say? Freelance."

Mischa frowned at that. "Then who is Mr. Bright to you?"

"I don't know that name."

"He knows you," Mischa countered. "He funds the operations that paid you to kill Zero."

"You are thinking of Mr. Shade," Krauss corrected her. "He is imprisoned, and I have never worked for him. I merely used his money to my advantage—"

"No," Mischa interrupted, irritated at being spoken down to like some child. "I am talking about Mr. Bright, out of New York. The business partner of Mr. Shade. He knows that you were contracted to kill Agent Zero—"

"And I told you, I have no employer—"

"He knows that you killed the wrong CIA agent and fled—"

"I did not *flee*, that is a bastardization of the truth—"

"And when I told him that someone wanted to kill you, for free, he gave you up willingly. Your name, your aliases. He said it was about time that you were put down. You'd outlived your usefulness. Patrick McIlhenney was easy to find after that."

"You listen here, girl!" Krauss snarled. For the first time since he'd opened the door, his gaze was hard, angry. "I have no employer! No one controls me! I control them! Do you hear me?"

Mischa stared right back at him impassively. "What I hear is a man that does not realize when someone is pulling his strings."

The elevator dinged and the doors opened. Mischa got out first, and then Krauss stepped out. The lobby was filled with people coming and going, flocking to the adjacent bar or heading out for a night on the town.

"May I ask," she said, "how you come by your information? Your contacts? Who you control and how you control them?"

Krauss did not answer, not at first. He stared straight ahead as they made their way toward the exit.

"A New Zealander," he said at last. "A smuggler. Or so he said. A man I thought I could trust."

"I would guess you thought meeting him was happenstance," she added.

Krauss nodded. "Though it would seem it was not."

They made their way outside. The night was cool, pleasant. Outside was the sound of honking horns and passersby, laughs and shouts and many conversations. Krauss led the way alongside the hotel to the courtyard he had mentioned.

"I don't often let my emotions get the best of me," he told her without turning. "If what you have told me is true, I have much to think about. Assuming I survive this night, that is."

They reached the courtyard and Krauss stopped. Mischa took a look around, surveyed her surroundings. It was not large, perhaps twenty yards by thirty, blocked from the view of the street on two sides by trees, on a third side by the hotel. The fourth side was open but faced the parking lot of the adjacent building. Benches dotted the perimeter. A small water fountain of concrete babbled in the center.

"This will do." She walked to the opposite end of the courtyard, pulled the revolver from the back of her pants, and placed it on a bench. Then she returned to the other side, from which Krauss had not moved. "The gun is there for whoever might reach it."

The man chuckled lightly. "A race?"

She shook her head. "I have no intention of going for it."

"You are an interesting child, Mischa Johansson." Krauss cracked his neck. "Now then, how to begin? As I said, I will not just strike a girl without reason, regardless of perceived threat—"

Mischa spun, lightning quick, and one foot came up and kicked out, striking him in the abdomen.

Krauss grunted and doubled over, and she jumped, bringing a knee to his chin. His head went back, and Mischa darted forward, under his arm, twisting it around so that when he fell, his own body weight would break it.

But he did not fall; Krauss caught himself on one leg and his other arm, and he pushed off, twisting back the way he came so that the arm she held instead tightened across her chest. He twisted at the hips and threw her easily. Mischa sailed and hit the pavement and rolled twice.

Breathing was hard but she still jumped to her feet, barely ducking a blow to her head, and responded in kind with two quick jabs to his ribs. It was like a toddler hitting a heavy bag; he barely moved, and an elbow crashed down on the top of her head.

Stars exploded in her vision. The pain didn't come, not at first, but it would. Until it did, she kicked out, aiming for his groin. He leaned and the kick hit his inner thigh instead.

Mischa leaned into the kick and threw a fist, but he caught it over his shoulder, pulled her in close. Both hands gripped her upper arms and he lifted her, and then threw her down to the ground.

Her own ribs screamed in pain. Her skull hurt. This was nothing new. It had just been a while. She rose and caught her breath, watching him as he did the same, both their chests heaving.

Behind him, a young couple crossed the courtyard, their arms linked and talking quietly to themselves. Mischa did not move and they paid her no mind. They waited until the young couple was around the corner, to the hotel, and then she launched herself at him again.

His rough knuckles split her lip. Her sharp fingernails opened cuts on his forehead. Her orbital bone cracked under his elbow. She threw him over her hip and dislocated his thumb.

He was tiring. So was she. Her body ached all over. She had underestimated this man, assuming him some two-bit assassin who used guns and knives, one who would underestimate her just as well and assume she would be easily bested.

They had both, it seemed, been wrong.

"You're quite good," he panted as blood ran into his eyebrows. He gritted his teeth as he yanked sharply on the thumb she had dislocated. "You've given more than ample reason to kill you."

He came again, rushing at her, faking a left and throwing right, an easy move to duck—but the slow right hook was just a distraction for the knee that came crashing into her sternum. The air was forced from her lungs and try as she might, she could not suck in a breath. He kicked out with one flat foot and sent her sprawling to her back.

Mischa coughed, and felt like she was suffocating as she struggled to catch a breath.

"This is the end." He stood over her. "For whatever it may be worth, I am sorry about your mother. But she got in the way."

*Your mother.*

A memory flashed through her mind, back when she was being held in the underground detention facility of the CIA, with its glass walls and no apparent exit. Maria would come and visit her, twice or sometimes even three times a week. On one of the occasions, she taught her a game called "Never Have I Ever." They each held up three fingers, and one would say something they had never done, and if the other person had done it, they would put down one finger.

*I have never met my mother.*

Mischa had won the game with that statement, at least insomuch that one could win such a game with such a statement.

But if she was playing that game here, now, she would not be able to say that. Not anymore. Because however briefly it had been, she did have a mother, maybe only on paper but still one who cared for her and respected her and had even loved her, all the while understanding that it would be difficult, maybe even impossible, for Mischa to love her back in the same way.

"What is this?" Krauss stood over her, and his face twisted to something like disgust. "What trick is this? Are you *weeping?*"

Mischa opened her mouth, and a breath came, and with it a sob bubbled out, a small one, but a sob nonetheless.

And then she kicked Stefan Krauss in the genitals so hard she was fairly certain she cracked a metatarsal.

He yelped and fell to his knees, and Mischa staggered to her feet. He vomited a small amount of something while her gaze flitted to the gun.

She had to get to it. That was the only way she would finish this.

She sprinted for it. Halfway across the courtyard she felt fingers close around her ankle and she sprawled forward, scraping both elbows raw. Krauss scrambled over her, nearly stumbled, and reached the revolver first. He grabbed it up, and he aimed it at her.

"I didn't want to do this," he said.

She stared at him from her place on the ground. She would not close her eyes or look away. She would face her killer, and he would remember her face—

A shape came out of the darkness, seemingly from nowhere, leaping, and delivered a cracking blow across Krauss's mouth. He staggered back and the newcomer kicked at the hand that held the gun, but still he managed to hold onto it. She struck again, once, twice, three times in his face, until his nose was flattened and bleeding down his chin.

Maya lurched for the hand that held the gun and twisted it, but Krauss snarled and twisted back, the two of them grappling for it. Mischa did not know how Maya was here, how she had found her, but she was there, fighting off Krauss, and she climbed to her feet to help her. Together they could do it. Together they could kill him. Together…

Krauss whipped his head forward, and the top of his skull struck Maya right between the eyes. She cried out and fell back, and before Mischa could get there he aimed the revolver down at her.

"No!"

He fired twice.

Maya's body jerked with each round that hit her, center mass.

Someone shrieked, an inhuman wail of despair that could not have possibly come from her own tiny lungs because she had never, ever made a sound like that before, had never felt misery like that before, as if a part of her own soul had been torn from her, and in that moment she understood Zero's pain, and what it would have been like to be there, and why Krauss fled, and why Sara hurt bad men.

She was frozen there, unable to move, as Maya gasped what would be her final breaths.

Krauss did not move either. He stared down at her, and then at long last he looked over at Mischa. He closed his eyes and sighed, and then he cursed softly in German.

Then he fled. He leapt between the trees that divided the courtyard from the street, gone in an instant.

She could chase him, she knew. She could follow. But instead she ran to Maya's side and knelt.

"Maya."

"Yeah."

"I'm so sorry. I am so, so sorry."

Maya groaned. "You'd better be. *Damn*, that hurts."

"…What?" Mischa ran her hand gently over Maya's chest. There was no blood. No bullet holes. "How…?"

Maya sat up with a grimace. She lifted the shirt, revealing two dark purple bruises that had already formed where the bullets had struck her.

239

"Graphene shirt." She winced. "From Penny. Bulletproof. But... hurts like a bitch."

Mischa breathed a sigh of relief. "How did you find me?"

Maya sighed. "You've got a tracker in your arm, kiddo."

She frowned. And then realized: "Oh. That was not a flu shot."

"No. That was not a flu shot." Maya looked her over and gently wiped some blood from her chin with a thumb. "Mischa, you're a mess. What were you thinking going after him alone?"

She shook her head. "I wasn't. Thinking, that is. I just wanted to hurt him. To kill him."

Maya nodded. "I get it. But you can't do that. We're sisters now. We have to rely on each other, not just for help, but also to not do stupid stuff like this. Yeah?"

"Yeah." She held out a hand, and she helped Maya to her feet.

"We could go after him," Maya said, though she sounded doubtful.

Mischa shook her head. "He will vanish again, I'm sure. But I found him before. I will find him again." She looked up at Maya and corrected herself. "*We* will find him again."

"Yeah." She put her arm around Mischa's shoulders and together they headed for the front of the hotel. "If anyone could."

# EPILOGUE

Zero kicked off his shoes, peeled off his socks, and stepped into the water. His pants were rolled up almost to the knee. His toes sank into the wet sand as he walked out further, until the water reached his knees and lapped at his rolled hems. He held the urn in both hands and looked out over the ocean.

He'd gotten married here a week ago. Now he was spreading his wife's ashes here, on the Chesapeake Beach with the first hill of the roller coaster just barely visible on the boardwalk to the north.

Anyone else would be in a prison cell for what he had done. Or maybe even a hole in H-6. But being Agent Zero gave him preferential treatment that even he had to admit bordered on unfair, even if he had found and recovered former President McMahon. Bill was back at home in West Virginia now, a trio of fresh Secret Service agents guarding him twenty-four/seven.

President Rutledge had pardoned Zero for his crimes. That's what they were—crimes. Not indiscretions or mistakes. Crimes.

They'd retroactively spun it as a covert EOT op. But he was done with EOT. He wouldn't go back without her. Alan had said the same. How and if EOT would continue, he wasn't sure; they still had Strickland and Penny, and Zero had personally recommended Preston McMahon if he wanted the job.

That was what they needed. Young blood. Fresh faces. Not him.

Zero was finished with it. He was retiring from the CIA and from that life entirely, and for good this time. Maybe he would go back to teaching. But not quite yet. There were still some things that needed doing.

The United States had narrowly avoided war with Iran; the relations between countries were intact. But there was a lot of work to be done domestically, in both countries, to avoid disenfranchisement and further division.

None of that was his problem anymore.

Zero reached into his pocket. In it was a ring, just a simple gold band, identical to the one he wore but for size. On the inner side two words were inscribed: *Never goodbye.*

*We don't say goodbye,* she would say before every op.

*Not ever.*

He held the ring to his lips and kissed it gently.

"Goodbye."

He turned his palm over and let the ring fall into the water. He lifted the lid from the urn, and he tipped it slowly. The ashes sifted out, caught on the breeze, and carried over the ocean.

Then he turned and waded back to the beach.

Maya was there waiting for him, watching. Her ribs were wrapped since two had cracked where she'd been shot twice. Mischa stood beside her, one eye swollen and Band-Aids covering almost a quarter of her face.

Sara was there, a little ways up the beach, separate from the rest. She'd been even more distant since he'd come back, and had explained her day and a half disappearance with only a shrug and the claim that since everyone else had left, she had gone to visit her friend Camilla. He didn't know if it was the truth, and if it wasn't he knew he wasn't going to get it.

Alan was there, staring at the sand with his big arms folded over his chest. Todd Strickland was there, standing closest to the tree line, his hand in the splint for his broken finger. Penny was there too, and it was she who came to him first as he reached the sand and wrapped him in a hug.

"I'm sorry, Zero." She held him for a long time, and when she pulled away, her eyes were moist. "Don't be a stranger, okay? Check in now and then."

"I will." He gestured to Todd. "Still doesn't want to talk to me, does he?"

She shook her head. "Not yet. Give him time. But it was important that he came to pay his respects."

"Tell him... it means a lot to me. And it would mean a lot to her."

"I will. Take care of yourself, okay?"

"Okay."

Penny treaded up the beach, and after one more glance over her shoulder she disappeared through the thin copse of pine trees, Strickland behind her.

Alan nodded to him once, and he followed as well. There was nothing to say between them; he knew how Zero felt and Zero knew how he felt. He knew that Alan wasn't exactly pleased with the way he'd handled things—but he also knew that Alan Reidigger was the last person on the entire planet who would turn his back on him.

Sara followed without a word. She had hitched a ride there with Alan instead of with them. Zero knew he would eventually have to address the chasm that had grown anew between them. But that would have wait for another day.

He stood there on the beach in early September with an empty urn in his hands and sand clinging to his bare feet, with Maya and Mischa nearby, silent, but he felt their eyes on him.

"I'm sorry," he told them. "For what I put you through and for what I made you feel you had to do."

"I would do it again if I had to," Mischa told him quietly.

"Me too," Maya agreed.

He looked up at them, but then looked back down at the sand, because seeing the bandages on Mischa's face and the pain in Maya's eyes was too much. They had gone after a deadly killer and nearly been killed, and he couldn't help but blame himself for it. He hadn't been there. Krauss had tried to draw him in and he hadn't been there.

But he would be next time.

"He ditched his alias," Zero told them. "His trail's gone cold. Penny has been scouring every resource she can, and no sign of him."

"I found him before without any of that," Mischa said. "I could do it again, I believe."

Zero nodded. "Fine. But we do it together. You understand? Together." He forced himself to look at Mischa. Her swollen eye. Her bandaged face. "We're a family. All of us. You're my daughter now. Not just legally but in every way that matters. You don't fight for us. You fight *with* us."

Mischa nodded. Maya's hand found hers and held it.

"So what do we do?" Maya asked.

"First, I have to go to Switzerland. I made a promise that I need to keep this time." Dr. Guyer was expecting him. He and Dillard had been collaborating on some sort of new plan, the likes of which Zero knew very little about except that it was an experimental procedure that might be Zero's best bet to salvage his brain.

243

And he knew now that he needed to. Because forgetting was not an option.

"And then, we're going to find him. We're going to find him, we're going to make a plan... and we're going to kill him."

They weren't girls anymore. He knew that. Maya was a legal adult. Sara had been mature beyond her years for a while now. Mischa... she'd lived an entire other life before this one. They weren't girls, but they were his daughters, and Maria's too.

He wasn't done yet with Stefan Krauss, and neither were they.

Zero tucked the urn under his arm and took Mischa's free hand in his. The three of them walked up the beach, across the sand, and through the trees, heading home. Together.

# NOW AVAILABLE!

## ZERO ZERO
### (An Agent Zero Spy Thriller—Book #11)

"You will not sleep until you are finished with AGENT ZERO. A superb job creating a set of characters who are fully developed and very much enjoyable. The description of the action scenes transport us into a reality that is almost like sitting in a movie theater with surround sound and 3D (it would make an incredible Hollywood movie). I can hardly wait for the sequel."
--Roberto Mattos, Books and Movie Reviews

ZERO ZERO is book #11 in the #1 bestselling AGENT ZERO series, which begins with AGENT ZERO (Book #1), a free download with nearly 300 five-star reviews.

**When Agent Zero visits his doctor in Switzerland, hoping to salvage his deteriorating health, he is met with a shocking surprise: another agent who has been given a memory implant, just like him. And, just like him, this agent has deadly skills—and a singular mission: to kill Agent Zero.**

**Agent Zero has met his doppleganger, a darker version of himself.**

**Who is he? Who does he work for? Who chipped him? What secrets does he hold about Zero's past? And why does he want Zero dead?**

ZERO ZERO (Book #11) is an un-putdownable espionage thriller that will keep you turning pages late into the night.

**"Thriller writing at its best."**
**--Midwest Book Review (re *Any Means Necessary*)**

**"One of the best thrillers I have read this year."**
**--Books and Movie Reviews (re *Any Means Necessary*)**

Also available is Jack Mars' #1 bestselling LUKE STONE THRILLER series (7 books), which begins with Any Means Necessary (Book #1), a free download with over 800 five star reviews!


**ZERO ZERO**
**(An Agent Zero Spy Thriller—Book #11)**

## Jack Mars

Jack Mars is the USA Today bestselling author of the LUKE STONE thriller series, which includes seven books. He is also the author of the new FORGING OF LUKE STONE prequel series, comprising six books; and of the AGENT ZERO spy thriller series, comprising ten books (and counting).

Jack loves to hear from you, so please feel free to visit www.Jackmarsauthor.com to join the email list, receive a free book, receive free giveaways, connect on Facebook and Twitter, and stay in touch!

# BOOKS BY JACK MARS

## LUKE STONE THRILLER SERIES
ANY MEANS NECESSARY (Book #1)
OATH OF OFFICE (Book #2)
SITUATION ROOM (Book #3)
OPPOSE ANY FOE (Book #4)
PRESIDENT ELECT (Book #5)
OUR SACRED HONOR (Book #6)
HOUSE DIVIDED (Book #7)

## FORGING OF LUKE STONE PREQUEL SERIES
PRIMARY TARGET (Book #1)
PRIMARY COMMAND (Book #2)
PRIMARY THREAT (Book #3)
PRIMARY GLORY (Book #4)
PRIMARY VALOR (Book #5)
PRIMARY DUTY (Book #6)

## AN AGENT ZERO SPY THRILLER SERIES
AGENT ZERO (Book #1)
TARGET ZERO (Book #2)
HUNTING ZERO (Book #3)
TRAPPING ZERO (Book #4)
FILE ZERO (Book #5)
RECALL ZERO (Book #6)
ASSASSIN ZERO (Book #7)
DECOY ZERO (Book #8)
CHASING ZERO (Book #9)
VENGEANCE ZERO (Book #10)
ZERO ZERO (Book #11)

Printed in Great Britain
by Amazon

16547555R00146